Al-Kabar

Al-Kabar

A NOVEL OF ILAURIS

LEE FRENCH

Myrddin Publishing

unique electronic & print books

Published by Myrddin Publishing
www.myrddinpublishing.com

First printing, September 2015

Al-Kabar is a work of fiction involving a fictional culture in a fictional world. People, places, titles, and incidents are either products of the author's mind or used fictitiously. No historical accuracy should be expected or assumed.

No horses were harmed in the making of this book.

ISBN: 978-1-68063-032-9

Cover copyright 2015 by Keith Draws
Ilauris map copyright 2013 by Miladoon

Acknowledgments

This book is dedicated to Megan Limke, a courageous woman and wonderful cousin whose light shined for far too little time.

Thanks to C.J., Rachel, and Ross for being excellent beta readers. Special thanks to Connie and Dave for mad editorial skills and to Shannon for reminding me that trauma is traumatic. I appreciate Bob as an excellent booth bunny who failed to make me want to murder him during a 16 hour drive. Jeff has my thanks for being my ConBuddy and an all-around awesome person.

I also wish to declare love for my dad, who can't stand this type of story but encourages my writing anyway.

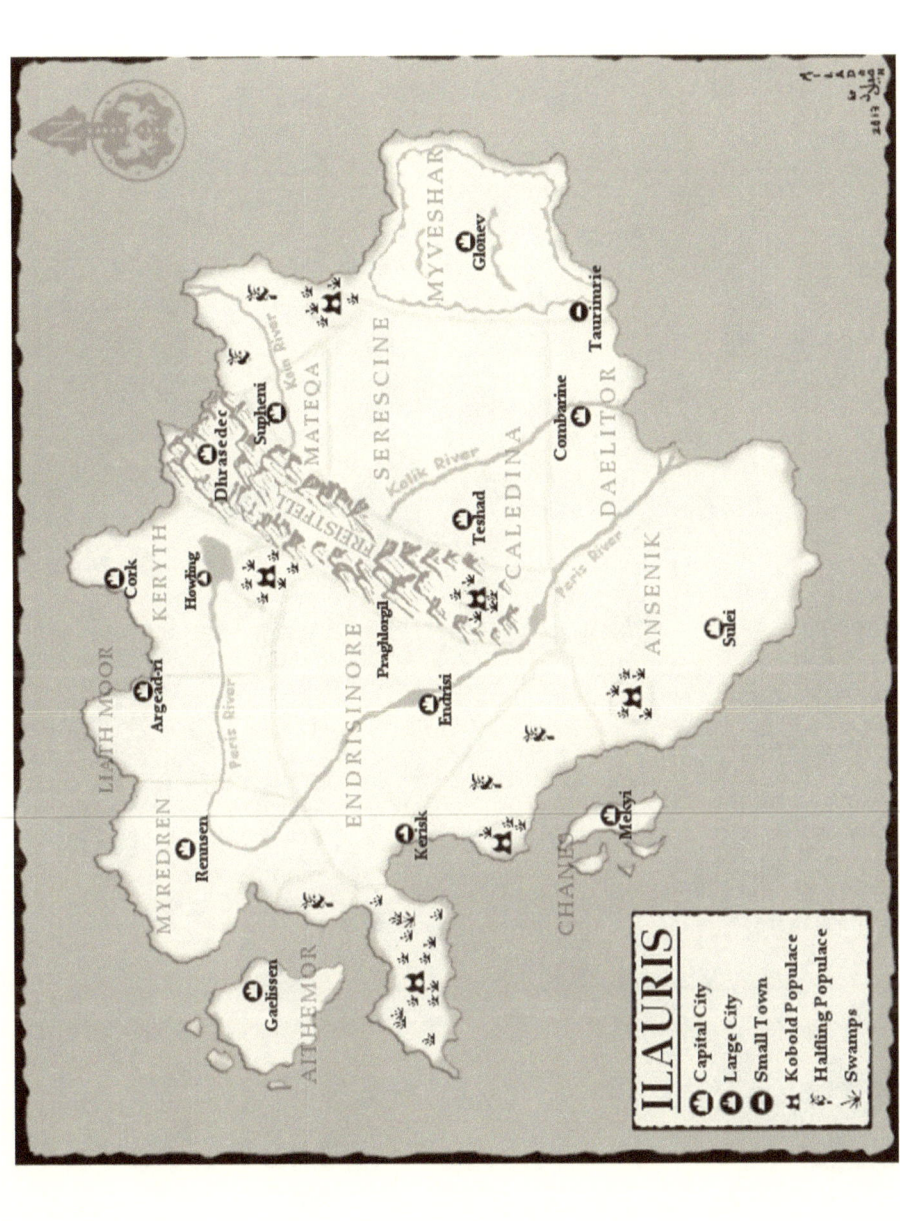

ILAURIS

Capital City
Large City
Small Town
Kobold Populace
Halfling Populace
Swamps

MYVESHAR
Glonev
Taurimrie
SERESCINE
MATEQA
Supheni
Dhrasedec
FRESTHELL
CALEDINA
DAELITOR
Combarine
Teshad
Kelik River
Kelin River
Paris River
Cork
KERYTH
Howling
Praghorgil
ENDRISINORE
Endrisi
ANSENIK
Sulei
LIATH MOOR
Argeadn
MYREDREN
Remsen
Paris River
Kersk
Melsyi
CHAMES
AITHEMOR
Gaelissen

Part 1:

Fakhira

Chapter 1

"Fakhira, this is Cyric." Father held his arm around the younger man's shoulders and presented him proudly. "I'll go tell your sister there's one more for dinner." He let go of Cyric and thumped him on the back.

With seven clean shirts from the nearby twine clothesline draped over her arm, Fakhira gave him a polite smile. "It's nice to meet you, Cyric." She nodded to her father as he left them alone in the dappled sunshine.

Cyric looked like her sister's husband, Shahan: tall, muscular, and bearded. Without the crisp white and blue uniform of Korval's Guard, the protectors of Aitrae Oasis, she thought they might seem less similar. "It's nice to meet you too." He took her small hand with his own rough, calloused one, bending to touch the back to his forehead. "I'm honored that your father thinks us a good match."

"I hope the Fires and the Waters bless this pairing." Nothing else to say came to mind and her attention drifted to the date palms nearby. They made her think about food and dinner tonight.

1

"I'm sure they will." He looked around the palm orchard and shifted his weight then reached up and scratched his head wrapping, its bright white sharply contrasting with his swarthy skin. "What do you do in the household?"

She pushed a lock of black hair behind her ear. "Laundry, cooking. I help Almiya with her new baby too, and go to market."

"That's good."

"Would you like to..." She shifted her gaze to the mud-brick wall separating the grove from the rest of town, to the varied-height trees with their giant fronds, to the brown stone well, then to the sandy earth. Nothing suggested an activity to invite him to. Looking at her bare feet led her to looking at the shirts still draped over her arm. "I need to put these away. Do you want to come inside?"

"Ah." He smiled at her in relief. "Yes, please."

She led him through the trees to the middle of five mud-brick homes hidden behind the grove. Inside the camel-hide curtain they used for a front door, Cyric pulled off his boots to leave them in the entry beside Father's and Shahan's. Fakhira kept going, intent on depositing her burden. Cyric would live here, so he might as well get used to being a resident and not a guest.

Passing into the large common space, she nodded to Almiya, who sat in Shahan's arms on the baked clay floor by the open window, feeding her baby. She hoped for her match with Cyric to turn out as well as Almiya's had with Shahan. Theirs had happened the same way, with Father bringing one of his men home to marry his daughter.

2

Half the shirts on her arm belonged to Shahan. She dropped them off in his and Almiya's room, hanging them off the back of their wicker chair. The other half belonged to Father. She found him moving baskets out of the spare room and into the room he shared with Mother and his unmarried children.

Father shoved a large round basket into a corner and chuckled at her. "Have you rejected him already, Fa-fa?"

She stuck her tongue out at him. "I have your shirts."

"What do you think of him?"

Fakhira shrugged. "I'm sure he'll be fine."

"Today, he's still a guest. If you can't stand him, I'll find you another man. He'll go home tonight, no matter what you think. Tomorrow, he'll bring his things and stay."

"Then you only need to move the heavy things." She set his shirts on his sleeping mat, knowing he'd want to change into one before Mother got home. "I'll take care of the rest."

"Yes, that's my plan." He winked at her. "Go, get to know him. Take a stroll."

"We should have a special dinner. I'll need to go to market."

He waved her off. "Leave it for tomorrow. Take five silvers and get whatever you want. For today, go pick some dates and make him feed them to you. See if you can talk him into stealing figs from Pakadi."

She laughed and shook her head, leaving the room. "You're wicked, Father."

"That's what your mother says."

3

Still smiling, she returned to the common space and found Cyric sitting on the woven rug with Fakhira's two little brothers, both filthy from their day's work. Harad apprenticed for the smith, and Granik ran messages for Korval's Guard. They must have run in from work and gone straight for the newcomer.

"Do you use a real sword, like Father and Shahan?"

"Yes, I have one."

"How many men have you killed with it?"

Cyric fixed each of them with a hard stare. "All the ones that deserved it."

"Does the Guard's mage play tricks on you?"

"No. He knows I'd punch him in the face."

"That's enough." Fakhira waded into the conversation and shooed the boys away. "Cyric's going to live here. You can ask him all the questions you want later. He's mine today. Go clean up or you won't get dinner."

As the boys groaned in protest and ran out of the room, Shahan chuckled. "You'd think they never saw Guardsmen before."

"It's alright, I don't mind. They're curious." Cyric got to his feet. "Boys are like that."

"Come walk with me," Fakhira said. She held out her hand, wanting him to see it as a request, and hoping he'd take it as a sign that she knew she had to do her part to make this work. It also didn't hurt to show him that she liked to be touched.

Cyric's gaze went to her hand and he smiled. He clasped it between both of his own, squeezing then letting go with one so they could walk.

Leading him out into the palms, she peered up at the bunches of fruit to check for ripe ones. "You've met everyone but Mother now. Are you ready to run away?"

He laughed. "No, it's quieter than my parents' house. I'm the youngest, and my four sisters are all married with their own kids. Four husbands and seven brats running around. My mother will be sad to see me go, I think. She says I keep her sane."

"You must have a big house."

"Not much bigger than yours. My parents like everyone close, so we all sleep in the same room. It'll be strange to have a room for just the two of us."

Pointing to the top of a tree at least fifty feet up, she suppressed a grin. "I see a ripe strand in that one. Will you climb the tree to get it?"

"So high?" Shading his eyes, he squinted where she indicated. "I haven't climbed trees since I was a boy."

"That was, what, a month or two ago?" She smirked at him.

Chuckling, he tugged on her arm to pull her close. "Oh, you want to see how much of a man I am? Is this a test?"

Suddenly, she stood with a hand on his broad chest and her eyes on his mouth. Her heart fluttered. She thought Father had chosen well. "It might be." His spicy scent filled her.

He brushed thick hair from her face then cupped her copper cheek. "If you want ripe dates, I'll fetch them for you, no matter how far I have to go to find them."

Her eyes danced around his face, unable to settle on any one part.

5

"There are some on the shorter trees."

"Minx." He grinned and let go of her, stepping away to wander among the trees.

His withdrawal surprised her, and she stood confused and gasping for breath. Did she want him to kiss her because she knew she had no choice, or because he said and did the right things? She turned her back to him so he wouldn't see her acting like a twit. Hands on her cheeks, she forced herself to breathe normally and to not be disappointed. They just met. There would be plenty of time to indulge in pleasures of the flesh.

Tucking her hair behind her ears, she turned to find he'd disappeared. How far away had he gone? "Cyric? Not all the trees are ours." She took a few steps, then a few more steps, looking all around. She called out his name again, her steps growing quicker as she went. Had she been dreaming when he held her close?

She hurried through the palms, searching everywhere, then ran out of the orchard. Down by the house, she saw him looking for her and laughed at her panic. He spotted her and held up a short strand of yellow dates.

"I called for you," she chided as they met halfway.

He wrapped an arm around her. "I must've wandered too far away, somehow. The orchard doesn't look that big."

"It's not all ours, we only own a quarter of it. You probably took someone else's."

"Then we should hide and eat the evidence." Grabbing her hand, he tugged her into a run and they dashed around the house to the herb garden.

She pointed at Mother's favorite spot to watch the sunset with Father. Five angled walls of wide lattice formed a hexagon with the west side open, and it had no roof. Grape and jasmine vines snaked through the holes making a long green curtain studded with tiny white stars. She brought him around to the opening and nudged him to sit on the clover covering the ground.

"Ah, a hidden oasis in the Oasis." He kept hold of her hand as he sat, bringing her down into his lap. "I got you dates. Do I pass your test?"

Hoping he'd kiss her this time, she nodded. "The first test, yes."

"You're as harsh a taskmaster as your father." He plucked one date from the stem and touched it to her lips. "I must admit I'm not sure how to feed you a date. The stone seems likely to get in the way."

She reached up and took the fruit from him. "Then maybe you should get me some figs. They have no pits." Taking a bite, she let the sweet juice rush into her mouth.

He let out a tiny sigh. "Or I could just watch you eat them. Watch you suck the flesh from the stone and roll it around in your mouth. Lick your fingers and lips."

"You could lick them for me." Her cheeks darkened with a dusky blush.

A slow smile spread across his face and he took her hand. "Once I start, I may very well get carried away." Bringing her hand to his mouth, he kissed her fingers. She still had half the date, and he took a bite of it.

"I don't think I'll mind."

Without swallowing the fruit, he gently pushed her hand away and kissed her. His lips parted, pushing hers open, and his tongue rolled the fruit into her mouth. Breaking off the kiss, he drew back. "That would solve the problem too."

She never imagined such a thing could be done. Chewing the fruit mechanically, she frowned and wished the taste could chase away how strange and uncomfortable his behavior made her feel. A kiss, so she thought, should make her feel wanted. This one brought to mind a bird feeding its baby. "I'm not sure I like that."

"No?" He frowned. "Should I try again? Maybe I did it wrong."

"No." Almiya liked to kiss Shahan and Father liked to kiss Mother, so there had to be something to it.

Furrowing his brow, he frowned at her. "Are you alright?"

"Yes, I'm fine." The mood had been lost, and she didn't know how to recapture it. She cast about for something to say, some subject to talk about, and found nothing. Sitting in his lap felt awkward now, and she wanted him to stop touching her.

"That bothered you, more than you'll say. I'm sorry. I thought it was clever." He wriggled out from underneath her, helping her move away until they sat side by side, staring out at the late afternoon.

That he didn't press on and force himself on her gave her some hope. "It's alright." She drew her knees to her chest and hugged them.

"I won't do that again."

"Thank you."

They sat together in a silence that Fakhira had no idea how to break. Even if she could think of something, it felt more comfortable this way. Almiya made it look easy with Shahan, but maybe it took more work in private than either admitted to.

"Fakhira! It's time to make dinner!" Harad's shout startled her out of her thoughts.

She huffed in annoyance and turned to apologize to Cyric only to find him hopping to his feet and offering her a hand up. The gesture made her smile. "Will you stay for the meal?"

"Am I welcome?" He pulled her to her feet without drawing her close.

"Father says you'll move in tomorrow."

"He told me that was up to you."

Her smile grew. Father had told her that, and he loved her enough to tell Cyric the same. She could almost feel his arms holding her and hear him telling her everything would be fine. "Then ask me later, before you leave."

Cyric took her hand and bowed over it again, touching it to his forehead. "I hope you find me worthy."

In the distance, thunder cracked across the desert.

Chapter 2

"Aren't you done yet?"

Fakhira bent past the fronds of the dwarf palm she'd spent the last ten minutes inspecting to see Almiya tapping her foot. A sling around her sister's body held the baby in place while he suckled and slept, allowing her to keep working despite him. In another year, that would be Fakhira.

"I was just making sure the sap goes into the jugs," Fakhira protested. "Some of the dates are ripe. I picked a few for dinner tonight." After last night's meal with Cyric, she wanted him to move in now. He'd complimented the cooking, entertained the boys, and made Mother blush. In so many ways, he seemed perfect. They'd figure out the kissing in due time.

Almiya rolled her eyes and waved for Fakhira to come inside with her. "You should leave them for the boys to collect."

Fakhira checked the jug strapped to the tree one more time to make sure it wouldn't fall or miss any sap, then climbed down. Circling around the side of the house, she padded through the small garden where they managed to grow onions and radishes with herbs and spices. She poked the sunflowers—tall enough to tower over her own five and a half feet of height—to see if any seeds would fall out and give her an excuse to delay following Almiya inside. None obliged.

Giving up on dallying, she pushed the front curtain aside and brought in her basket of dates. Cooler air greeted her and she followed her sister into the large space that held their cooking tools and provisions, and a woven mat of palm fronds for sitting and eating. Mother sometimes talked about the amazing enchanted things her employer's kitchen had, and Fakhira dearly wished they could afford a few here. Even one tiny light would make a difference.

Almiya grabbed a fresh dung-brick and dropped it into the cooking fire pit, then she took Fakhira's basket and settled on a low stool to examine the bright yellow dates. "Make the bread," she said with a dismissive wave toward the bowls and grains.

Fakhira wanted to work with the limes and dates and opened her mouth to say so. Almiya raised an eyebrow and pointed to the bread board. Knowing her sister wouldn't change her mind, Fakhira fetched a clay bowl, filling it from the sack of flour, jar of bread seasoning, and pitcher of water. As she returned to Almiya's side, she swished the bowl to mix it then stuck her hand in and used her fingers.

"These are good dates," Almiya said as she swallowed a bite from one. "We'll save two for Father, and chop up the rest. They'll go well with the lettuce and—"

Outside, someone shouted from far enough away that Fakhira couldn't make out the words, or who it might be. He sounded male and afraid. It filled her with dread. "What did he say?" Her voice refused to raise any louder than a whisper.

"I don't know." Almiya put a hand on her baby and stood. "Stay here, I'll go check."

Fakhira gulped and nodded, grateful she didn't have to go. "Be careful."

Almiya waved in irritation and left the cooking room.

Fakhira heard the the creak of leather as her sister pushed the front curtain aside and it fell back into place. Heart pounding in her chest, she focused on the dough in her bowl, squeezing it between her fingers and turning it, then squeezing and turning it again. Her ears strained to hear every sound, hoping to pick out footsteps among the rustling of the palm leaves and buzzing of flies. Unwilling to risk Almiya's wrath if she ignored instructions, she moved on to spreading the dough out on a clay tablet to go into the oven.

As she rose to start the fire for making dinner, she heard a shrill scream and froze. It came from someone nearby. Mother would be at work. Her two younger brothers should be at their apprenticeships. Shahan and Father should still be at their posts. No one but she and Almiya should be that close. Panic sending sparks through her body to her fingers and toes, Fakhira lurched to her feet and ran to the front curtain. A woman's whimper and a baby's squall made her pause before she ripped the curtain aside. Instead, she peered through the gap between the curtain and the wall.

Through the palm orchard, she first saw the baby screaming as a man held him up without regard for his safety. Almiya struggled against something, squirming and reaching for her son. Though she stood too far away to hear words, Fakhira understood Almiya's pleas well enough. All her instincts told her to charge out and fix the problem, to stop whatever threatened her sister and her nephew.

Fakhira yanked the curtain aside and took one step before she noticed what she would charge into. The first man wore a curved sword, the same kind Father and the rest of the Guard used. Instead of Korval's blue and white, his clothes and head wrapping had brown and maroon. Another man pushed Almiya back, holding her by the neck. Fakhira's breath caught in her throat as she saw the third man, and the fourth and fifth. Their horses waited nearby, maroon tassels on their reins catching her eye.

She ducked back inside, hoping the men hadn't seen her, and covered her mouth to keep from screaming. Darting her eyes around the room, she wished for a way to save her sister. Almiya sobbed and begged, and a man's voice rumbled. Fakhira jumped when she heard a sharp, meaty crack, and again when Almiya wailed.

Fakhira needed to know what had happened. She flicked the curtain aside enough to see the silent baby on the ground and Almiya collapsing in a heap, hands covering her face. Shock kept Fakhira staring until one man pointed at the doorway and walked toward it. She jerked away and gasped for breath.

They already had Almiya. Fakhira could do nothing about it. Five men would have no trouble dealing with her. Even if she had a weapon, she didn't know how to use it. If she hid well enough, they wouldn't find her, and she could tell Father and Shahan what happened and who did it. They would go find these men and chop their heads off. But only if she hid now. Tearing herself away, she ran deeper inside and searched frantically for something they wouldn't suspect.

In the main sleeping room, she found the line of clothes baskets. If they opened the one she picked, they'd kill her. Standing there, frozen in indecision, she heard Almiya's wailing draw closer. She grabbed the lid of her mother's basket and climbed in. Once she pulled the lid back on and covered herself with clothes, her body shook with the effort to keep her grief and terror in. Later, when they were gone, she could afford to weep for the baby and for Almiya. Now, she needed to stay alive.

"Please, no." Almiya had been brought close enough for Fakhira to make out the words, and she wished with all her heart to block it out. Boots clomped closer. Something wooden crashed.

"Thank you for cooperating," a man's cold, cruel voice said. "I want all these hovels looted for supplies. You can have this one, but if you find any other girls, bring them to me."

Fakhira covered her ears, willing the sounds to go away. Her body trembled and she struggled to breathe without crying. Too much noise would give her away and she'd become one of those "other girls." What would happen to them seemed clear.

One man walked into the sleeping room and Fakhira heard the creaking as he pulled the lid off a basket. "Captain, do we want clothes? Linens?"

"Men's clothes, sure. We won't want any *women's* clothing." Deep, dark laughter followed this, echoed by the other men, then drowned out by Almiya's cries.

The lid of Fakhira's basket flipped open, and a hand groped in the cloth on the top. She froze, begging the Fires to make him pass her by. The man left it and moved on, not noticing her under Mother's dresses.

She stayed hidden while he picked up a different basket and walked out.Another girl shrieked outside. The man came back and took another basket. More screams filled the air, then cut off abruptly. Men shouted in anger and greed. Fakhira held her head, wishing it would all stop. It seemed like a long time passed before she heard voices speaking again.

"By the Fires, *stop already,*" a woman snarled. "You've done enough. Put her out of her misery and move on."

"Yes, my Lady," a man growled. "You heard Fire Dancer Anahita. Let's go."

Fakhira heard a wet ripping sound she didn't want to understand, then boots tromped away.

"I'm so sorry," the woman said, her gentle words carried on an errant zephyr. "Those men are jackals. May the Fires take you and your child. Be at peace."

For many more heartbeats, Fakhira stayed in the basket and wept. She only stopped and peeked her head out when she noticed a burning smell. Flames licked at the roof. Smoldering bits of palm fell through to the floor, setting the sleeping mats alight.

Knocking the basket over, she scrambled to get free. Her black hair splayed out in her haste and caught fire. She smacked her hands on it, brushing the fire off in a panic, then ran for the kitchen. Almiya lay on the floor in the entry hut, clothes ripped off her body and eyes glassy and still. Fakhira stared, heedless of the danger all around. Sucking in ragged, wheezing breaths, she took in the savagery done to her sister.

Her stomach heaved. She turned away and threw up. The shuddering of her own body brought her attention back to the flames and she coughed up bile as she dashed through the burning curtain. Outside, the bright, sunny world had turned to an ash-filled nightmare. Those men had set the palms on fire. She fled through them.

She stopped at the gate and gazed in horror as she realized the entire town burned. The Fires gave life. They also took it. Alone in a vast sea of destruction, she turned around and around, hugging herself and choking on tears. Everywhere, black smoke roiled into the sky, blotting out the sun.

Chapter 3

Something came toward her. Fakhira froze, staring at the shape hurtling through the haze and destruction. She saw a horse's black eyes, firelight reflected in them, and a burning, blazing swathe of steel. It bore down on her, and she knew she wouldn't have to mourn her family for long. Closing her eyes and covering her face, she waited for the cruel cut of the blade that would send her to the Fires and the Waters to be reborn.

A force slammed into her from the side, knocking her down. Her shoulder hit first and took the brunt of the fall. Opening her eyes, she saw Cyric standing over her in his uniform, smudged with soot and blood, his curved sword out and ready. His eyes glowed with rage, daring anyone to come near and try to hurt either of them.

"Are you hurt?" Cyric asked.

She sat up, unable to answer through her tears and pain. Looking past him, she saw the man on the horse pull his beast to a stop and turn it to run them down. Cold fear gripped her, even in the heat of the flames all around. "What do I do?" she choked out.

"Stay down. Keep away from the swords. Watch all around and call out if you see others coming." Cyric stalked forward, his steps precise and measured, those of an experienced swordsman.

She didn't want to watch yet couldn't look away. The horseman goaded his mount into charging. Cyric screamed a defiant challenge and ran to meet him. The horseman's blade cut a wade arc. The man who would be Fakhira's husband ducked under it and hacked at the horse's two front legs. With his mount crashing to the ground, the horseman leaped clear and tumbled.

The horseman rolled close enough for her to smell the stench of his sweat. Grasping for something to hit him with, Fakhira scrambled back, eyes wide with fear and pain forgotten in favor of survival. The man hopped to his feet and rounded on her, dark delight twisting his features into a terrifying mask. Hands still empty, she turned to crawl faster and found herself face to face with a wall of flames. Her pursuer stabbed down at her, and she managed to roll enough that he caught only the fabric of her dress, pinning her in place.

He lashed out with his hand, striking her across the face and knocking her to the ground again. Raising her hand in a feeble attempt to ward off a killing blow, she saw Cyric come and shove his sword into the man's back. Her attacker stopped, dumbstruck, and stared down at the bloody metal point sticking through his belly.

Cyric ripped the blade across, cutting him nearly in half. The horseman crumpled into a pile of things Fakhira didn't want to see. She scuttled away, only stopping when Cyric crouched in front of her, blocking her view.

"Fakhira." He gripped her arms. "Look at me, not at him. I'm here. I found you. I'll keep you safe."

She found his eyes and couldn't hold back tears. "They're all gone."

He looked down and nodded, his mouth taut. "I know." With a deep breath, he met her gaze again and showed her fierce determination. "It's not safe here yet. They wouldn't want us to let the fire claim us when we still have two feet. Let's go find someplace to rest and mourn."

Nodding, she took his hand and let him pull her to her feet. She wiped her face as he picked up his sword. They ran through the streets, finding everything burning or knocked down. Bodies lay strewn about, some already burned beyond recognition. The enemy spared no one, leaving babies and young children discarded like broken toys.

Near the edge of town, Cyric grabbed her and spun to hide them both behind battered debris. He held a finger to her lips and flicked his eyes in the direction they'd been heading. Over the crackle of flames, she heard distant shouting and screaming. Worse, she heard a nearby woman whimpering and moaning in pain, and a man grunting. Other men laughed.

How many suffered the same fate as Almiya today? She lurched against Cyric's arms, needing to stop these monsters. That woman could be saved, she knew it. Cyric should be saving her, but if he wouldn't do it, she would. She grabbed for the hilt of his sword, struggling against his arms. He clamped a hand over her mouth and pinned her arms, holding her down.

"Ssh," he whispered next to her ear. "I know it's awful, but there's

21

too many of them. We have to survive, Fakhira. We won't if you give us away."

The truth in his words cut through her rage and she collapsed against him, burying her face in his neck to keep the jackals from hearing her sobs.

"Anybody else want a turn?" The man drawled with satisfaction.

"We don't have much more time for this. The fire will reach here soon. I saw the Captain with girls tied up in a line, so there'll be plenty for everyone at camp."

"I'll take a turn."

The woman let out a fresh sob of agony. Fakhira covered her ears. Cyric covered her hands and held her close. At least the woman would be sent to the Fires when they finished with her, and she wouldn't have to live with the memory of this. Fakhira, on the other hand, would carry her cries as a wound on her heart. Her mind flashed on Almiya's body, knowing the same would happen to this woman, and she wanted to throw up again.

Cyric took his hand away an eternity later, moved her aside, and peered out. He threw himself back around the corner and gripped his sword, getting his feet under him and coiling to lurch into an attack.

"Did you see something over there?" the man asked.

With no weapon, Fakhira shoved herself back, digging herself in to hide under the rubble. She hid her face and prayed for the Fires to guide Cyric's sword. At the same time, she patted the ground, hoping to find a big rock she could lift.

"No, but I heard something."

That poor woman moaned softly, her voice fading to nothing. Boots crunched on stones and gravel, moving toward them. Despite the burning heat marching closer to her, Fakhira shivered.

More stones shifted nearby. She lifted her face to see Cyric jumping up and skewering a man with maroon on his clothes. Cyric's sword sank into the man's belly and ripped out. The dying man fell only to be replaced by two more enemy soldiers. Frantic to defend herself, Fakhira shoved her hands through the debris and found a large chunk of stone-studded earth. It held together as she hefted it and threw it at a soldier.

The soldier cringed away from the impact and snapped his head around to see where it came from. He took two steps to loom over her as a wall of swarthy muscle with a sword ready to claim her. Fakhira scrabbled back from the terrible monster and knocked a board loose. Broken pottery and cracked mud bricks rained down on her. Clawing at the rubble to free herself, she heard grunts and ripping cloth and tearing meat.

Too soon and not soon enough, the wretched noises stopped, replaced by one man panting. "They're dead," Cyric said. "The fire is close."

Fakhira wriggled to free herself. Somehow, it seemed she only dug herself in deeper and she thumped her fist against the wall at her back in frustration. Dust fell, making her cough and choke. "I'm stuck," she mewled.

He heaved a board aside and she saw his head in shadow with a halo of firelight. "Take my hand. Push as hard as you can with your feet."

She grabbed his wrist and pushed while he pulled. Something

23

scraped her thigh, searing a line of agony across it. Her leg buckled and she fell. Broken rock inches from her face and cutting into her arms, she pushed with all her strength to raise to her hands and knees. The effort proved too difficult and she sagged against the debris. "I can't," she whimpered.

Cyric swore under his breath then he tugged on her hand. "Yes you can. Only a little farther. I won't leave you behind."

Though she wanted to stay and let the fire win, she knew Almiya wouldn't want that. Father wouldn't want that either. The ache inside had to wait. She wiped her face and tried again, this time able to wobble to her feet. Ducking under Cyric's arm, she clutched at a shallow cut in his side to help him staunch the bleeding. "We're going to make it."

"Yes, we are. You're very brave, and you're doing great."

"Why did they attack?"

"I don't know. It doesn't matter. What matters is that we survived."

"No one else did." Tears blurred her vision.

"We have each other. Look, that spot's already burned out. We'll be safe there until morning." He jutted his chin at a charred, barren pile of rubble. "It even has a bit of shelter. We won't be too cold tonight."

They helped each other shamble over and settled into an intact corner. Ripping pieces of their clothes, they bound each other's wounds as best they could, and lay down together. Clutching her to his body, he murmured soothing noises. She finally dissolved into tears, weeping for everyone and everything, especially herself.

24

Chapter 4

"All of you survived. This is a blessing and none should question that." Caliph Korval stood, tall and proud, surveying the ragged group of twenty-one that included Fakhira. He wore a helm of bronze with blue stripes and a leather cuirass with a white linen shirt and pants underneath. His wide, curved sword with a scalloped golden hilt hung from his blue sash belt in a black scabbard.

This morning, Korval's men had ridden into the Oasis and put out the few fires still burning. The rest of Fakhira's family had been killed, one way or another. Father and Shahan had been cut down in the fighting. Like so many others, their bodies had been tossed into the fires. Her brothers and mother surely had perished, though she hadn't seen their corpses. Trimar's men had no reason to spare any of them, especially not an ordinary woman past childbearing age.

"Caliph Trimar's cowardly raid on our fair city will not go unpunished," Korval continued. "As we speak, riders have been dispatched to my other holdings to call my army to readiness for war. Though Aitrae Oasis may be rebuilt, such an effort will take more than a handful of women and children, and all our able-bodied men must now turn their attention to the war effort. I am sparing four men to escort you all to Kamrik, where arrangements will be made to see to your well-being. Before you leave, you will each be given one of my markers. Take care to keep it safe. When you reach Kamrik, this marker will identify you as a survivor of Aitrae Oasis. I wish you all good fortune and hope you can settle in Kamrik despite your sorrows and hardships."

He turned his back on them, striding away with his blue cloak flapping in the wind. Four of his guardsmen—one of them Cyric, favoring his left side—stepped forward, herding the small group to a wagon laden with supplies. One man barked out, "I am Captain Ekral. The smallest four children may ride in the wagon. Everyone else must walk. If we leave now, it will take us until tomorrow noon to reach Kamrik at the wagon's pace. We will take you to Korval's Palace. Should anything unexpected happen, follow our directions without fail. Wait your turn for food and water, which we must ration even for this short trip. We will tolerate no fighting."

Ekral and the other two men mounted horses. Cyric gave Fakhira a longing look, then climbed into the driver's seat of the wagon. Its enchanted wheels, recognizable by their wide, flat shape, would carry it over the desert dunes surrounding the oasis. Though she still had to limp, Fakhira picked up the smallest child and hefted her into the wagon, settling her between a barrel and a stack of blankets. Captain Ekral handed her a skin of water, then she fell into line and began the long walk with everyone else.

Others had small packs of belongings they'd rescued or looted. She had nothing but the ripped brown skirt and linen shirt she'd worn that nightmare day, still smudged with soot and blood. Trudging along with the wagon, she wondered why she didn't think to grab anything from that basket she'd hidden in. Maybe she should have let the Fires take her. She was no one special, no one worth saving, no one who would change anything in this world. Then she wouldn't have to remember Almiya's grotesque fate.

The hot sands begged her to stop and bask in them, to lie down and close her eyes and forget while the sun burned away her flesh. Sand flew everywhere as they plodded across great dunes. She tasted grit—it scratched her eyes, it ground into her thighs as they brushed together, and it grated at her joints. By the time an hour had passed, she followed the boy in front of her for no reason other than the fact he walked in front of her.

Captain Ekral called a halt as the sun drifted down to the horizon. The guardsmen passed out dried meat and dates, and refilled water skins. Fakhira sat and ate, in no more mood to chat than anyone else. She heard the four guardsmen moving around the refugees, murmuring to them. Cyric finally had a chance to be near her.

He knelt beside her, a hand brushing hair out of her face. "Can you keep going tonight?"

"Yes," she nodded, not looking away from the patch of sand she stared at.

He draped a blanket over her shoulders. "Ekral says we'll go on for another few hours, then rest. Make sure you drink all your water and eat all your food. I can't show you favor with rations or other supplies. I'm sorry for that."

27

"I understand."

He brushed his rough fingertips on her cheek. "I'll stay with you in Kamrik for as long as I can. The caliph is calling for all his guards to muster for war against Trimar. Since I still have to heal, I can delay a few days, but no more than that."

A single fat tear rolled down her cheek. She wanted to go home. She wanted to have Mother tell her everything would be fine. She wanted Father to make a joke.

Cyric tilted her chin up and kissed her forehead. "Marry me before I leave. We can start a new life. Leave the past behind."

Afraid of the prospect of being alone, she nodded again and stuffed jerky into her mouth. He patted her shoulder and left her, moving on to the next person. She pulled the blanket tighter. With her eyes closed, she imagined it to be Mother's arms, holding her tight and chasing a bad dream away with whispers of reassurance.

The sun's warmth faded away and her head drooped forward with weariness. When the night refused to cool, her family would lie outside to sleep, staring up at the myriad flecks of brilliance in the night sky. Father knew stories about them, and his deep voice would rumble in her breast as he explained why the stars moved or why that one sparkled brighter than the rest, or how they got there in the first place. The Fire Dancers never spoke on the subject, so he had no one to contradict him.

With that thought, she realized the Oasis's three Fire Dancers were not among the survivors. Had they succumbed to the Flames they served, or did they enjoy more pleasant accommodations? She could well imagine such important women spirited away by the caliph before his men went looking for any other survivors.

"Let's go," Captain Ekral called out.

Watching him swing into his saddle, Fakhira had a thought to lie down and let herself be left behind. Someone tapped her shoulder, dispelling the impulse. She stood up in response, clutching the blanket around her neck. Walking became a reason to walk and she fell into line behind the boy again. Every step followed another step because it followed another step.

"Does anyone else hear that?" The Captain's voice cut through the blank fog in her mind.

Fakhira raised her head and blinked. All the horses snorted and refused to walk in straight lines. The two pulling the wagons strained against their harnesses. In the distance, she heard a low growling sound, one that made her stomach clench.

"Halt." Captain Ekral pulled on his horse's reins, and it whinnied in protest. The other horses likewise didn't want to stop. He peered all around, and Fakhira watched him. She saw when his eyes widened. "Storm," he breathed. "A storm is coming! Everyone stop now. Men, hand out the blankets. We shelter the best we can against the wagon."

Had they all survived the enemy and fire only to die in a sandstorm? Fakhira hung her head and dropped to her knees, covering her face with both hands and letting the blanket fall from her shoulders. A strong breeze blasted sand hard enough to blow the fear of death back into her. Gusting wind picked up her blanket and snapped it out of reach. Without thinking, she jumped to her feet and chased after it.

"Leave it," Cyric called after her.

She reached out and snared a handful of cloth. Another gust slammed into her, knocking her down and filling her mouth with grit. Wrapping the blanket around her head to protect her face and keep breathing, she peered around to try to find the wagon in the darkness. Sand flew in every direction, blocking her view; she'd ventured too far and the wind had kicked up too strong. It sounded like Cyric called out again, and she struggled to crawl in that direction.

Sand buffeted her, forcing her head down. She pushed off her feet and smacked her skull into something hard. Dazed and dizzy, she lurched to the side and tumbled down a slope. When she hit the bottom, the ground cracked and gave way under her weight.

She fell.

Chapter 5

As she dropped through empty air in total darkness, she knew her death waited at the bottom. Her back hit the water first, a solid slap that knocked the air out of her. She plunged into a pool of frigid water, too stunned by the impact to react. The water pressed on her body, shocking her alert, and she flailed. Scrabbling at her face, she tore the blanket away only to feel something grab her hair. Unseen hands wrenched her mouth open and shoved water down her throat. Coughing and choking and drowning, she kept thrashing.

Blue light flared in front of her face and she reached for it, hoping it would show her the way out. Instead, her hand wrapped around something hard and cold. The light filled her vision and her mind. She heard whispers. Straining to hear the words, she failed to notice when her lungs stopped burning and she started breathing the water.

The words refused to become clear, but the light in her mind resolved into a vision. She saw a man standing on the crest of a sand dune, looking down at a bustling city straddling a river. Wrapped in clothes the color of sand, he gripped a strange silver sword with a blue stone set into the pommel. A blue scarf covered his face, the fringed end flapping in a breeze. Other men, their faces also shrouded, stood waiting for his orders.

Using the sword, the leader pointed toward the city. Though his voice came out garbled, she understood. In that city, they would find the object of his hate and kill that odious, despicable man. The other men made comments and asked questions, their words also too distorted to understand. Their leader had answers and a plan.

The light flashed and everything went black. Something pushed on her back until she broke the surface and sputtered, sucking in air and coughing up water. In the darkness, she had no idea where to go. Buoyed by the certainty that she would find her way, she picked a direction and kicked toward it. Never having learned to swim, she bobbed underwater and pushed off the bottom several times until she could walk with her head above the surface. It grew shallower and shallower until she fell to her knees and crawled out of the pool. Soaked and exhausted, she collapsed onto flat rocks at the water's edge.

She woke with water lapping at her knees and something warm in her hand. Both sensations filled her with peace. Breathing deeply, she opened her eyes and saw only darkness again. Whispering voices echoed in the cavern.

"Cyric?"

No answer came. She groped the thing in her hand, trying to understand what it could be. The long cylinder felt like solid metal. One end seemed to be heavy, as if it extended into the distance. Her imagination supplied the idea of a pole she might use as a walking stick.

"Is someone there?" She waited while her question echoed across what must be a large space. It mingled with the whispers as it faded. "I can hear you. I fell in by accident. If you show me the way out, I'll leave you be."

The whispers gained volume and she once again strained to understand them. One became clear.

"Al-Kabar."

She'd never heard such a word before. It sounded like a title for an important man who deserved respect. Had she fallen into this man's hall without knowing? "My apologies, Al-Kabar. Please, which way is out?"

The voices laughed at her.

Clutching the thing in her hand, she pushed herself to her feet. Whoever this Al-Kabar might be, she had no intention of kissing his feet. "I didn't ask to come here! If you mean to make me your prisoner, then I'll fight you to get free." Hoping the object she held could be used as a weapon, she brandished it.

The laughing cut off abruptly. "You would fight for your freedom?"

Something about the way it asked made her think it weighed and judged her. "I did not survive the destruction of my home and a sandstorm only to be caged by a coward who refuses to show his face."

"Would you do the same for another?"

Fakhira gulped and thought of that woman on the other side of the wall. She and Cyric hid rather than face them. Had she been able to fight by his side, would she have demanded they rescue that woman? "Yes. If I had the power, I would save them all."

Air swirled around her, tousling her hair and ruffling her clothes. It brushed her cheeks and neck, reminding her of Cyric's touch. The breeze rushed to her hand and enveloped it. A pale blue glow pulsed in time with her heartbeat, letting her see her hand. With a start, she realized the breeze had been water, not air. A long arm of water reached out from the pool to hold her hand.

"I don't understand."

"Go forth and fight for freedom, Al-Kabar."

The water fell to the rocky ground, yet her hand continued to glow. She held it up and saw that the object in her other hand was a sword. The simple silver handle had no guard and the blade stuck out straight. A flange ran up the center on both sides, and the line of the edge curved in, then out, then in again to the tip. In the pommel, jagged silver lines ran across a familiar blue stone.

She stared at the sword and blinked in confusion. "*I'm* Al-Kabar?"

"The Waters bless you."

The simple statement took her breath away. The Fires had their Dancers. She'd never heard of anyone wielding power for the Waters before. Everyone invoked the Fires for fortune and blessings, not the Waters. She didn't know why, other than tradition. More than that, she had no idea why the Waters would choose *her* to fight for anything.

Fakhira held her glowing hand out to shine the dim light ahead. It swept over glistening rock and revealed a dark shadow in the wall. "Al-

Kabar," she said, rolling the word around in her mouth to get the feel of it. She also thought about that word, "freedom." Caliph Trimar brought war to her home and her family, and she had no doubt the reason would turn out to be nothing more than an excuse. Caliph Korval came too late to prevent the slaughter. He now raised his army to get revenge. More people would die like hers had, this time in the name of retribution. Both men needed to be stopped before they drowned the sands with blood.

Caliph Korval would never listen to her, and Trimar would probably throw her to his men for sport. She needed a way to stop them indirectly. If she joined Korval's army, she could stop him with false scouting reports or changed maps and other sabotage. But women didn't fight. Women tended the family and the hearth. Men made war and kept peace. To join Korval's army, she had to be a man.

Her new title sounded like a man's name. Looking down at her body, she thought she could bind her breasts and wear loose clothes to complete the fiction. Like the man in that dream earlier, she could... That dream must have been the Waters showing her what to do. The sword now gripped in her hand was the same.

Fakhira squared her shoulders. Never mind why the Waters chose her. She would remake herself as a man and collect men to follow her. "I accept this challenge. The people of the desert will be set free by my hand, or I will die trying to make it so." Her death would be no great loss. Cyric would mourn and move on, and she had no one else to care about. If she could keep another family from such a fate, she would.

Striding forward, she found that the dark place in the wall hid a tunnel with a tiny stream trickling down the center. She plunged into it, eager to leave her losses and pain behind. Trimar would pay for what his men did. He would pay with coin. Then he would pay with blood. She would be Al-Kabar, the champion of the Waters, and nothing would stand in her way.

The tunnel narrowed, forcing her to walk hunched over. With every other step, the sword flashed in the light, and she wondered where men used such weapons. Men of the desert used curved blades, not straight ones. Less strange, it lacked a scabbard. Father had never used one, and neither did Shahan. She recalled finding one for Father's blade in a basket of old things. When she presented it to him, he refused it, explaining with pride that only a novice needed such a thing, to keep from cutting his own leg off. As a novice herself, she hoped to somehow find or fashion a scabbard. Until then, she would exercise caution and hold it away from her body.

She continued, light held out and sword held aside. After some time, a hissing echoed to her. She came upon a writhing pile of sand-colored cloth. It froze as her light advanced, then she heard more hissing. To her surprise, the cloth reared up, alive of its own accord. Before her eyes, it filled with water until it formed the shape of a man in the shirt and pants she'd seen in the dream. This man had no head, hands, or feet, and she stared at it, unsure how to kill it without damaging the clothes.

Heedless of her concerns, the sleeve lashed out. Water slapped her across the face, snapping her head to the side and forcing her to take a step back. Her light flickered and shrank until she could barely see the cloth man as he turned the first strike into another with the second sleeve. She felt a blow to her belly and curled up to protect herself.

"No, child, do not cower." The voice of the Waters flowed up from beneath her. "Learn. See how it moves and evade."

This foe had been sent to teach her to use the blade. She straightened as much as the tunnel allowed and watched the cloth man. Its sleeves lashed out at her, pushing her back step by step, leaving bruises the size of dates. Yet, she suffered no true harm. This creature had no power to kill her. Watching its sleeves and pants legs, she noticed it shifted this way before a thrust from the left, that way for a right sleeve. When its leg lashed out to kick her, it moved just so.

By the time she took her first try at ducking away from its strikes, she ached from head to toe. Her dodge went astray and she took the full force of its punch. It knocked her against the wall, and she shook her head to clear it. The cloth man let her take a moment to gather her wits, then it lunged again. This time, she hopped out of the sleeve's arc and flung an arm back to try delivering her own blow.

The cloth man paused as its arm collapsed from her slash, having to take the time to re-inflate it. Bolstered by this small success, she waited for it to swat at her again and leaned out of the way, sweeping her leg to kick its knee. It dropped down, no longer able to use that knee for support. Again, she waited for it to recover and attempt to hit her before throwing her fist at its center. The water on her hand shot out in a forceful stream, throwing the cloth man away from her.

Fakhira gasped and pulled her hand back. More water streamed up her body from the trickle on the floor, bringing more blue light with it. As the cloth man ran to re-engage her, she set her jaw and thrust the heel of her palm into its chest. It recoiled from the impact. Following with an upward slash of her sword, she watched it deflate, the water returning to the stream. She panted and stared down at the cloth, her mind already replaying the fight to glean everything she could from it.

She slid down to sit beside the puddle of cloth, leaning the sword against the wall beside her and watching the water swirl over her hand. "Al-Kabar will be a name to make Trimar tremble and hide." The words echoed down the tunnel. Her voice, she realized, would give her away as a girl. For the next several minutes, she played with the pitch and tone, finding something she could use without hurting her throat. Many other things occurred to her as potentially giving her away. She would need to relieve herself, and couldn't do it in sight of others. Cleaning her body would be difficult. Her monthly courses would need to be managed. She would never be able to go shirtless like men often did when the sun beat down. Any injury could reveal her.

"This may be a mistake."

"No, you will succeed. The road will be difficult, your path will be one of pain, but you will not fail unless you refuse to try."

She rubbed her face and sighed. "There is no other choice," she told herself. "I must do this. For my family." Picking up the clothes, yellow-brown like the sand, she undressed and took a deep breath. The cloth of her skirt would work well to wrap around her chest. Balancing the sword between her knees, she dragged the coarse fabric across it, cutting it into six wide strips. Never again would she show herself as a woman, not until Trimar lay broken or dead.

It took several tries before she managed to wrap the strips so they did their job and refused to fall when she twisted. When she stood again, dressed as a man, she looked herself over and wished someone could tell her if she'd done a good enough job. She gripped the sword, resolved to do this, and continued up the tunnel.

Only a short time later, her foot caught on something softer than stone. The unknown cloth swiped at her ankles, knocking her to the ground and sending her sword clattering away into the darkness. She yelped at a sharp sting on the bottom of her foot, curling up and holding out her hand to shine light that way.

Heavy blue cloth covered in a thin layer of water glimmered in her light, the strip rearing like a charmed cobra. Another teacher had come for her. She scrambled to her feet and watched, waiting to see what it would do. The end slammed down onto her foot, forcing a howl out of her. When it raised to attack her again, she used the lessons her clothes had taught her and tried to move her foot out of the way.

Again and again, the cloth snapped at her toes, forcing her to shift back and forth, to balance on the balls of her feet, and to find the rhythm of a strange dance. When she went ten strikes in a row without being touched, she noticed the way her body moved seemed to make it easier to swing her arms and backed away from the cloth to pick up the sword. Without its interference, she combined what she'd learned so far.

The cloth strip slid across the tunnel floor to her and she knew it judged the lesson learned. She marveled at it spiraling up her leg to encircle her waist. There, it cinched and tied itself, and she found the knot perfect to hold her sword. The water animating it fell to the ground with a tiny splash and joined the stream.

Only a few more paces up the tunnel, she found another long cloth strip, this one in sand yellow. Instead of attack her, it lay in a heap. Wary of a trick, she nudged it with the tip of her sword. When nothing happened, she squatted and crept closer, keeping the blade ready. She poked the coarse cloth and waited, then picked it up and ran it between her thumb and fingers. The fabric reminded her of her father's head wrapping.

She remembered him coiling it around his temples and forehead, telling her men did that to protect their scalp from the sun and keep cool. At night, it kept their head warm. Some men stored small skins of water inside for emergencies. Women, on the other hand, showed their hair to be able to dance wild and free whenever they wanted. The memory made her crumple to the ground, holding the cloth to her face.

"I want him back," she whispered through her pain. "I want them all back."

"Hold their memories close," the echoing voice said, "and avenge them."

Nodding, Fakhira wiped away her tears with the wrapping and sniffled. "They deserve justice." Her voice quavered, so she cleared her throat and said it again, this time firm and strong. "I'll be the one who delivers it for them." She took a deep breath and held up the wrapping then gasped as cool water flowed up her body to take the cloth slithering across her arms.

Standing, she felt it slide over her shoulders and watched it coil around both her arms. With the sword in hand, the wrapping twisted and pulled to move her. Grasping that it meant her no harm, she yielded. As it moved her arms, slashing the sword through the air and keeping her counter-balanced, she fell into using the lessons she'd already learned, combining all the movements until she thought she understood how to fight.

When she began to stumble, it let her go to catch her breath. She sat leaned against the wall, thinking about those men who murdered her sister. Never in her life had she genuinely wanted to hurt someone. The path to finding them would be long and hard and she would walk it, no matter how long it took. She gathered her hair and used the wrapping to hide it, determined to see this disguise through. In the dream, she had only two other things: boots and a scarf to cover her face. She hoped meeting them would be less exhausting, but would never find out if she stayed still.

Hauling herself to her feet, she groaned at her aching muscles, then she pushed herself to jog as far as she could. When she paused to catch her breath again, she noticed movement out of the corner of her eye and turned to see the water gathering in the shadows. She gulped and stepped toward it warily. The water echoed the light on her hand, revealing the blue scarf she'd been expecting to find in the center.

The water made no move toward her, it only built in mass until a wall blocked forward progress. Surface rippling and sparkling with bright blue light, it remained stationary while she watched. As she had with the head wrapping, she crept close and touched it with the tip of her sword.

41

The blade sliced through without effort. When she pulled the sword out, the water sealed the gash she'd created. She then reached out and poked it.

Pleasant and cool, the water covered her fingertip. Able to pull it back out, she decided it meant to teach her something without attacking and pressed her palm to the wall. The water engulfed her hand and flowed up her arm until it reached her shoulder. It soaked her sleeve and drenched her skin. She thought about slogging through the rest of the tunnel while soaking wet, an exhausting prospect.

To her surprise, the water pulled away from her arm and sleeve, leaving both dry. At the same time, she felt a press on her mind, proving her own thoughts had made the water behave this way. She experimented with wanting the water to recede and advance. It obeyed her wishes. The water swirled and splashed to the beat of her demands.

This effort left her buoyed. Though she still craved rest, her newfound power offered a glimmer of true belief in her ability to walk the path she'd chosen and been chosen for. Releasing the water, she squared her shoulders and continued on her way.

Chapter 6

Finally, the tunnel ended in a shaft extending upward. Several feet above her head, the light dancing on her hand showed a mass of rocks blocking the only way out. Water dripped from the center, and she thought a single jab with her sword ought to open it up.

With her arm fully extended, the tip of her sword missed the lowest rock by less than an inch. She jumped, hoping to gain the distance that way, but found she couldn't thrust hard enough to cause any effect. Since she would have to find a way to climb out regardless, she resigned herself to being pelted with rocks from above and braced her bruised and battered back against one side of the shaft. Using her arms and legs on the other side, she scraped her way up, inch by agonizingly slow inch.

By the time her head hit the rocks, she felt an hour or more must surely have passed. Held in place by her legs, she gripped her sword and punched upward. The rocks shifted and tumbled down, striking her bent knees and ankles and shoulders. In the tumble, a gush of water made the tunnel slick. She lost her grip and fell, hitting the curve and sliding several feet with the stones. Her first instinct had her squealing in pain. After a few seconds of that, she forced herself to grunt in a lower register.

Scraped and aching, trembling from head to toe from the effort, she returned to the shaft—now bathed in sunlight—and set her back against one side again. Nothing would stop her but herself, and she refused to do that. Each inch upward in the heat took longer than it had before. At the top, she heaved herself to the side and lay panting in thick mud for several minutes.

At the point when she convinced herself to get up, she discovered she'd come up in a small pond. Without the rocks there, it would never be a pond again. She could only hope nothing relied on this water source that couldn't find more elsewhere. The thought of replacing the rocks flitted into her head, but she didn't have the strength or skill to make a new dam, and couldn't see enough stones to attempt it anyway.

Shrubs surrounded the pond, and small huts lay beyond them. Seeing that people lived around this spot, she heaved herself to her feet. They would notice soon, and if she still lay there, they would blame her. If that pond had served as their primary water source, the repercussions would be swift and harsh. As she scurried away, she tripped over a pair of well-worn boots. Though it seemed wrong to take them, she couldn't go on barefoot. She grabbed them and stuck her feet inside to find they fit.

Emerging from the tiny oasis, she found the dusty fringe of a city. Though she had no way to be sure, she suspected it must be Kamrik, as it had been the closest city when she fell into the Waters. If that turned out to be true, she could find the caliph's palace here and present herself as a refugee to get supplies. Then again, if she claimed her refugee status, there would be questions about why she hadn't joined up with the army already. Such questions would have no answers.

Pulling the caliph's marker out of her pocket, she held it between a finger and thumb and stared at it. Fakhira could use it. Al-Kabar couldn't. She'd already made her choice and knew she couldn't use it. If she kept it, the coin might be found in her things. If she discarded it, someone would gain a favor meant for her. Though she couldn't use it, this struck her as fundamentally unfair. The caliph granted this boon as the only reparation he could offer for the loss of everything but her life.

Not sure what to do with it, she tucked it back into her pocket. Such a decision could be made later. Now she needed to figure out where to go to sign up to fight Trimar. As she walked through the dingy alleys of the outskirts with buildings leaning haphazardly against each other, she checked signs and found one proclaiming its shop had the "best spice deals in Kamrik." She wondered if the seasonings found inside could cover the stench of offal and rotting meat in the narrow streets.

Seeing a stooped figure in rags scuttling away from her, Fakhira remembered she had to play the part of a man now. Lifting her head, she did her best to affect a swagger. Shahan had a good strut, one that spoke of confidence and certainty. Though she had little of the first, she thought she could muster enough of the second.

As she walked, other people reacted to her by either skirting around her or offering polite, respectful nods that she returned out of habit. Some gave her odd, sidelong glances, which bothered her until she remembered the mud. Most of it had come off with a little effort. The rest still stained her sand-colored clothes. They could be put off by the mess, or they could merely be intrigued by the foreign shape of her sword.

The important buildings in Aitrae Oasis had all been in the center, and she assumed it must be the same here. She struck for the city center, using the sun as her guide. Kamrik, however, would not be so easily conquered. It swallowed her up, confusing her with its zigzag streets and unexpected dead ends. Turned around and utterly lost, she wandered from place to place, finding herself on the same street lined with brothels and taverns for a third time.

"I think we got someone looking for trouble here." A large, burly man stepped into her path.

She glanced to the side and found two more men watching her. Her first thought told her to duck her head, back up, and seek safety through one of the doors. That's what Fakhira would do. Her eyes did drop to the ground, then she clenched a fist and put the other hand on the hilt of her sword. "No, that's not what I'm looking for."

"No? I've seen you walking through here this afternoon, your face covered up. You got something to hide?"

Fakhira stifled a gulp and shook her head. "Not used to the smell."

The leader chuckled, deep and dark enough to remind her of Trimar's men. "Boys, we got a foreigner here. He doesn't think much of our city."

Behind her, the other two closed in. One cracked his knuckles. The other produced a thick stick and patted his hand with it.

She didn't know what to say or do. The Waters hadn't taught her anything about fighting three men at once, and she suspected using her sword on these men would get her into serious trouble. It might even land her in jail, which would foil her plan to join the army. Hoping to ward them off by escalating the situation, she pulled the sword out of her belt. "I have no interest in fighting you."

The leader's eyes narrowed and he took half a step back. His arms spread in preparation to fight her, not in conciliation. "That'll make this a lot easier."

The one with the stick swiped it at her. She ducked into the knee of the leader. The third man drove his elbow down into her side. They moved in concert, used to fighting together, and she couldn't watch them all at once. Her wraps offered one small blessing by lessening the blows somewhat. It mattered little, as the leader stepped on the back of her leg, forcing her down to one knee. The stick went up to come down on her head. In a stroke of what felt like luck, she raised her sword in time to catch it.

Throwing herself back against the nearby wall, she squawked in surprise when she fell through the cleft that hadn't looked big enough to swallow a person. It dropped her down into a small, dark room, where she landed on packed earth with a groan. Above her, she heard the men grunt in irritation, kick and whack the wall, then stop.

Not sure if she'd had a stroke of luck or fallen into a worse place, she took a deep breath and summoned light to her hand. This small amount of water could be carried with her, she suddenly knew, but if she wanted to use more, she needed a source to draw it from. Perhaps this explained why the Waters rarely had a champion. Few would be pleased to have these magical powers with such a harsh limitation.

The blue light showed her filth. Muck and rags had been packed into the corners of the small chamber, everywhere except in one corner. A jagged rip in the wall showed her another chamber beyond it.

"Who's there?" The male voice sounded older than a child, but still fearful and timid. "The curse of a thousand ants in your nose if you try to hurt me!"

Ignoring the new bruises on her side, Fakhira crept to the hole. "If you don't hurt me, I won't hurt you." In the next hollowed out space, she found a nest. Cloth rags and stained rugs covered the floor, deep enough to be at least as comfortable as her old sleeping mat.

Dark eyes squinted at her from the middle, suspicious and fearful. "What do you want?" Holding the blanket tight to his neck as if it could protect him, he stared at the light on her hand.

"Nothing. I fell by accident from above." She stayed at the hole, hoping that would help him relax. "Three men tried to hurt me for being lost."

His eyes rolled. "Darius and his thugs. They'd beat an old woman for making too much noise while shuffling to buy her dinner."

The image he inspired in her head made her sneer behind her scarf. "They sound charming."

"The neighborhood would be better off without them, but someone else would take their place if they left." He shrugged and sat up, letting the blanket fall. Something squeaked by his hip and he picked up a brown rat. The rodent went to his shoulder, where it brushed its whiskers on his cheek, which he seemed to like. Seeing more of him, and especially noting how little beard he had, she guessed him to be near her own age of eighteen years, but thin and worn.

Fakhira recoiled, knowing rats only as thieves who took her family's food and bit babies and small children. "Why do you have that?"

"Brumble? She's my little sister." He petted the rat, treating it like a cherished pet. Then he put his hand over the rat's ears. "Not really. Neither of us is a shapeshifter, but she's like enough to a sister I call her that. Don't tell her."

Madness had taken him. His parents must have turned him out when he lost his mind. "Ah. Is there another way out? I don't mean to trouble you. Just point me, and I'll leave you be."

"Oh, you have a sword!" He hopped to a crouch on his feet, wrapped in rags like the rest of him. "Are you good with it?"

If she had any hope of escaping this hole, she needed to humor him. Otherwise, she'd have to find a way to climb out that hole, and had no idea if Darius and his thugs waited nearby. "I'm still learning." The words came out and she wanted to grab them and pull them back in. How foolish, to tell him such a thing!

"Oh. You probably couldn't defend the neighborhood, then."

"I didn't come here for that."

"No?" He sat back on his behind with a disappointed sigh. "That's a shame. We really could use a defender. What did you come here for?"

"Korval is raising an army to fight Caliph Trimar. I wish to join it."

49

He laughed. "Girls can't join the army."

"What?" She couldn't imagine how he saw through her disguise, and blinked at him. "But...how...?"

"Your hands. Also, there's nothing between your legs."

She sat with a groan, despair pouring over her in an icy rain. Dropping her sword, she pulled the scarf from her face and covered it with both hands. "Then all is lost."

"All?" The rat squeaked, then the boy tapped her arm. "Everything can't be tied up in joining an army to go die for a man who owns you."

"What else do I have?" Raising her face, she saw he'd leaned forward to offer her a piece of cheese from a larger wedge. The rat already nibbled on a piece held in her front paws.

"You're alive. That's something. That's always something. What's your name? I'm Tahjis the Rat."

His simplicity made her take the cheese and bite a corner off it. Pungent and strong, it pushed away the stench of the area. "Al-Kabar."

He took a bite of the cheese and raised his brow at her. "If you say so. That sounds like a man's name to me."

"It is. I have to be a man to join the army."

Tahjis shrugged. "Is it so important to pretend to something you're not to get yourself killed?"

"I won't be killed until I avenge my family and bring justice. After that, it won't matter anymore." She took another bite and chewed it slowly. The first hit her belly, which had been empty for almost an entire day now. Something lighter would have been better.

"Ah." He took his own bite of cheese and stuffed it in a pocket or the rags, or someplace else she couldn't see. They sat with the sound of chewing filling the space. "You need to be a man, then. If you help me, I'll help you."

Given his obvious madness, she thought this might be a bad idea, yet she asked anyway. "What do you need help with?"

"Not Darius—that's a waste of time." He dug around in the cloth until he found a skin and let Brumble lick the mouth until she got her fill. "My sister is a prisoner of Black Abhar. He runs loan scams, protection rackets, brothels, and that sort of thing. Our father borrowed money from him and died with debt. Black Abhar took our mother and Santrice, along with most everything we owned, and still claims the debt is unpaid.

"I don't believe him, but he has ledgers. Mother died soon after she was taken, Fires watch her soul. But Santrice is strong, and he makes her work in one of his brothels to pay him back. I steal as much as I can to speed it up. That's why we live down here. I won't waste money I don't have to for an apartment when I can sleep down here."

The story struck a chord with Fakhira. He wanted revenge and justice, just as she did. "I'll help you as much as I can. I'm not sure how long the caliph will be recruiting, though."

"Bah." Tahjis dismissed the problem with a wave of his hand. "Something like that always needs people to volunteer to go get themselves killed. No number is ever enough, no time is ever long enough. I'll send Brumble to see if she can find out how long until the caliph's army moves out, and we'll get to work."

51

The rat on his shoulder squeaked.

"Yes, and be quick. We need to know as soon as possible." Rising as tall as the chamber allowed, about four feet, he stepped past her and tossed the rat up at the hole in the wall Fakhira had fallen through.

She leaned aside to let him past, uncertain about this deal. "You can...understand her?"

"It's crazy, yes?" He returned to his nest and patted the space beside him. "Come here, let's fix your costume."

She gulped, not knowing if he would try to fondle or otherwise molest her. Gripping her sword, she found the hilt cool, and felt the Waters approve of this. It gave her the courage to cross into his sleeping space and sit beside him. If he tried anything she didn't like, she could always chop his hand off. She sank into the cloth, finding it surprisingly squishy and comfortable.

"Your breasts are fine. I didn't notice them until I knew to look. Which I knew because you need something between your legs." Leaning over, he peered at the spot.

His pointed scrutiny made her blush. "Like what?"

"Hm." His attention turned to the floor, which he rooted around in. "You need something more like..." He pulled his hand up with a rock, gave it a dirty look, then tossed it into the other chamber. After that, he produced an old sock and stuffed it full of rags.

When he offered it to her, she felt her cheeks burn fiercely. "Um, what do you think...how should I...?"

"You know, if you keep blushing like that, you'll give yourself away

52

no matter what kind of disguise you put on." He fished around in the rags more and produced a strip long enough to be tied around her waist.

Her blush deepened. "I've never— My sister has a baby, and I sleep in the same room as my parents, but I always just turn my back and ignore them." Her face fell. "Had. Almiya *had* a baby. They're all dead now."

"Fires watch their souls," Tahjis murmured. He shook his head. "You're alive. Let's focus on that so you can go die in the army after we rescue Santrice. Would you rather chance that blushing gives you away, or see one for real right now?"

She stared at him, the offer strange and unexpected. "Um."

He chuckled at her. "We'll worry about that later. Who knows what you'll see or do before we're done here. Pull your pants down, and let's get this tied on."

Now convinced he would do nothing untoward to her, she did what he said. To stop herself from flinching at his touch, she held her breath.

When he sat back and examined his handiwork, he shrugged. "Your belt should hide the tie well enough. Try to forget it's there as you move around. Get used to it."

Pulling her pants back up, she had no idea how she would get used to having a stuffed sock tied to her hips. Still, she'd gotten used to stranger things, like sleeping through the squalling of a hungry baby. "What do you think we need to do to free Santrice?"

He shrugged. "Kill Black Abhar, or kill enough of his lackeys to take away his power."

Fakhira sat and blinked several times, staring at the wall. If she wanted justice for her family, she had to get justice for his. "I've never killed anyone before."

"Me neither. I've seen a lot of corpses, though. Once the Waters take their soul, there's nothing but a bag of meat left behind. It bloats and stinks and attracts flies, just like any other kind of dead thing."

She sighed and finished for him. "The Fires cleanse the soul and send it back to be shaped by life again."

"We're just going to take a bad man and give him another chance to try to be good."

"What's the point of living, then?" Before the attack, she never thought to ask.

"To make people happy. To change things so your next life is better." His answer came automatically, without thought. "This isn't important. Since you're still practicing with your sword and manhood, we won't be able to kick Abhar's door down and slit his throat. We'll have to think of a more clever plan than that. Something he wouldn't expect that'll let us ignore his usual defenses."

Since she had nothing to add, she stayed quiet, leaned against the wall, and listened to him. All her aches and bruises throbbed, growing worse as she relaxed. In the absence of danger, the efforts of the day caught up with her, sending her head drooping to his shoulder and pulling her eyes shut.

Chapter 7

"Al-Kabar," someone hissed. Her shoulders shook. She snapped her eyes open in dim light to find Tahjis's face inches from hers, the brown rat sitting on his shoulder.

"Good. Wake up. Brumble says we have three more days before the army moves out." He sat back on his heels, watching her rub her eyes and struggle to sit up. "I have an idea about how to get to Abhar. It's complicated, but I think it'll work. We'll have to ask someone else for help. She won't listen to me, but she respects a man with a sword."

Her body demanded she stay still. She told it to shut up. "What?"

"The Scorpion will help us if you can prove yourself a worthy ally. We should be able to do this in three days."

"Who's this Scorpion?"

Tahjis offered her a thick piece of bread torn from a larger loaf. "Well, she's kind of like Black Abhar, actually. Except the city would be a better place with her running the underbelly. She's willing to bargain and keeps debts honestly. She also doesn't treat people like cattle. So things would be better. She can't take over because Abhar has too much muscle and power. If we tell her our goal, she'll most likely offer what help she can. Except we'll have to prove we mean business first."

Sitting up against the wall, Fakhira closed her eyes and worried about the mess she'd gotten herself into. A simple quest to join the army had become something much more complex. The Waters set her on this path, though, and she felt certain she'd fallen into Tahjis's bolt hole for a reason. "What should we do?" She took the bread and nibbled off a small bite, finding the thought of food repulsive but knowing she had to eat anyway.

"We'll go see her. Let me do all the talking and agree with whatever I say. Come on." He beckoned for her to follow him out through the crack in the wall.

It took effort to haul herself up with screaming muscles, and she panted when she rolled onto the ground outside. Looking back at the cleft, she had no idea how she'd fit through such a small opening.

Tahjis grabbed her arm and tugged her to her feet. "Never show weakness. Get up, shake it off, keep going."

She pulled her hand back before she touched the wall to use it for support. "Never?"

"No." He smacked her hand. "When you pull back, don't bring your hand so close. Let it fall to your side or cross your arms."

She dropped her hand to her side and took a deep breath. "This is going to be harder than I thought."

"Don't think about how small you are. You're the biggest, baddest man ever. No one can beat you, no one can put you down. You're the king of your hill. Head up, eyes forward, walk like you own the street and you'll fight to defend it." Despite his words, Tahjis seemed to cower away from everyone and everything, including her.

Squaring her shoulders, she scanned the street and thought about the idea of every spot she placed a foot on being somehow hers. No one could take her space away from her. She belonged here, and nothing would change that. Her gait took on a swagger, with her head high and her arms out and ready to hurt anyone who came close.

Like yesterday, people gave her polite nods of respect. Unlike yesterday, she got no odd, sidelong glances. The mud had dried and caked off, leaving the normal stains of life. With the scarf covering her face and the sword at her hip, no one had reason to question her scruffy, disheveled appearance. Tahjis led her along, giving the impression of a boy showing his master the way to a new place.

They arrived at a tavern, closed for the morning. Tahjis pushed the door open and she followed him. The place smelled of nutmeg. All the chairs had been stacked on the round tables, and a young girl in plain, drab clothes used a small broom with stiff bristles to scrape the floor clean. Though she couldn't have more than seven or eight years on her, the girl planted a fist on her hip and gave them a stern glare.

"We're closed. Go away." The corner of Fakhira's mouth twitched at the girl's slight lisp, caused by her missing front teeth.

Tahjis hunched his shoulders. "We want to see the Scorpion."

The girl huffed. "Come back later."

"It's important," he pleaded. "Time matters. Can't wait."

"Oh, fine." The girl returned to her scrubbing with a roll of her eyes. "Don't blame me if they throw you out on your ear." She jerked a thumb at the back door.

"Thank you, miss." Tahjis dipped his head in a bow to the girl then nodded to Fakhira and led her to the back. He pushed the door open and they walked into a kitchen with the hearth fire banked and everything clean and put away. Selecting the farther of two doors in the side wall, he revealed a small office. The desk had papers strewn across it, and the shelves held stacks of ledgers and ink. The spindly man in the chair behind the large wood desk yanked his head up and blinked rapidly.

"Who? What? Yes, I'm awake!" He peered at them and frowned through bushy black eyebrows. "Who are you?"

"Nobody." Tahjis looked down and scuffed his foot wraps on the floor. "We want to see Scorpion. Let us through."

Fakhira didn't see another door, so she didn't understand. Despite that, she focused on Tahjis's instructions, confidently looming as much as her small frame allowed.

"Oh, I see." He leaned back in his chair and folded his hands over his nonexistent belly. "Do you have the toll?"

Tahjis rolled his eyes and slunk to the edge of the desk, setting his shoulder to the base. Brumble walked onto the desk and squeaked. "There's no toll," he told her. He shoved with all his might, and managed to barely shift the heavy piece of furniture with a groaning scrape. "Well? Help already."

The man sighed and waved to make the rat move. "It's always worth a try." He reached under the desk and shoved something upward, causing a click noise.

Tahjis slid the desk aside, the effort made easier by whatever the man did. In the space now revealed, he yanked on a trapdoor. He scooped up Brumble and hopped in. Fakhira followed him down a ladder. As soon as her head cleared the floor, the trapdoor thumped down, cutting off the light.

"How will we leave?" In the darkness, she felt compelled to whisper.

"That's not the only way in and out. Stay quiet." It seemed they climbed down for a long time, then Tahjis's hands on her waist helped her find the floor. He held her close from behind, and his breath warmed her ear. "From here on is real danger. Scorpion is no fool, and takes care with her security. Don't make eye contact with anyone, and don't get into anyone's personal space. This is someone else's domain, and you need to walk like you understand that. You're a man who is not to be trifled with, but you respect Scorpion and are not here to challenge her. You're here to ask her for help. I'll do the talking. Agree with me if you're asked. Understand?"

"Yes."

He took a step away and she heard him pat the wall, then knock three times.

Light poured in when a door opened. A large, beefy man stared down at them, holding a curved blade and wearing stiff leather armor.

"Hand over your weapons."

Tahjis pulled a slim dagger from somewhere and offered it, hilt first. Fakhira gulped and held her sword out, the blade balanced on her palms.

"What kind of sword is this?" He grasped the hilt and picked it up, then his lip curled in disdain. "Feh, it's too light. All looks and no brains for the both of you." He got no answer, as Fakhira had none. "You'll get them back when you leave. Now, why should Scorpion see you?"

Tahjis nodded and clapped his hands together. "We come with a business proposition, about Black Abhar. We want to help her kill him."

The man laughed, hearty and full. He took a step back and waved them in. "Two boys with a rat and a piece of pot metal are going to kill Black Abhar!" Behind him, other men joined in his laughter. "Scorpion will always see jesters to brighten her day."

Fakhira and Tahjis stepped into the lamp-lit rock chamber, finding five other men sitting on cushions, playing cards for money with swords near at hand. Their escort, still chuckling, beckoned and led them through a curtain, up a tunnel, and to a door. He rapped it twice, then opened it and stood aside for the pair to enter.

Tahjis scurried in and Fakhira strode in. Despite not having much skill with her sword, she felt exposed without it and had to think more about following Tahjis's instructions. She echoed his gesture of getting down on his knees on the thick rug covering most of a rock floor that matched her clothes. The rug's tiny floral pattern used a deep, rich red and a bright, bold blue, both of which Fakhira knew to be made with expensive, foreign dyes.

The person they offered this fealty to lounged on a wide, velvet chaise of bright, spotless white. Loose satin pants of baby blue with golden cuffs at the ankles covered long, athletic legs. A matching brassiere covered her full breasts, leaving her flat, toned stomach bare. She lay with her head propped on a hand, a thin sleeve of gauze covering the arm braced against a velvet cushion. A dark, gold speckled veil shrouded her face and hair.

Two men, each well-muscled and wearing only a beige loincloth, sat on the floor in front of her. Two knives and a sword lay arrayed on the floor in front of them in easy reach.

Fakhira stared at the woman, wondering why such a desert flower kept herself hidden away and had to resort to criminal enterprises when she could easily command men for legal pursuits. Working through a husband and with enough sharpness to earn her 'Scorpion' for a nickname, she could have anything she wanted.

"A thousand pardons for the interruption, Scorpion. " Tahjis bowed his head and clasped his hands together. "I am Tahjis the Rat. You may have heard of me. Or not. This is my friend, Al-Kabar. I hope for him to become my brother. You see, I have a sister who was taken by Black Abhar and put to work to pay off debts of our dead father. Al-Kabar has met her and fallen in love with her, and would storm the place to take her, were it not for the fact this would get him killed as surely as the sun rises. We seek your assistance to free her.

"In exchange for whatever help you choose to provide, we offer our own services, as a thief and a swordsman. Our ultimate goal is to kill Black

Abhar, because he will not allow us to finish repaying the debt, no matter how much we give him. Al-Kabar and I will pursue this no matter what you say, but we hope that in combining our efforts, we may have a better chance to succeed than by going alone."

Scorpion let Tahjis talk without interrupting him. She reached out and stroked the bald head of one of her men with delicate fingers. The silence stretched until Fakhira felt certain they would be thrown out to the sounds of more laughter. "This sounds like a deal I shouldn't refuse, which makes me suspicious of it." Her sultry alto voice had an odd lisp that spoke of a mild deformity in her mouth.

"We, of course, expect you to task us with proving our worthiness." Tahjis bobbed his head up and down, reminding Fakhira of a chicken. "Allow us the chance to perform some deed that will aid in this cause, something you don't have the manpower to do and would rather not be blamed for no matter how it turns out."

Her hand swirled on the man's head, raking her fingernails across his flesh. His lips parted in pleasure. "Very well," Scorpion said. "Your failure would cost me nothing, and your success would win me much. Abhar uses a warehouse at the docks for his goods. Steal the keys and ledgers and bring them to me. To prove they are the true keys, also bring me the pearl-handled knife he keeps there. Take whatever you wish of his goods. We will use the ledgers to send the caliph's guards in, so don't free any captives, and avoid letting Abhar's people discover you."

Even without knowing what went on at the warehouse, the task sounded impossible to Fakhira. She tried not to let that show. The Waters would help, and it might be easier than it sounded.

"We can do this, Scorpion, I swear it. You won't regret meeting with us." Tahjis bowed again.

"We shall see. You may use the Market door next time." She lifted her hand and waved to dismiss them.

Tahjis hopped to his feet. Fakhira stood, following in his wake. The guard at the door still smirked and shut the door behind them. "You're lucky. She threw out the last man who tried to convince her to help him kill Black Abhar."

Fakhira didn't need the glance from Tahjis to know she shouldn't respond to that. They walked through a maze of tunnels. Tahjis fit in here —a rat in a rat warren. They came to a chamber with more guards sitting around and were ushered through a door to a small room with only a ladder up. The beefy man tossed their weapons in and shut the door behind them, plunging them into darkness again.

"Why do they use such places for their doors?" Since she knew they wouldn't open the door again, she conjured light in her hand and picked up her sword. A brief inspection showed it hadn't been damaged by the rough handling.

Tahjis picked up his knife and tucked it out of sight. "Choke points are good for defenders and bad for attackers. The guards can stand there and cut down anyone trying to pile through the door one at a time. Standing out in the open, you can be surrounded, which never goes well."

Following him up the ladder, Fakhira thought about times when she'd found herself in the middle of a swarm of children begging for dates and then imagined them to all have small swords they wanted to stab her with. She shivered and recognized the wisdom of his words. The Waters surely must have put her on the path to finding him, because she would need his knowledge to survive in the army.

"This warehouse we're going to break into, it'll have better security at night, but more people around during the day. Since we don't have to do anything but get the keys and ledgers, we'll see if we can blend in now. Sooner we get that stuff back to Scorpion, sooner we get my sister back."

"Why did you tell her that I'm in love with Santrice?"

"I figured that would explain why we came together. Besides, who doesn't like a story about a man trying to save his woman?" The moment he cracked a trap door open and let in sunlight, she banished her light.

He had a point, again. She needed to not question him about these things, because he clearly had a good head on his shoulders and knew how to deal with people. "I hope she won't expect any displays of affection from me."

Tahjis chuckled and climbed out, then offered her a hand up.

Chapter 8

They emerged from a door in a shaded alley. At the end of the alley, they found the marketplace, an open square filled with tent stalls. The vendors hawked fruits and vegetables, grains, beans, and herbs and spices. Women and children flowed through the lanes like water in canals, minor pools forming when someone stopped to haggle. The din of chattering and shouting mixed with music and the snorts of restive animals swept down the streets, audible for several blocks all around.

Tahjis plunged into the crowd, Fakhira struggling to keep sight of him. She had no idea why they came here when the goal involved robbing a warehouse. He threaded through the market, weaving between people and ducking to the side over and over again. They emerged from the throng on the other side, and he offered her a small sack.

"What's this?" She opened it and peered inside.

"Lunch, and maybe dinner. Don't eat it now. Tie it to your belt."

Inside, she saw a lime, lily roots, figs, and peas. "Did you just steal all of this?" The lime in particular must have cost far too much for him to waste on food.

"No. I didn't steal any of it." He gave her a sly grin. "I somehow found the money to buy it."

She stopped and stared at him. "You just walked through the market and—"

"Shh!" He cut her off with a hand over her mouth. "It's never a good idea to give any guards nearby the idea you might be doing anything wrong." He let go and nudged her forward again. "We need to eat, and those people all had plenty. The first rule of stealing is to take from those who can afford to lose it. Never steal from the poor. It's also a bad plan to steal from the very rich. They usually can afford to have guardsmen hunt you down and cut off your hand."

"There are rules for that?"

"There are rules for everything."

"What are the rules for breaking into a warehouse?"

Tahjis chuckled. "Always assess your target before making a plan. I know some about this warehouse, but we can't decide how best to get inside until we get there and have a chance to watch the workers and guards."

Fakhira looked down into her lunch bag again. "Caliph Korval is a good man."

Stopping, Tahjis barked out an incredulous laugh. He held out a hand to keep her from continuing

while he laughed and laughed and laughed. His mirth forced him to bend over, gasping for breath.

Fakhira watched him in alarm that changed to annoyance. "What?"

He wiped away tears, leaving clean streaks on his brown skin. "You know nothing. Too innocent for words. Be careful what you say, Al-Kabar, because there are people who would gut you for saying that, thinking you must work for him."

Frowning, she pulled the caliph's marker from her pocket. "If he's not a good man, why did he give me this for nothing more than surviving the destruction at Aitrae Oasis? He tasked four of his men to guide us to his palace here, and they did their job without complaint."

Tahjis plucked the coin from her fingers and examined it. "If you had this, why not just use it?"

"I want to join the army. If they see me with this, they'll know I'm not a man."

"Right, back to your crazy plan to die someplace exotic."

"How is it any different from going to kill Black Abhar? Didn't he destroy your family and home? I want to kill the men who destroyed my family and home." She held out her hand for the coin.

"And can you do that?" Still holding the coin, he met her eyes. "Kill men, I mean. Can you take your sword and plunge it into their hearts or cut off their heads?"

Such stark terms made her flush. The idea of killing bad people didn't include how they would die. She only knew they would cease to live and go back to the Fires. Could she drag her sword across the neck of a living, breathing man and watch his blood spill out? "I...I don't know."

He deposited the coin back into her palm. "Then we should go

67

find out. Watch yourself, though. There's no such thing as a powerful man who's also good. He may do good things, but that doesn't make him a good man. If the caliph cared about all his people, would there be slums? Would a man like Black Abhar be allowed to sell children to the highest bidder? Would he be allowed to press women into whoring against their will? Don't fool yourself into believing the caliph doesn't know what's going on in his cities. He knows. He knows and does nothing."

"Then why did he give these to us?"

"Because he looked you in the face? Because he wanted to keep track of you? Because presenting it would get you into his service to pay off the debt he would saddle you with to set you up here? I don't know. I do know that there's no such thing as a free meal."

His words made her want to find out what happened to those who turned in the coins. She tucked it into her pocket and hurried to keep up with Tahjis as he led her to the riverside. A branch of the mighty Koin river, called the Tebru river, flowed through here, making the area ideal for settlements. Someone once told her the Tebru went to the ocean, but she didn't understand the concept of "ocean" and had no way to know if it was true. Here in Kamrik, it flowed in a wide, deep cleft of the earth and made the ground brown and fertile.

The closer they got to the water, the more Fakhira smelled wetness. She knew the scent from home, but it felt cleaner there, like damp earth. This aroma carried rot, spoiled fish and a sharp, foul tang she couldn't identify. They came to a street filled with people and wagons pulled by horses. Tahjis led her up the side, dodging waste in the gutters and bucking the traffic.

Warehouses lined the road, each with its own contingent of men lifting and carrying boxes, crates, barrels, and sacks. Horses stamped, wagons trundled and jangled, men shouted and laughed and grumbled. He pulled her to a stop at a spot with a narrow alley for waste and water to run between the buildings, and pointed across the street.

This particular warehouse had nothing special about it that Fakhira could see. The men loaded one wagon and unloaded another at the same time. Large crates covered with thick black cloth went onto the loading wagon. The unloading wagon held barrels and large sacks. As she watched, she noticed the sacks had an odd shape and flopped strangely. She saw one of the men drop a sack on the ground and kick it, then throw it back over his shoulder.

Her hand went to cover her mouth as she realized with horror that the sacks must contain people. She judged the sizes of the barrels and crates and thought they might hold the same thing. Black Abhar moved his shipments of slaves in daylight, and a simple inspection would reveal it. Yet he had no fear of such a thing.

Tahjis grabbed her arm and yanked her hand down. "Stop doing that. It makes you look like a girl."

"How can he...? I don't understand."

"No one cares. The inspectors sit in their offices and get fat off of bribes to look the other way. Their bosses take a cut and proclaim the dock safe and free of corruption. Their bosses know bribery is going on, but have no reason to do anything about it, because they get fees from the usage of the port. Anyone who tries to raise a stink gets killed or captured. Black Abhar doesn't even have to do it. The port inspectors send the city guard to arrest someone for imaginary crimes, and they do it."

"This is awful."

"This is how the city works. Give anyone the chance, and he'll take the easy way over honesty every time."

"It wasn't like that at home."

"That you know of. Tuck your sword into your pants."

"What?" The abrupt change of subject confused her at least as much as the order itself.

"Laborers don't carry swords like that. Put it inside your pant leg."

She slid the blade inside her pants with a gulp. "What if I cut my leg?"

"Then you'll bleed. Let's try to blend in." Tahjis grabbed a fistful of her pants and tugged, getting her to follow him across the street.

She tried not to think about the steel bouncing against her leg. Instead, she ruminated over what else he'd said. Had Aitrae Oasis been like that? She didn't want to think of her father and Shahan and Cyric as pawns of corrupt officials working for the benefit of criminals like Black Abhar. The entire Oasis had less than one thousand souls, and she knew everyone in her neighborhood. Did one of them buy and sell people without her knowledge? Did the Magistrate know about it and ignore it so long as he received a cut of the profit?

Tahjis walked directly to the unloading wagon and offered himself to take a barrel. Since each required two men, Fakhira stepped up to help him. As the least burly of the men here, they struggled under its weight while tracing the path of the men in front of them. She couldn't tell if she actually heard or only imagined a groan from inside the barrel as they dropped it into place beside the others.

Two large men with their arms crossed watched the laborers move both the barrels and the cloth covered crates for the other wagon. With their attention divided, and focused more on the goods than the people, Tahjis found a moment to slip deeper into the warehouse. Fakhira followed him, aping the way he walked as if he belonged.

Grabbing her hand, he darted behind a pile of boxes. The sword threatened to rip through her pants as she ducked down, so she drew the blade and held it tightly. Two and a half feet of steel would shield her. Tahjis patted her arm and pressed a finger to his lips, warning her to stay quiet. Then he pointed to her and to the ground, and then to himself and to the door in the wall some twenty feet away.

Thinking she understood, she nodded and watched him pull Brumble out of his shirt. He set the rat down and together, they slunk along the wall to the door. Seeing him do this, she had no idea why he'd brought her when he clearly didn't need any help to steal something. Perhaps he thought she'd be good for a backup plan if things went sour. Or, more likely, he had nothing better to do with her while he took care of this. Stashing her someplace would have taken time and effort.

Brumble wriggling under the door surprised Fakhira. From her hiding spot, the door appeared to fit well into the frame. Tahjis waited several seconds then he turned the handle and slipped inside the room. Fakhira had no idea what to do with herself and crouched there, waiting. She considered what her father would think of his little girl doing these things and had to stifle a mirthless laugh. He'd be torn between pride at her for taking up vengeance in his name and horrified by her pretending to be a man.

This deep in the warehouse, noises from the loading and unloading filtered to her, muffled by distance and shelves full of goods. Standing out in sharp contrast, boots on the stone floor clacked toward her and interrupted her musings. She peered out, searching for the owner of the boots and his destination, only to see him as he reached for the handle of the door Tahjis had used. If he went in there, Tahjis would be captured.

Her mind blanked with no idea how to stop him. "Hey," she called out with no idea what else to do. Something about him—his build, maybe —reminded her of Shahan, which made her think of times he'd fallen into his cups. Lurching up, she purposely staggered into the barrels she hid behind, causing enough of a clatter to echo in the large space. With a drunken slur, she called out, "Aren't you a pretty pony?"

The man stopped in front of the door, the handle turned and the door cracked open already. He turned to stare at her in confused surprise. "What? Who are you?" Letting go of the handle, he walked toward her. His clothes marked him as having some wealth, enough to put tassels on his yellow and brown tabard.

Unable to think of anything else to say, she laughed at him.

The man stood taller than her by a full head. He made to grab her arm, then saw the sword and took a step back. "Did you come in here looking for shade and more drink? Get out and be on your way."

Fakhira squinted at him and blinked. "You're the ugliest woman I ever saw." Behind the man, she saw Tahjis ease out through the door, flashing her a thumbs-up sign and slipping away from the door. "Where are the pretty girls?"

The man rolled his eyes and pointed, staying far enough away to avoid being skewered on her sword. "Out there. One block that way. Go find them."

"Thanks. You're alright." She shambled out, bouncing from shelf to shelf on the pretense of needing the support. The man didn't follow her, though she suspected he watched until she stumbled past his guards and workers to blink in the sunshine. Cringing away from it, she put a hand on her belly and hurried back to the alley. Tahjis crouched in the shade, waiting for her and petting Brumble.

"Good thinking." He hopped to his feet and led her away.

"Did you get all of it?" She straightened and tucked her sword back into her sash belt.

"Yep. Easiest job I've ever done. Thanks to you. Are you sure you want to get into the army? You'd make a good thief with some practice and training. Your instincts are good."

She shook her head. "I want justice, not coin."

"Who says you can't have both? Steal from the caliph, squeeze him until he bleeds."

"Fight him by...taking his money? How does that bring justice?"

"You seem so smart in one moment, then you turn around and say

73

something really stupid. Look, when you kill someone like Black Abhar, someone else steps in and does all the same things. Nothing really changes. Someone better has to be put into place, like Scorpion. Caliphs work the same way.

"But," he raised a finger to emphasize his point, "if you steal from him, you affect him. Not only can you steal things other than money, you can use whatever money you take to help others. Like, take me, for example. I steal some money and buy food. I give half of it to you. Why? Because you can't get food for yourself. Imagine if I didn't have to pay everything to Black Abhar. I could help more people eat every day. Maybe I would do it by giving them money or food directly, or maybe I would buy something from a vendor on the street, making it so he can then turn around and buy something, and so on and on."

Fakhira knew that people buying her family's dates meant that they could buy other things, but never thought about how it had a place in the whole of the Oasis community. This would take more time to think about and really understand. "What are we going to do now?"

"Take these things back to Scorpion and see what she says. We did it fast and clean, so there's no reason for her not to help us." He turned and led her to the marketplace. When they reached the edge, he ducked into the crowd and she lost track of him.

Knowing where to go, Fakhira didn't worry and instead focused on being Al-Kabar. He owned the place and needed no guide. Al-Kabar swaggered with purpose. People got out of his way.

On the other side of the market, she leaned against the wall at the mouth of the alley, enjoying her lime and waiting for Tahjis to reach her. The small fruit burst with juice and flavor, delighting her palette and quenching the thirst that had been building in her throat. A scruffy little boy watched her eating it, licking his parched lips, and she offered him both partially eaten halves. He took them with reverent gratitude and disappeared.

After far too long had passed in the hot sun, a brown rat ran to her and squeaked madly. Guessing it must be Brumble, she picked it up and ducked into the alley. If something happened to the rat's master, she didn't know what she'd do. "Where's Tahjis?" Talking to the rat felt silly, since she had no way to communicate with Brumble. She still did it. Watching the rat shiver and squeak with obvious fear and urgency, Fakhira gulped. "He's in trouble, I take it. Can you show me where?"

The rat ran down her body, making her shudder, then hurried into the crowd. Fakhira followed, falling over people to keep her eyes on Brumble and expecting the worst. They zigged and zagged, leaving her thinking the rat had no idea where she was going. When they broke free of the market, she wondered why Brumble didn't just take her around it. Then again, the poor thing couldn't be very smart. Perhaps the smell of food proved too distracting.

Brumble turned down an alley and scampered to a pile of rubbish. Uncertain what she'd find there, Fakhira closed the distance warily, eyes darting around in every direction to spot an ambush or other trap. Five steps away from the heap, she saw it move and froze. Brumble squeaked at it. A hand reached out of the refuse and pushed a limp, rotting head of let-

AL-KABAR

tuce away.

"Tahjis," Fakhira breathed, rushing to his side. "What happened?"

His voice strained, he gasped in pain. "Just had a chat with some of Black Abhar's goons. Curse of a thousand spiders in their shoes," he spat.

"How did they know it was you in the warehouse?"

"They didn't." He shoved more of the garbage away and she saw the skin around his eye had already turned purple. "I was supposed to pay them last night. Once a week. When we decided to go to Scorpion, I decided to not pay him. I think they meant to take me to him and do more, but I got away and hid under here. We can't stay or they'll find me."

Fakhira bew out a breath in relief. Yes, he'd been in trouble, but he got himself out of it, and now only needed a little time to heal. "We have what Scorpion asked for, so we can go to her."

"No, we can't," he moaned. "I lost the ledger."

"Did the goons take it?"

"No, it fell out of my shirt. I don't think they saw it. We'll have to steal it from whatever merchant's tent it slid into. Brumble can find it, you can be a diversion, and I'll slip in and grab it." He leaned against the wall, holding his side. "We have to steal it without them thinking we're stealing any of their stuff, and without anyone noticing what we're taking so Black Abhar doesn't get wind of it. His men are notoriously good at noticing thievery."

The more Tahjis said, the more complex this sounded. Not only that, but he clearly couldn't do any of the things he felt he needed to. "You stay here, Tahjis. You're in no shape to do any of that. Ask Brumble to lead me to the ledger, and I'll figure something out."

"You don't know how to steal," he protested.

"Black Abhar's people also don't know me. Rest, stay hidden. I'll find it."

He tried to stand, failed, and sighed. "Brumble, find the ledger, show Al-Kabar to it then come back to me."

The rat squeaked and led Fakhira back to the market. She sniffed around the edges of the tent stalls until she stopped and ducked under one edge. A few seconds later, during which time Fakhira pretended to be interested in the wares of a different stall, the rat poked her head out, squeaked once and tore away, heading back to Tahjis.

This particular merchant, a plump, friendly looking woman, sold dry beans and seeds by the scoop. Fakhira couldn't see any reason to pursue a ruse. The woman didn't sell paper or books of any sort, and if she had her own ledger, it would be tucked away someplace safe. With a shrug, Fakhira walked up, wishing she had some money to buy something from the poor woman.

"Excuse me. I've dropped a ledger here, and I think it was kicked into your tent, near that corner."

The woman's pleasant smile faded, but she bent down and patted the ground, then came up with a book. "Is this it?"

How many books could be under there? Fakhira smiled and nodded, knowing her eyes would still show her pleasure, even with her mouth covered. "Yes, thank you. Sorry to trouble you."

"Have a good day."

"You, too." Fakhira tucked the book under her arm and walked straight to Tahjis. She found him cowering behind the garbage and crouched to help him stand.

"You got it! How did you get it so fast?"

"I asked politely." She helped him hobble back to the trap door into Scorpion's lair.

Tahjis blinked and stared at her. "You...what?"

"It clearly didn't belong to her." She related the exchange with the woman.

"Oh. That was good thinking." He cracked a pained smile. "We make a good team! You should forget this army stuff and stick with me. We'll become invaluable members of Scorpion's organization and have everything we want."

"Can she get me revenge on Trimar and his men?"

He huffed in exasperation. "Always back to that. You know, I only want to kill Black Abhar because it's the best way to free Santrice. You have no one to free and only memories to keep promises to. Maybe you're too focused on revenge. Besides, what happens when you get it? Will that make you happy or keep your belly full?"

She didn't have an answer for him yet. At some point she would, but not now. "Can you climb down the ladder, or do you need help?"

He peered down through the door and into the darkness. "I can manage it, but maybe you should go first in case I fall."

Chapter 9

"Aside from Tahjis getting beaten up, you did well. This is faster than I expected, certainly." Scorpion leafed through the ledger, the keys and letter opener on a platter beside her. "It appears to be useful to me. Did you see any signs he has people chained up in there now?"

"Hard to say, mistress. He takes pains to cover them up. It was clear he removed some this morning, but not clear what was in the barrels arriving. I saw some covered cages in the back. Couldn't say if they had people or animals." Tahjis avoided looking directly at her. Fakhira did the same and kept her mouth shut.

"I see." She set the ledger on the platter and waved at it. One of her scantily clad men picked it up and took it away. "That will cripple him, but not enough for me to dare to strike at him directly. Since you did so well with this one, I have another for you. While my people get the city guards to move on this, you will attack one of his gambling houses. He has several, and we will pick the one where the lower floor includes a gladiator pit."

Fakhira blinked, stunned. Gladiatorial combat had been banned several years ago in this caliphate, after a scandal with the recruitment methods surfaced. Caliph Korval didn't tolerate slavery. She considered Santrice's plight and realized he might not be quite so strict about such things as he pretended. Later, she would ask Tahjis about it.

"You will first rig the gambling, then reveal it to the customers. In the resulting chaos, you will free the gladiators. Conduct them to me. I will give them better choices than Abhar has. Promise they will be able to do as they please, so long as they understand I expect to be repaid somehow." She waved a hand in dismissal.

Tahjis bobbed a bow to her. "May I see your healer?"

"Yes. Go."

They backed away from her and left the room. Tahjis led Fakhira to a different room, one with a curtain separating it from the hallway. When he drew it aside, an elder woman reclining on silk cushions looked him over and tsked. "Boy, what have you done to yourself?" Her voice creaked with age to match the steel gray of her hair and wrinkles in her face.

"I had a disagreement with some men." He hung his head and shuffled to her.

"They wanted your blood on the outside and you didn't?" She patted the cushion beside her and dunked a white washcloth into a bowl of water.

"Something like that."

"This will hurt. And then it'll feel better." She wrung out the cloth and touched his eye with it.

Tahjis yelped and squirmed.

She slammed his shoulder down, pinning him with strength beyond appearances. "I said it would hurt, didn't I? You, hold him down or this'll never get done."

Fakhira gulped and put her forearms across his chest. "Why did you ask to see her if you knew it would be like this?"

Tahjis whimpered, trying to wriggle out from under her weight.

"He came to me because he knows I'll make the pain go away, he just doesn't like what has to happen to get there. Have you never seen a healer?"

Fakhira gripped his shoulders and held him down with all her strength. "No, Elder. We didn't have one where I grew up. Only a midwife."

"Either you've been lucky or your midwife had more skills than she let on." The healer swiped her cloth against Tahjis's eye again and he howled. "Such a crybaby. I'll bet he isn't that much of a whiner." She jutted her chin to indicate Fakhira as the "he" in question, then swiped Tahjis's eye again, making him flail and whine.

With the next swipe, he stopped and moaned. Fakhira sensed something else in the room, something familiar. When she lifted her head and looked around, she saw nothing. Confused, she turned to see the healer set her hand on Tahjis's brow. That other presence swirled around Fakhira, then flooded up her arms to course through her body.

The healer had called the Waters, and they recognized Fakhira. Tendrils of warmth spiraled around her and she closed her eyes, drinking the sensation in. It covered her from head to toe, and she knew if she hurt, it would wash away the pain.

"Al-Kabar?" Tahjis's voice pulled her back from the bliss she'd found.

Her eyes opened and she discovered she'd gotten to her feet. Sparkling droplets of water swirled around her body from head to toe. At her command, they closed in around her and sank into her clothes. Though the cloth appeared dry, she could tell the water remained there, waiting to be called when she needed it.

"Oh. My." The healer sat back and gaped at Fakhira. "Al-Kabar, was it? I'll remember that name. When you learn to control that, you'll be unstoppable."

"How do I learn to control it? All I can do is make light."

The healer shook her head. "That's your journey to take. I can't help you."

Frustrated with such an unhelpful answer, Fakhira scowled. "Not even a bit of advice?"

"Do what feels right," the healer shrugged. "When you need it most, it'll be there for you."

Turning her attention to Tahjis, Fakhira saw he looked fine now. "We have work to do." She spun on her heel and walked away.

He scurried after her with Brumble on his shoulder again. "That was perfect. And incredible. You have to stay here. Together, we can free everyone. Imagine it!"

"Why is it that the only option you can imagine is for me to stay here and help you get what you want? Maybe you should come with me and help me get what I want."

Tahjis's mouth opened and shut. He looked down and said nothing as he guided her to a way out. The heat of afternoon pressed down on them from the moment they returned to the surface, demanding they stop to rest. He took her around the edge of the marketplace, passing her a fresh lime that she ripped in half and sucked dry. They went down a different alley and he hunkered down in a patch of shade.

"Where is this place?"

"On the edge of the slums." He didn't look at her. "I'm not sure how to do what Scorpion wants."

"Why do they call her that?"

He shrugged. "I heard a scorpion stung her in the face and she survived. The poison ate part of her face away, so she wears a veil."

Fakhira grimaced in disgust. "That's awful. How did it happen?"

"According to the story, her husband thought she cheated on him, so he put it in the bed, expecting it to kill both her and her lover. There was no lover, and though she cried from the pain, she managed to keep it from stinging her a second time, trapped it in a box, and unleashed it on her husband. It killed him. Now she keeps several men as pets."

Fakhira admired the strength of such a woman, and had no idea what she would do in Scorpion's place. The sting probably would have killed her outright, as she didn't think she could handle such venom. "We still need to figure out how to do what she wants."

"Yes. The gambling part isn't illegal, it happens in the open. I don't know how he cheats any worse than anyone else does. The caliph is supposed to monitor the places to make sure they're fair, whatever that means. Abhar probably bribes or beats the inspectors to keep them from looking into his places."

"Could we get to an inspector and threaten him to get him to expose Abhar to the caliph?"

"It would be exposing himself to the caliph, too, since he'd get into trouble for never stopping it before. The inspectors don't want to get caught any more than Abhar does. We need to think of some way to show the customers that the inspectors are so dishonest they get outraged by it. At the same time, they need to see they're being cheated worse than they think."

Fakhira leaned her head against the wall, no ideas coming to mind. "We could steal the ledgers and let a customer find them."

"Hm. I don't know that he'd keep a ledger there, or if it would make sense to anyone who stumbled across it." Tahjis shook his head. "We need a grand gesture that any idiot can understand."

"How do they cheat at those places? Can we use a mirror to show it, or pull a cloth away to reveal something?"

Tahjis sat and rubbed his temples. Brumble walked around his neck to sniff at Fakhira. Her whiskers quivered in the air, and she squeaked.

"She's trying to learn to be a man," Tahjis said. "Going in as a woman won't help that."

"What's the idea? If it can work, we should try it."

"Brumble's idea is that you slip in as an employee and circulate while serving drinks, watching to find a time when you can 'accidentally' drop something in a man's lap to show him he's being cheated."

Fakhira blinked several times at the man and the rat. "She said all that with one little squeak?"

One side of his mouth quirked into a grin. "No, but I got the idea from what she said."

She chuckled. "I'm willing to try it. While I do that, you can sneak downstairs and do your thing to free the gladiators."

"You probably don't know how the employees there behave. You need to not blush down there, because they'll pounce on you for it, like hyenas on meat." He rolled to his feet and offered her a hand up. "They'll realize you're a virgin and want to fix that."

She blushed. "How can you tell?"

He rolled his eyes and pointed between her legs. "I had to fix that for you. And the blushing."

"How am I supposed to not blush?"

"I don't know, but figure something out. Come on, let's find you some clothes and stash your sword. You won't be wearing enough to hide it, and shouldn't need it anyway." He grabbed her hand and dragged her to the marketplace yet again.

This time, she recognized a few of the stalls as they walked through and stopped Tahjis at the bean seller. "Give her something, she helped earlier. She could've been difficult, but instead cooperated." She took the steel coin he handed over and approached the woman. "Thank you for your help earlier." Offering the gift, she gave the woman a small bow.

"Oh." The bean seller smiled and tucked the coin into a pocket. "If you ever drop anything near here again, you're welcome to have a look at anything you'd like." She gave Fakhira a once-over and winked.

Fakhira needed a moment to realize the woman had just flirted with her. She fiercely fought back the color that threatened to rise in her cheeks. "I'm spoken for, miss. In fact, I'm working to free my love right now." She stepped in closer to take the woman into confidence, not sure where the idea to do this came from. "She's a prisoner of Black Abhar," she whispered.

The woman went from disappointed to sympathetic in a flash. "Oh, you poor thing. She must be a pretty girl for that bastard to take her. He takes a cut from all of us, says he'll wreck our wares if we don't pay up. It's awful. I wish we could kill him. He's the reason my kids sleep three to a room and my husband has to work so hard on our plot. We can't even afford to keep enough to eat for ourselves! Ask anyone here. They'll tell you a similar story."

"I mean to kill him for what he's done to my lady love. Offer whatever you can to the Fires and Waters for me, because I'll need all the help I can get."

She took Fakhira's hand and patted it. "I'll make an offering tonight. What's your name?"

"Al-Kabar."

"Al-Kabar, Champion of Kamrik. You have allies and friends. Do what you need to do."

Fakhira bowed her head and backed away, returning to Tahjis. They continued in silence and Tahjis stopped at a stall to buy clothing.

86

From the gauze and fake gold, she expected it would be more revealing than she liked or found comfortable. Neither had anything else to say after he haggled for the costume until they reached his bolt hole.

"What did you tell that bean seller?"

"She flirted with me. Without using her name, I told her about Santrice. She said there are allies to be found here."

Tahjis handed her the clothing, face closed and unreadable. "Change into this."

"Should I not have done that? It felt like the right thing to do."

"I don't know. I'm not the one that the Waters favor. Maybe she meant it, and maybe she'll tell Abhar about you. It could be a reward or a trap. Put the clothes on and let's get going."

The costume had only three small pieces of red satin, held in place by thin gauze anyone could see through. With it, he gave her cheap gold collars for her wrists, neck, and ankles. Never had she worn anything like this before. The caliph had women who dressed this way, put on display at the Feast of the Fires. Fire Dancers, though, wore more. But then, Fire Dancers had respect as arbiters for the Fires.

With a start, Fakhira realized she ought to have such a status. The Waters chose her, and everyone knew the Waters were equal to the Fires. But they had no Feast of the Waters and no Water Dancers. Until this moment, she never thought to question that.

She frowned at the skimpy clothes. "Are there no shoes?"

"No. The steps out are serrated metal, which cuts bare feet, but not shoes. It keeps the girls from leaving. You'll wear your regular clothes over all this to get in and out." He sat and gestured for her to hurry and change.

She could ask him to turn around and not watch. In his own home, that seemed rude. Besides, she'd probably need his help to put all these things on properly. With a shaky breath, she turned her back on him and tried to ignore him. If she pretended he didn't exist, and he stayed quiet, she could do this.

Pulling the end of her scarf out, she unwrapped her head, freeing her black hair. It fell to her shoulders, damp with sweat. She untied the neck of her shirt and pulled it off, then set her sword aside and removed her sash belt. Another tie freed her pants, and they dropped to the ground. Standing in only the wrap around her chest and the short pants that held the sock in place, she covered her face and wished she could make her blush go away.

Tahjis cleared his throat, startling her. "We don't—" His voice cracked and he coughed. "We're kind of in a hurry."

She stammered an apology and fumbled through removing the last layer. Despite the heat, she shivered in the dim light and wanted to curl into a ball. She jumped and squeaked when Tahjis's warm fingers touched her bare hip.

"They'll do worse," he murmured. He moved closer, his clothes brushing against her skin. His breath, hot on her neck, raised prickles on her flesh. "Smack your butt, grab your breasts, slap your face, stick fingers in all kinds of places. You have to brush it off. Forget where you are, forget what you feel, forget who you are. Your role is to be their servant, their toy. They have to pay extra for sex, so you need to be able to slip away before they can find someone to give the money to."

"How do I do that?" Her voice came out as a hoarse whisper.

He cleared his throat. "Santrice told me she pretends they're pick-pockets, trying to steal coins she keeps in unusual places. But don't swat their hands away. Just slip aside. Let them grab empty air. Keep moving and never stop long enough to let them do anything more than a bare touch." He sighed, sending a puff of breath swiping down her neck and shoulder. "I forgot you were a girl." Pulling his hands away, he took a step back.

At once, she wanted to both step close and run away. Her skin longed for his touch. The rest of her wasn't so sure. She stood there, frozen with indecision, until she heard Tahjis move again. Looking over her shoulder, she saw him sitting against the wall, face turned away from her. Not sure what to think, or even what to feel, she crouched and shrugged into the ridiculous clothing. It hung low on her hips and the gold band marking the lower edge of the top hung only half an inch below her small breasts. Between the two, bare flesh showed. She felt exposed, only marginally better than wearing nothing at all.

She struggled to fasten the last few clasps, then gave up with a huff. "I can't reach the hooks in the back."

Tahjis turned and stared up at her. He opened his mouth to say something, then closed it and hopped to his feet, his gaze directed at anything but her. Without a word, he tugged her pants straight and adjusted her sleeves. After he dealt with the offending fasteners, he snapped all the collars into place before stepping back and gesturing at her old clothes.

"Cover up with that. Don't forget the boots."

She tossed the shirt over her head and stepped into her pants. There would be no binding of her breasts or sock in her pants this time. "Are you sure I'll fool them until we get inside?"

"Those clothes are bulky enough, and it won't be well-lit. Not even in daylight. Walk like a man and they'll accept you as one, because no woman would go down there of her own free will unless she's rich and likes girls."

Fakhira nodded and took a deep breath. She avoided Tahjis's eyes as much as he avoided hers and they stood in awkward silence for several long seconds. Brumble squeaked and he scrambled to get out of the hole. The gauzy material swished between her legs as they traveled through the city, calling her attention to her thighs. The strange sensation made her want to slow down and experience it fully.

"Stop doing that," Tahjis hissed. "You look like a girl. Remember, your personal space is your domain, and you have no hips."

Duly chastised, she made fists and forced herself to swagger. That type of movement had already become natural with the lump between her legs. Without it, she had to relearn the swing of her arms, the bend of her elbows, and the bounce in her step.

They walked for a long time, long enough for the sun to cast long shadows from behind the tall buildings. Tahjis stopped in front of a blank building where a large man sat with a coconut and a deck of lacquered paper playing cards at a small table. Tahjis laid four gold coins on the table and pushed them at the man. The man covered them with his hand and nodded, his eyes directing them to go around him to the side of the building.

Tahjis grabbed the handle of a door set seamlessly into the wall. All around it, high walls barred passage into this apparent dead end from any other direction. Fakhira guessed the man in front would get up and stop anyone who didn't pay, and might have a way to signal to more guards inside.

Tahjis pulled cloth down from the wrapping on his head and covered his face with it, then wrenched the door open and gestured for her to go first. Fakhira stepped in and he heaved it shut behind her. They stood in a room lit only by two low burning lamps on the wall, each dueling with the other to create flickering shadows. Four more large men, all dressed in black leather and carrying curved swords, stood at attention. A fifth man sat at a table blocking passage to the only other door.

The fifth man barely noticed them, leaning back in his chair with his eyes glazed over. Fakhira approached the table side-by-side with Tahjis and discovered the reason for his distraction: movement in his lap. From the silky black hair on the head there, she guessed it must be a girl pleasuring him with her mouth, and wondered if Black Abhar appreciated his employees behaving this way. It certainly distracted this man from his duties.

Without bothering to stop, Tahjis tossed some coins at the man and walked around him. Several bounced to the floor, and one hit the girl. Fakhira followed, averting her eyes from the spectacle and cringing at how much worse it must be inside. Since the guards didn't stop them, she guessed the coins appeared to be enough. On the other side of the door, she took a deep breath and vowed to herself that she could do this.

"You'll be fine. Remember to move your body instead of your hands. Slip away, don't jump." He took her hand as they walked down the wide spiral staircase and squeezed it, then dropped it. "Do whatever you can to expose the methods Abhar is using, then get out."

She noticed the steps had been carved out of the earth, then fitted with a sharp, cross-hatched metal top. Tahjis had explained about it, but she hadn't been able to picture it. A bare foot on such a surface would be cut. With even a light shoe, the danger vanished, though she suspected running in anything less than a boot would still cut through. Her own shoes wouldn't manage running on this surface, she guessed, and neither would Tahjis's. Getting out would be difficult if they had to flee.

Chapter 10

As they descended, Fakhira pulled her outer layer of clothing off. She saved the shoes until they'd nearly reached the bottom. Tahjis threw her over his shoulder with a grunt and stumbled down the last turn of stairs. He laughed heartily while she whimpered and squirmed.

Though she couldn't see them, Fakhira expected the two guards at the bottom of the steps gave Tahjis some sort of strange look. "What are you doing?" one of them asked, incredulous or shocked, or maybe both.

"They said upstairs," he threw in random hiccups and slurred his words, "that I can't take her home, and I had to bring her back. Here you go." Setting her onto her feet on the bare stone floor, he shoved her at the guards.

She stumbled and fell, doing her best to make the tumble hide her face under her hair. As Tahjis had recommended, she cried softly and otherwise kept her mouth shut.

"How did you get past us with her?"

Tahjis gave them a hearty, drunken laugh and stumbled his way back up the steps without answering. He said he'd find a way to the bottom somehow, and she had to trust him to do what he promised.

"Some days, this job isn't worth what we're paid," one guard grumbled.

"No kidding. Get up, whore." The other guard grabbed a handful of her hair and yanked her to her feet. "Stop whining and get back to work." The door opened and he tossed her through it.

Catching herself on a table, she avoided hitting the floor while managing to knock over two drinks. The man sitting with a girl dressed like her in his grip made an angry noise and she ducked away. Lamps on the small tables scattered about the room created pools of dancing light in the dark sea. The crowd babbled and chattered and whined and laughed. Under that, she heard the sounds of dice and card games: rattling and slapping and tumbling and clunking. Glasses clinked, leather creaked, cloth swished, wood groaned. It smelled of sweat, alcohol, and sex.

She had to take a deep breath to steady herself under such a sensory assault. Someone touched her arm and she pulled it away, forcing herself to keep moving. So long as she kept moving, no one would get her. Her eyes darted around while she put one foot in front of the other and spun in a circle.

Hands reached out and touched every part of her body, some with a light brush, others with pinching fingers or slapping hands. None of it felt half as intense as Tahjis's hands resting on her bare hips. These people meant nothing to her, which gave her the sudden realization that he *did* mean something to her. What, she couldn't say, but definitely something.

Several heavy curtains hung along the walls for no apparent reason. Perhaps guards stood behind them, ready to quell any hint of rebellion by the girls or in case of other disturbances. Or maybe they held passages down to the gladiator pit. It seemed an excessive number of stairwells for such a thing, but she had no idea how this kind of place might work.

Keeping her eyes open, she got the idea of how the girls were treated. No one cared if they cried or smiled, struggled or cooperated. She noticed one man grab a fistful of a girl's hair and wrench her head down to his crotch. His mouth moved, she assumed with instructions the girl scrambled to obey under penalty of a punishment worse than his treatment. It seemed a popular way for the men to pass their time here.

She paused near a table with men throwing dice, watching to see what happened. Someone grabbed her neck and yanked her close. "Bring me red wine," a man shouted in her ear, then he shoved her away. She stumbled into another man who turned and slapped her. Without waiting for him to do worse, she hurried to the bar in the back, a thick, polished stone counter with two men in black uniforms behind it. No customers sat here.

Girls ran to the bar, leaned over and shouted their orders, then waited for the tenders to fill them, and hurried away. After waiting in a short line, she shouted for a red wine and got a full glass pressed into her hand. She hadn't seen his face, but that man would find her again, she expected, and would be harsh if she didn't have his drink. Returning to the same table, she stood and watched for a few seconds before a hand closed around her neck again.

"Good job." Like Tahjis, he breathed into her ear. Unlike Tahjis, this man filled her only with dread. "You'll do." The hand squeezed her neck, cutting off her air. Automatically, she reached for it and tried to pry his fingers away. "No, no. Bad girl." A sharp swat on her rear stung. "Don't spill my wine or I'll have to punish you." Something about his voice struck her as familiar.

He dragged her away from the table and walked to a curtain. Pushing it aside with his wine hand, he revealed an alcove with satin cushions. Once he had her behind the curtain, he let go and snapped the curtain shut. "Up against the wall," he ordered.

Panic kindled in her belly. With even less light here, she still couldn't see his face. Something moved in the dark and cracked against her cheek. Pain exploded in her eye and she cried out, cringing away from him.

"I said up against the wall. Do it now, whore." He tossed the wine at the cushions and advanced on her.

She put up her hands to ward him off as she backed up. It took her only two shuffled paces to run into the solid, cool stone wall. A shiver began in her shoulders and worked its way out to her arms and legs. His hand snatched her wrist and flung it at the wall, then something clicked around it and she couldn't pull it away.

"Still full of fire, I see." He chuckled, the sound dark and dangerous. "Go ahead, struggle. Scream. Kick. Flail." He slapped her again, on the other side of her face. The blow knocked her head against the wall, dazing her long enough for him to grab her other hand and wrench it into a second restraint. "I thought Abhar broke all his girls before they came down here, but I see he missed one. All the better for me."

His hands grabbed her thighs, wrenching them apart. The act crystallized in her mind what he intended to do to her. The flickering panic turned to a rush and she closed her eyes, willing the Waters to come and help her. She felt their chill embrace her and rush in. Distantly, she heard someone scream.

Opening her eyes, she saw the man backing away from her, swatting at something. Blue light flared and she recognized someone she never expected to see in a place like this: Caliph Korval. He stumbled into the curtain. It ripped away from the wall. He slipped and fell, crying out as he hit the floor.

Rage boiled in her, and she called the Waters to her wrists. The restraints froze and she jerked her hands away, shattering the metal rings. Eyes flicking over the alcove, she spotted a small lamp on the wall and jumped to reach it. Her hands caught the bottom and the Waters froze it, letting her wrench the sconce down and smash it against the curtain. The oil inside splashed and the flame spread on the fabric.

The caliph shrieked and scrambled to get away. In his haste, he dragged the curtain with him. Fakhira grabbed two wine-splashed cushions and threw them at the fire, hoping to create smoke and chaos. If she could cause enough of both, she could escape. One cushion hit the flames, caught fire, and bounced away. The other hit the caliph in the face.

Guards rushed in and pulled the caliph away. More guards followed them in, running to her. She guessed they had no intention of rescuing her when she saw swords in their hands. Running for her life, she twisted away from a blade slashing through the air and dove at the burning cushion. The gauze of her costume let her slide across the stone floor and she took the cushion with her.

The Waters protected her from the flames. She ran into a patron, knocking his drink aside, and the alcohol made it easy to set his pants on fire. Desperately wanting the fires to burn more, she shoved the cushion at another patron and called the Waters to help her. It seemed backward, to want water to make fire, but it was the only power she had to call.

Water coalesced around her body, cooling her as the air heated. She tripped over someone and his clothes burst into flames. Screams rang out. Still she called the water, and realized she called it out of the air, out of the drinks, even out of the people. Everywhere around her, fire leaped from cushion to curtain to clothes. People stumbled and fell.

It took so much effort. She panted and wobbled to her hands and knees. The world spun and something hard hit her stomach, knocking her aside with a burst of pain. Another flash of agony exploded in the back of her head and she blacked out.

Chapter 11

She woke with something glass in her mouth and a cloth covering her face. Pressure pushed against her from every direction at once. Confused, she pulled on her hands and couldn't do anything but wriggle and writhe. Something held her feet, too. Opening her eyes, she felt grit in the darkness and shut them again. Every movement felt strange.

In the distance, wood scraped against something else, then she heard boots clack on a floor. "Tell the caliph she's awake."

What did he mean to do to her? Judging by her current position, he wouldn't rape her, at least. His intentions might still be more than she could survive. Yet, if he wanted to kill her, why not just do it in that club? Bringing her here spoke of some other plan. If he meant to torture her until she agreed to do what he wanted, she didn't know what she'd do.

She couldn't tell how much time passed before she heard boots approaching. Something heavy hit the floor and creaked.

"Don't bother struggling, my dear," Caliph Korval said. "You're buried in sand. If you move your mouth too much, that sand will choke and smother you. This precaution has been taken because you tried to kill me. If you swear not to use your powers now, I'll have your face uncovered so we may speak. If you agree and you try to kill me again, I will pull out the breathing tube and more sand will be poured in. So, shall we have a conversation? Make one noise for yes and two for no."

Panic surged through Fakhira, making her thrash. This man not only defied his own laws to satisfy his base, carnal needs, he also buried people alive. Tahjis was right. She had been so horribly naïve.

"I realize this is distressing and frightening, so I'll ignore that. Yes or no, child?"

She swallowed around the tube, feeling tiny grains of sand scrape her throat. Her will to live forced a single sound out of her.

"Good. Stay still until I tell you."

Something plunged into the sand and lifted her head. The tube was pulled from her mouth and the cloth removed. Stiff bristles brushed her face, stinging her eyelids and lips.

"Ah. There we are. Open your eyes and tell me your name."

She found herself in a dimly lit room covered in cobalt blue tiles. Her body lay in a steel bathtub filled with sand, chains plunging into the bottom where they must be connected to her feet. Korval sat beside her with two of his beefy guardsmen in the background. He smiled at her and sat casually in the chair.

His pleasant demeanor confused her after his threats. "Fakhira."

He propped an ankle up on his knee and placed his hands on his leg, presenting a picture of calm confidence. "Well met, Fakhira. My Fire

Dancers have looked you over, and they've decided you're not one of them. Which leads me to the mystery of what you are." Though it didn't sound like he'd asked a question, he paused and waited, looking at her expectantly.

After what he said, she didn't trust him with her story. "I don't know."

"Oh, Fakhira." He sounded disappointed. "That's not true. One doesn't just fall into something like this."

"I don't remember." She sagged against the hands holding her head up and closed her eyes. Now that she knew her position, she noticed that she'd been stripped bare before being buried. The sand grated in places it shouldn't be.

"I see. I'm a reasonable man, Fakhira. Be fair to me and I'll be fair to you. I'll let you consider that while we discuss other things. You see, it's curious for you to have been in that particular place at the same time as me. A woman with command over some kind of unknown power happens to show up in a place where I happen to be at a time when I'm vulnerable to attack. This doesn't seem like a coincidence to me."

She snapped her eyes open, realizing he meant to accuse her of trying to assassinate him. "I didn't know you were there until I saw you. I didn't go there for you."

"No? Then who were you there for?"

She tossed out the first name that came to mind and made sense. "Abhar."

Korval leaned back and stroked his chin. "What did he do to you?"

101

"He took…" She couldn't call Santrice her love, that didn't make sense. What was the woman to her, then? Tahjis's sister, of course, but then she had to figure out what Tahjis meant to her. Deep down, she had no idea. He felt more than a friend, yet she hadn't kissed him or said anything, and she'd only known him for a day. Still, she needed to answer. "The man I love, Abhar took his sister and killed his mother."

"Ah, young love. No wonder you reacted so strongly to me. Or, should I say, against me."

"You went there to rape girls. Without my power, you would have raped me. And now, I'm chained in your bathtub."

He sighed, the sound full of regret. "You're chained here for my protection. My mage thinks I should have let my guards kill you on the spot. I disagreed. Since they thought you came to kill me, specifically, we took precautions. If you give your word not to use your power on anyone or anything here, I'll have you cleaned up as my guest."

She noticed he'd neatly skirted the other part of her complaint. "Are you more attracted to girls than women?"

He made a sour face. "I'm a man. My wife is uninterested and so I go looking elsewhere. It was my impression that all Abhar's girls are paid and willing, no matter how they behave."

"Is that what you tell yourself to sleep at night?"

"It's what I was told. If my desire to believe that clouded my judgment, then I'm to blame for it. I'm not your enemy or your tormentor. I have no interest in harming you."

"Yet you visit Abhar's clubs."

The caliph sighed again. "Abhar is a cockroach. He's the kind of man you have to set boundaries for and learn to live with. There's one in every city, and I manage five of them, so I know this to be true. When a population reaches a certain size, someone like Abhar inevitably rises up. I could have him killed, but another will step into his shoes. I could have all his businesses shuttered, but he'll find a way to open different ones. Instead, I manage him and we trade services. He's effective at keeping crime low in the slum areas where no one trusts my guardsmen."

She laughed, finding his argument absurd. Tahjis said the same things, yet he saw it from the other side. Korval spoke as a man who didn't want to be bothered to do his job well enough. "It's hard, so it's not worth doing?"

"Perhaps." He rose from the chair and waved to the person holding her head. "My duty as the caliph is not to control everyone and everything, it's to keep the city safe for most people. The majority of Kamrik has no idea about Abhar."

She thought of the bean seller. "You mean the majority of the people you care about. Everyone in the slums knows who he is." The man behind her pushed to help her sit up.

Korval moved to the foot of the tub and crossed his arms, expression thoughtful. "I'd like to speak on this subject more with you. No one ever challenges me on my decisions. Perhaps not finding someone who will has been a mistake." He crouched and the clank of chain suggested he released her feet. "Amil will help you to a place you can wash the sand away and relax. When you're ready, we'll share a meal and I'll listen to anything you have to say."

She looked up at him, wanting his words to be real and true. His smile convinced her to hope and to try. "I accept."

"Good. I will be honored to share my table with you." He nodded and swept out of the room, his guards following on his heels.

Amil pulled the bindings off her hands and averted his eyes from her chest. "I've been blessed by the Fire Dancers so your magic won't harm me." Clean-shaven and about her own age, he wore a crisp uniform of blue and white, Korval's colors.

"I have no reason to harm you."

He lifted her feet and snapped the chains off her ankles. "I'm glad. I've been assigned to serve you for as long as you remain the caliph's guest." He offered her a hand and helped her stand. Without looking, he held out a fluffy white robe that she stepped into and slipped on.

The soft smoothness against her skin came as a relief. "The caliph is a strange man. One moment, I'm an assassin. The next, I'm an honored guest."

He gave her a hand as she stepped out of the tub, then guided her out of the room. "It's not my place to comment on such things."

As they walked down a wide marble hall with a high ceiling, she gawked at the paintings and vases and statues. Scorpion's opulence had been more than she'd seen before. Korval's destroyed her pathetic illusions about how the rich lived. They passed glass doors open to a balcony, cool evening air brushing past her.

He took her to a suite of rooms, decorated in blue and white. It had a room with a couch and chairs, then a bedroom beyond that, and a bathing chamber with a private toilet. "While you are the caliph's guest, this is yours. The door has a lock, and he has said to tell you that you will not be punished for using it. I'm also to tell you that anyone who harasses you will be executed on your word. Please tell me if I'm harassing you, as I like my head attached to my neck."

She blinked and stared at him. Every line of his face pointed to sincerity. "I'll be sure to say something to you, yes." She gulped at the power Korval had given her.

"I will be stationed outside your room at all times. Whenever you're ready to eat, I will conduct you to the caliph's table." He bowed and left her alone without giving her a chance to respond.

Last night, she slept in a cramped hole in the ground with rags for a bed. The night before that, she slept in a cavern on rocks. Now, she found herself in a palace, a guest of the caliph. She didn't understand his treatment. Why did he choose to leave her alive? Why did he treat her this way? He confused her even more than Tahjis.

Would she ever see Tahjis again? Did he escape with the gladiators? Would he find her somehow, or could she find him? Did she love him? What did that even mean? She never expected to love anyone the way she loved her family. Almiya never claimed to love Shahan. Father never suggested either of them should go find boys they liked. She never thought she'd love her husband.

Then she met Tahjis and spent a night and a day with him. They made a deal and nothing more. She saved him, twice, and he insisted upon deriding her beliefs and ideas. Worse, he had a lunatic obsession with rats, and even believed he could talk to one. He cared so much about that rat. And yet... When he touched her, she liked it. When he pulled his hands away, she knew she could trust him. When he told her what to do, she found it to be right every time.

As much as he used her, didn't she also use him? Everything he wanted her to do had a purpose: to make them both feel that helping her act like a man and get signed up for the army turned out to be a fair trade. Deep down, she didn't know if she believed Santrice was a real person, and she also didn't think she cared. Whether Abhar had really done those things to him, or Tahjis had some other reason to hate the man, she helped him willingly.

Because she liked him a lot. Time would tell if this turned out to be "love" or not.

Chapter 12

It took her several minutes to make water come out of anything in the bathing chamber. She'd never experienced a shower before, and the spray from above startled her. It came out warm and pleasant, and washed away the grit from everywhere. Lavender soap sat on a ledge, and she used it, unable to remember the last time she'd truly been clean. She found thick, fluffy towels and wrapped her hair and body in them.

On the bed, she found a white linen shirt beside a blue silk dress and chose to wear both. The tall mirror on the wall—which in itself must have cost a fortune—showed a young woman she barely recognized. Her parents had a piece of polished steel she'd seen herself in before, but it had much less clarity. The girl in this reflection looked like her mother, slimmer and without the wrinkles and gray. They had the same wide mouth, the same sharp nose, the same dark eyes.

Her smile slipped away and she turned from the mirror. On the floor by the front door, she found thin white stockings, but ignored them. All her life, she'd gone around barefoot, and only wore shoes in the city because it became clear she needed to. In a place like this, she needed nothing to cover her feet.

Outside the door, she found Amil waiting on a cushioned chair, sitting up straight and doing nothing. He jumped to his feet, bowed, and conducted her through the halls to a dining chamber larger than her parents' house. White magical light shone down on a long table with enough chairs to seat twelve. Ten places sat empty. The head at one end had a place setting of gleaming white china, and the seat to the right had the same. Amil brought her to that right-hand seat and pulled the chair out for her.

"The caliph will arrive shortly. Would you like anything to drink?"

"Oh. Yes, please."

He looked at her, waiting. When the pause stretched long enough to become awkward, he asked, "Water, juice, wine, beer?"

The choices surprised her, except for how a caliph's palace would naturally have many options for everything. She felt stupid. "Juice, please."

The boy nodded and left her alone in the cavernous room, most of which sat empty and dark. What purpose could so much space have? With nothing to occupy her, she peered at the plates, noting the delicate silver whorls around the rims. To one side, a knife, fork, and spoon of genuine silver sat on a folded white napkin. In less than a minute, the boy came back and handed her a silver-rimmed glass goblet full of cloudy orange liquid that turned out to be a tangy citrus blend.

Another minute later, the caliph walked in and took the seat beside her. "I hope you didn't wait long."

"No, not long at all. This juice is incredible." She set it down and folded her hands in her lap, not sure where to look or what to do. Her eyes found her plate and stuck to it.

"It is, isn't it? I have some every morning at breakfast. Everyone else I know prefers wine, but that juice is remarkably refreshing, and leaves me feeling much more awake."

Amil appeared again, along with a second servant. They deposited small bowls on the plates, full of steaming red soup. Korval took the napkin from under his silverware, snapped it out, and draped it across his lap. "Tell me about this young man who stole your heart." Picking up his spoon, he dipped it into the soup and blew to cool it.

Fakhira echoed his actions, hoping he didn't take it as an insult. She hesitated, searching for words and worrying about how much to say. Would the caliph use any of this against her, or somehow find Tahjis and do something to him? From his behavior now, she didn't think so, but the man who grabbed her neck earlier surely would.

"Oh, come now. I thought girls your age liked to gush about their boys."

She frowned into her soup. "I wasn't raised on stories of love. To me, this is all very...strange and new."

"Ah, you were caught off guard by a chance encounter?"

"Yes, that's a good way to put it." She dipped the spoon in and watched the soup swirl, trying to sort out her feelings enough to explain.

"Where are you from that tells no tales of love and romance?"

She looked up at him with no idea what to say, or how he would react to the truth. If she said nothing, would it be worse. "The slums." The lie tumbled out of her mouth, and she imagined Tahjis's hole as the place she called home. She constructed an imaginary history out of the things she'd seen since she got here, the things Tahjis had told her, and pieces of her own life.

"Ah. A difficult place for a young woman to be. My predecessor once tried to solve that problem, then more sprang up in a different part of the city, where they are now. Much like Black Abhar, I've accepted them as a fact of city life."

She sipped at the soup, tasting savory flavors she'd never before encountered and had no names for. "What do you think the problem is that makes slums?" Not knowing much about the subject, she hoped he would enlighten her.

Korval showed her a sad smile. "The problem is that the problem is complex. It would be easy to say that poor people are lazy, but this is simply not true. Very few adults able to work resort to begging or stealing. Even of those who do, from what I've seen, they put a remarkable amount of effort into begging or stealing. It's unclear to me how they begin on such a path, and once they have some skill at it, turning them to something else is an uphill battle. Learning new skills is hard. Sticking with the old ones is easy. In my experience, humans tend to choose the easiest path."

Almiya had chosen to go along with the plan to marry Shahan because resisting would have been hard. Fakhira took the hard path now, and she'd spent the last few days confused and exhausted at nearly every turn. She nodded her agreement. "I think you could reduce the problem if you helped the children. Have them taught things that will help them succeed later."

Korval lifted a hand and snapped his fingers. "What do you think of that suggestion, Zavin?"

An older man with a short beard appeared at Korval's elbow as if he'd been waiting in a shadow to be summoned. Fakhira thought she caught him giving the back of Korval's head a glare, but the expression smoothed into bland neutrality too fast for her to be sure. The deep-blue silk of his gold-trimmed robes brushed her arm and she couldn't remember the last time she'd touched something so smooth and soft.

"Educating the street children, my Lord?" Zavin's voice rumbled in Fakhira's chest as he stroked his dark beard with long, thin fingers. "How...creative." He stretched out a hand to clutch her shoulder, his fingertips pressing into her flesh. She couldn't tell if he tried to push her down on purpose or merely used her to steady himself. "There may be a small segment of the population that would benefit from such an initiative, my Lord. In my experience, the strong hand of a parent is the best tool to guide young people. Even so, finding the financing for such a project would require a great deal of effort."

The caliph huffed in amusement. "Always comes back to money, doesn't it?" He leaned over and patted Fakhira's hand with a smile that made her recoil. "Zavin, make a note to consider the suggestion anyway and figure out how much it would cost."

"Of course." Zavin squeezed Fakhira's shoulder too hard and let go. "I'll give it all the attention it deserves." He bowed and backed into the shadows.

To avoid appearing rude, Fakhira stifled the urge to rub her shoulder. She ate another spoonful of the soup, hoping it would wash down the oily taste Zavin put in her mouth. It didn't.

Korval set his spoon down and wiped his mouth. This seemed to be a signal, because another servant stepped in and took his bowl away, replacing it with a plate holding wide noodles in a thick white sauce, studded with bits of a strange green vegetable and chunks of white meat.

"Back to the matter of Black Abhar, if it's your intention to kill him, what do you think will happen when he's gone?"

"Someone else will step into the void and fulfill similar functions," Fakhira said. "But we'll be able to free his prisoners, which will make things better."

"Especially for your boy's sister." He stuck his fork into the noodles and twirled it, winding them onto the tines. "What's his name?"

She didn't dare tell him that until she had more reason to trust him. "Shahan." Using this name seemed safe, and she'd remember it.

"But your true concern is Shahan's sister, isn't it? Does Abhar need to die for that? What if I could find a way to get her released?"

She set her spoon in her bowl and pushed it to the side. Amil sprang in, replacing it with noodles. "Why would you do that?"

He set his elbows on the table and clasped his hands together, the fork dangling from them. "I'm a devout follower of the Fires, Fakhira. The Fire Dancers live in my palace firstly because the Lead Dancer is my wife, but also because I've decided that's the best way to protect them. You may not be a Fire Dancer, but you've clearly been chosen by the Fires and

Waters for some task, and I mean to do my part to make sure you can attend to it. That's my part to play in such matters. If rescuing this girl means you can focus on your true calling and path, then I'll make it happen."

She blinked and stared at him in disbelief. "I almost killed you."

"Yes, and I almost raped you. I think we can look past that situation now, don't you? For my part, my brush with danger has made me realize it's stupid to put myself in that position. What I need is a steady mistress, not a series of escapes in Abhar's dens of iniquity."

She stabbed a noodle and stuck it in her mouth, confused again. The sauce tasted of cheese and butter, things she rarely ate at home. Pangs of homesickness clenched around her heart, forcing her to take a few deep breaths before speaking again. "Shahan wants Black Abhar dead for what he's done to his sister in the time she's been his prisoner. I pledged to help him make it happen. I'm sure he'd be happy to have her back, but it would break my vow."

For half a minute, the sounds of Korval eating—clinking, slurping, chewing, and swallowing—filled the room for Fakhira. All of it rang oppressive and demanding in her ears. "I can't let you risk yourself on such a foolish idea." The words dropped onto her, lead weights tying themselves to her feet.

What he offered had nothing to do with freedom. He would be nice to her, he would protect her. He wouldn't let her do anything that needed doing. "What if that's my path?"

"It's not." With a slice of his fork through the air, he gave the statement finality.

"But what if it was?"

He swallowed the food in his mouth and met her gaze. "Black Abhar is what I said: a cockroach. He's beneath the concerns of the Fires. The Fire Dancers believe this. That makes it true."

The Waters, on the other hand, might have noticed him. Korval clearly thought the Fires mattered more. "Am I prisoner here?"

"You're *protected* here. If you leave, I can't guarantee your safety. That makes leaving a very foolish idea. With no money, a woman alone on the streets or even with your Shahan, won't get far. Besides, look how well I'll keep you. This food? We eat like this every day. All the water you could ever want. You'll meet the Fire Dancers, and they'll keep you company. You can explore what powers the Fires grant you and learn to use them properly, at your beck and call. Invite Shahan to stay with you. He may be a good fit for my Guard, or perhaps the army. Then you'll have everything you could ever need. His sister can stay here as well, if you like."

Without a doubt, he knew how to present an attractive offer. She sat in silence, eating and thinking about it. The way he spoke, he didn't offer her a choice so much as explain what her life would be like from now on, whether she agreed or not. Were she truly from the slums, it would be irresistible: cared for, fed, surrounded by friends. Her life, however, hadn't been devoid of these things. Her family had had little, but they'd never starved or went without anything they truly needed.

"I'm tired," she said after a long pause. Setting her fork down, she put her hands into her lap. "I think I should get some rest."

"Go ahead. Amil will get you whatever you need. He'll show you back to your room."

Standing, she thought she understood the meaning of his statement: Amil would watch her and report on anything she did. "Thank you." She bowed her head to him and walked toward where she remembered the door being. It opened for her, letting light from the hallway in, and Amil shut it behind her.

"Are we actually going to your room?"

"What will you do if my answer is no?"

"Try to subtly suggest that might not be a good idea, then report back to the caliph when you go elsewhere anyway." He bowed his head in apology. "I work for him. What he demands is what I do."

She understood. "Then take me to my room, please. I have no need to make your job difficult tonight."

He let out a relieved breath and led her up the hallway with a grateful smile.

Chapter 13

Fakhira woke in gloom provided by dark blue linen curtains covering her windows. For the first time in her life, she slept on a real featherbed
with real feather pillows and soft, smooth sheets. The thin fur blanket covering her provided just the right amount of heat for the cool summer night.
Her eyes adjusted to the hazy light and she wondered if the caliph was
right. This life could suit her. Black Abhar didn't matter, not really.
Despite what Tahjis said, Scorpion probably would be as bad, and would
do all the same sorts of things.

Amil had laid out fresh clothes for her, this time including the
undershorts she requested. It bothered her that he moved about in her
room while she slept, and she didn't wake or see him. For all she knew, he
pulled the fur back and ogled her body. So far, she couldn't tell if he could
be trusted not to do such a thing. Tahjis wouldn't do that, not without permission. Korval, she felt certain, would.

Sliding off the bed, she dressed quickly and found food in her
smaller room. Amil left her a bowl filled with more foods she'd never seen

before. Little balls of orange, green, and red had been stacked with chopped dates and lime wedges. Beside it, a small plate held a thick slice of yellow bread studded with more chopped dates. She tried the balls, finding them to be fruit so juicy they nearly melted in her mouth. The mild flavors mingled on her tongue, soothing away thirst.

She took her time with the meal, enjoying each flavor and texture, and trying them all separate and in combinations. The bread turned out to be a rich lemon cake, and she discovered those bits of fruit had little in common with dates. Another new flavor greeted her as the small berries popped on her tongue. Drinking down the ice water provided with the meal, she sighed and wanted to crawl back into bed.

Hiding under the blanket would get her nothing and nowhere. She forced herself up out of the chair and opened the front door to her suite. Amil stood from his chair beside her door and smiled at her.

"The Fire Dancers have asked to meet with you today. I'll show you the way." He gestured for her to come with him.

"I want to see the caliph."

"I'll let him know while you sit with the Fire Dancers."

She stifled back a pout. "I don't want to see them."

Amil's smile faltered. "When the Fire Dancers call, it's unwise to refuse. You'll invite the wrath of the Fires. On both of us."

"I see." She had no desire to cause Amil harm for doing nothing more than following orders. "I guess I should go then." Stepping out of the room, she shut the door behind her and walked with him up the wide hall. "How many rooms like that does the caliph have?"

"The palace was built to house several visiting dignitaries and up to eleven Fire Dancers, all at once. We rarely need all the space." He guided her around a corner, then down a set of wide marble stairs. "It has three wings, one for the caliph and his personal guards, one for servants and staff, and one for guests. You're staying in the guest wing. The Fire Dancers are in the personal wing."

She noticed he didn't answer the question, but didn't press. He might not know the number. "Where did I eat last night?"

"In the casual guest dining chamber. The caliph thought you might appreciate not having to walk very far after your ordeal."

The stairs opened into a grand chamber with so many arches leading to rooms or hallways it must be a hub for everything. More than two dozen people passed through laden with trays, cloth, sacks, papers, or boxes. Amil slipped through them with ease. It looked like chaos to Fakhira, and she kept her hands close as she dodged people. He took her down a smaller hallway, one without displays of art or wealth.

"Where did they get all this beautiful stone for the floor?"

"There's a quarry near Peshtir."

Fakhira had never heard of Peshtir. It didn't seem to matter much. The caliph had a quarry, so the stone belonged to him. She made a small noise so Amil knew she'd heard him.

They walked until they reached another large room of halls and doors. Amil took her up another set of stairs and another wide, ornamented hallway. He stopped at a set of double doors and knocked. A young girl —perhaps twelve years old—opened it, her black hair braided and coiled around her head. She wore a bright red silk dress and a pleasant smile. Fakhira thought she resembled the caliph around the eyes.

"This is Fakhira. The Dancers asked to see her."

"Oh!" The girl beamed at her, grabbed her hand, and pulled her into a large room full of soft things. It had couches, chairs, cushions, furs, and silks in bright colors, all scattered and draped around the room. "Come in, come in." The girl dragged her to a couch and waved at it for her to sit. "Mama! Fakhira is here!"

Fakhira threw an alarmed glance back at Amil, who shooed her inside and closed the door. On her own now, she lowered herself into the chair and, like her bed, it swallowed her up in comfort. With a little sigh of pleasure, she surveyed the room and realized some of the colored fabric covered the bodies of women lounging on the furniture.

Seven of them, a full troupe of Fire Dancers, stood and approached her. Each took her breath away with their beauty. As dancers, all had athletic bodies, though not the same kind as Fakhira. She'd spent her days working and cleaning and cooking. These women spent their days communing with the Fires and practicing ritual dances. Their duties made them critical to any leader who wished the populace to follow him. A wise ruler pampered his Fire Dancers to keep them happy.

Each had a head of shiny, full-bodied hair, some straight and some curly. None had scars, blemishes, freckles, or other marring. All moved with liquid grace. It seemed to Fakhira that these women must have been sculpted to perfection, or chosen because of their looks.

"Thank you, Adiya," said the tallest of them. This Dancer had

120

wavy hair and wore a peach dress with slit on the side to her hip. Her smooth, perfect bronze thigh peeked out higher than Fakhira would consider allowing. She waved the girl off, and Adiya skipped away. "Welcome, Fakhira." She held out soft hands laden with gold and gemstones to take Fakhira's plain, calloused ones. "I'm sure this is all confusing and frightening."

The woman's clear soprano voice enticed her to stay, to speak of whatever she wished. How such things could come from mere pleasantries, she had no idea. She didn't care, either, so long as the woman kept talking to her. Since she seemed to be waiting for a response, Fakhira nodded.

Tugging gently at her hands, the woman pulled her back up to her feet. "I'm Mahdis, the lead Fire Dancer for Korval's domain, and his wife. Come, let us speak of the Fires."

Fakhira trailed along behind Mahdis, an obedient dog following her master. They moved to a long couch, and a different Fire Dancer pulled her close, her arms wrapped around Fakhira's waist. Mahdis sat beside her. A third sat at her feet, body pressed to her legs and hands on her knees. The fourth and fifth stood behind her. One ran her fingers through Fakhira's hair and scraped her scalp with her fingernails. The other rubbed her neck and shoulders, digging thumbs into places in her upper back that cried out in joy at the ministrations. The sixth knelt in front of her, rubbing her feet. The last offered her a cup of juice.

All the closeness should have been stifling. Instead, Fakhira felt loved, cared for, and pampered. She relaxed into their hands and the cushions, a small sigh escaping her lips. Her eyes fluttered with the pleasure.

121

After all the trials and confusion and aches and loss, she needed this and reveled in it. Even when they stopped actively caressing her skin and muscles, she wanted to lie there and do nothing.

"Fakhira." Mahdis whispered next to her ear. "Wake up." Fakhira opened her eyes to find Mahdis's perfect skin close. Mahdis touched her cheek to Fakhira's in a cat-like gesture, then pulled away enough for Fakhira to see the smile on her full lips. "Tell us about the Fires."

Whatever Mahdis wanted to know, Fakhira would answer. Something about that seemed wrong, but she didn't care. "Fire..."

"Show me, Fakhira."

The command plucked a string deep inside her and she held up a hand. Languid and sleepy, she called to the Waters. Nothing answered. "It won't come."

Mahdis chuckled. "We've relaxed her too much. No matter. Rest, Fakhira. We'll speak later."

"No," she protested. "Don't send me away."

"I won't." She kissed Fakhira's forehead. "You're staying with us for now." She gathered Fakhira into her arms and held her close. Her mother had held her this way, a long time ago, and Fakhira curled up in the memories. Tears welled up in her eyes and spilled out onto the soft peach cloth.

She stroked Fakhira's hair. "You poor thing. The Fires took you after a tragedy. Who did you lose?"

"Everyone."

"Let it out, Fakhira. Mourn them."

In Mahdis's arms, she wrung her heart dry for her parents, her sister, her nephew, her brothers, her friends, and her home. They'd left her alone, in a world that didn't care about her. The Waters wanted her, but the Waters couldn't hold her or tell her a story, or smack her rump when she did something to deserve it.

None of these things came out in words, and when she'd cried herself dry for the second time, she lay there, staring at nothing. Warm skin and soft cloth surrounded her and she wanted to stay like this forever.

Chapter 14

"Fakhira," Mahdis murmured, "it's time for lunch. After that, we'll brush your hair and braid it for you, then we'll find your best colors and have clothes made just for you. When your Shahan comes for you, you'll be the most beautiful woman he's ever seen, and he'll want you with the desire of a thousand suns."

She sat up and nodded, willing to do anything for Mahdis. Without leaving the couch, they ate salads in folded flatbread with lime yogurt and date wine. The women fussed over her, brushing her hair and braiding it down her back. They washed her face with something cool and spicy, then brushed powder over it. They slathered something cool and thick over her fingers and toes, then they trimmed her nails and painted them. Cloth flew all around her as they argued about the perfect color for her. In the end, they wrapped her in cobalt blue silk.

As they worked, they chattered about names and places Fakhira had never heard of. She let the voices drift through the air, their words passing her by. When they finished with her, she twirled for them, the skirt of her dress flaring out. Someone provided applause, and she stopped to see the caliph near the door.

"Bravo, ladies. I see her time here was well spent." His boots clacked as he approached.

Adiya ran to him with a squeal of delight and hugged him. He tousled her hair.

The Fire Dancers each gave him a polite incline of their head. "She needed a day of rest, Korval," Mahdis chided. "She should go to bed after dinner, and she'll spend tomorrow with us, as well."

"As you say, so it shall be." He bowed to Mahdis, then straightened and offered his arm to Fakhira. "Come, child. Dinner and then to your bed."

"Papa, can I come?" Adiya gazed up at Korval with adoring eyes.

"Not tonight." He kissed the top of the girl's head and pushed her away. "I'll come for breakfast tomorrow."

When Adiya sighed and let go, Fakhira nodded and took Korval's arm. He led her to that large dining room and seated her at his right side again. Another parade of new flavors teased her mouth. As they ate, Korval made a few remarks about her appearance without inviting questions or conversation until Amil set a mound of chocolate cake piled with frothy cream and sprinkled with sugar in front of her for dessert.

"I've thought a great deal about Black Abhar and your interest in seeing him dead. If you tell me who Shahan's sister is, I'll have her released, but I don't think this is a good time to deal with Abhar in such a final manner. Tomorrow, I leave to lead my army against Caliph Trimar, and an upheaval as tumultuous as the one Abhar's death would cause will need a firm hand on the city. When I return, that would be a good time to pursue the matter."

Such a practical reason had her nodding in agreement. She tried to think of how to make sure Korval had the right girl released without revealing Tahjis's true name. "I don't know where she's being held."

"Where can we find Shahan? He'll know the details, I expect."

As much as she trusted Mahdis and liked the caliph, it felt like a betrayal to reveal where Tahjis lived. "He doesn't trust guardsmen. Let me go find him."

Korval scratched his cheek and leaned back, chewing a bite of the cake. He swallowed it down and shook his head. "I can't let you risk yourself like that. Write him a letter?"

She dropped her eyes to her lap. "He can't read." If he wouldn't let her out, and she wouldn't tell him Tahjis's real name, this wouldn't work. "Her name is Santrice."

Korval shrugged. "I'll get him to release any girl named Santrice. That should resolve the matter." He snapped his fingers and Zavin appeared, startling Fakhira.

Zavin's spindly fingers brushed across her shoulder. "My apologies," he said to her. As before, his touch made her uncomfortable, though she still couldn't explain why.

Mustering a weak smile, Fakhira looked up at him. She stared into his light brown eyes and felt dizzy. Turning away, she tried to come up with something appropriate to say. Nothing seemed right.

127

"I'll take care of it," Zavin said with a shallow bow, now ignoring her.

Korval nodded and waved to dismiss him. He turned his attention to Fakhira again as Zavin ducked into the shadows and disappeared. "While I'm gone, I expect you to get to know the Fire Dancers and develop your connection to the Fires. If your Shahan comes to the palace, the guards will let him in on your word."

She took a deep breath and shook her head to clear it. All the rich food had to be muddling her. With a few seconds of concerted effort, she pulled her thoughts together. "What will you do to Trimar?"

His brow raised and he clasped his hands together over his plate. "He laid waste to Aitrae Oasis, destroying vital supplies and killing hundreds of people. We'll return the favor twofold."

Thinking she misunderstood, she furrowed her brow. "Won't you kill him?"

"Assassinating a caliph is dangerous business, and we need to be careful not to invite someone worse into his position in his stead. It's a matter not unlike that with Abhar. Such men must be managed, and it's always easier to manage a man you know than one you don't. I've met Trimar before, and I know his type. As much as I'd like to indulge my own desire for revenge on him for a few things, it would be counterproductive."

Korval took one last bite of the cake, then set his fork down and pushed it away. "I expect to be gone for two weeks, three if the campaign proves troublesome. When I return, if Shahan hasn't come for you yet, I'll take you into the city myself so we can find him."

"Thank you." She bowed her head.

Wiping his mouth with his napkin, he stood. "Sleep well, Fakhira." He dropped the napkin and left the room.

Fakhira took another bite of the cake, wondering if the unfinished food would be eaten by someone else. She also wanted to laugh at her foolishness for thinking that killing these men—Black Abhar and Trimar—would have any useful effect. Though she still yearned to see someone punished for her loss, and knew Tahjis must feel the same, one man here or there wouldn't make any difference in the bigger picture. The Fires and the Waters would see them dealt with, one way or another.

Chapter 15

"Fakhira," a voice hissed.

She opened her eyes and saw someone looming over her in the near darkness. When she opened her mouth to scream, a hand covered it.

"Shh. It's Tahjis."

Stunned, her eyes snapped open wide and she surged up to wrap her arms around his neck. "What are you doing here?"

He tensed with the embrace, then relaxed and put his arms around her. "Did you think I'd leave you to rot in the caliph's prison?"

She laughed. "Such a terrible prison it is."

"Without a doubt, it's the softest one I've ever seen or heard of. Come on, I can get you out." He slid his hands under her arms and pushed, forcing her to let go.

"Out? I don't want to get out." She pulled the fur blanket up to cover her bare breasts. "Do you want to take a bath? He'll get you new clothes, just like he did for me. We can be safe here, and he'll have Santrice released."

In the dark, she had a hard time making out his face, but she thought it crinkled in confusion. "You're saying crazy things, Al-Kabar."

"Fakhira. My name is Fakhira."

"Whatever. Scorpion expected something different, but the fire at the club was good enough and she's ready to help us kill Abhar. We have a plan, but we need your help. I have your sword and your man clothes. Come on, I'll help you change." He took her hand and tugged.

"No, you don't understand." This didn't match how she thought seeing him again would go. He was supposed to sweep her into his arms and kiss her, not talk about plans for murder that needed her to pretend to be a man. "Abhar needs to be managed, not killed. He's not worth killing."

Brumble squeaked and Tahjis nodded. He slid off the edge of the bed without Fakhira, pacing to the window and peering out around the curtain. "Scorpion is ready to take the position from him. She's a step up from Abhar, I've already explained that. It's a step worth taking."

"But you don't know she'll really be that way." She followed him, pulling the fur with her. "She could be worse, for some reason you don't know yet. What about the way she treats those men? Is that better?"

He glanced at her, then back out the window. "Are you coming or not?"

"But the caliph is going to free Santrice. He promised. You don't need to do any of this."

Tahjis froze. He let the curtain rush back into place. She could tell he turned to look at her. "What? Why would he do that?"

She gulped, hoping she hadn't done anything seriously wrong. "He thought I went down there to try to kill him, so I told him I was there to kill Abhar, and he wanted to know why. I said you were—I said I loved you, and Santrice is your sister, and that's why we wanted to kill Abhar. For her. He said he'd have her freed."

"You told him about me?" He sounded so angry and incredulous that she feared he might attack her. "Why would you do that?"

"I gave him a fake name. I called you Shahan, my sister's husband's name. I told him I grew up in the slums and he's given me everything I could want: food, clothes, a place to live, even friends. You could stay with me. He said you'd be welcome here, and he would even find you a job, if you want."

Tahjis thumped his back against the window, crossing his arms and looking down. Brumble squeaked again. "What's the catch?"

"Catch? I don't understand."

"Nobody gives away everything for nothing. What does he want?"

"Nothing." She said it, knowing it to be a lie. Her shoulders slumped. "I can't leave. He says it's too dangerous."

He snorted. "That part I already figured out. I knew it was a prison the second I got here. A nice, fluffy, pampered prison, but still a prison. If you put a rat in a cage, it doesn't become less of a cage just because you give it food and toys." Huffing in frustration, he shook his head. "What happened in the club? I heard there was a fire, and I saw them hauling girls out, but I didn't get any details."

"Someone...got hold of me and tried to—" She couldn't finish the sentence, not for him. "The Waters...I somehow started a fire. I think it took too much of me to do it, because I blacked out."

"I never should have sent you in there alone. It was dumb. You're pretty, and they can smell virgins at twenty paces. It was—"

"You think I'm pretty?"

He scratched at the wrapping on his head, shifting from one foot to the other. "Do you want to kill Trimar, or not?"

She didn't know how to take his abrupt change of subject. "He's no different from Abhar. Kill him and another one takes his place. There's no reason to. It's a waste of time."

Silence filled the space between them for a long time. "I know I said that, and I'll bet Korval said the same thing. But there's more to it than that. I don't want to kill Abhar because he has my sister. If all I wanted to do was free Santrice, I could have done that by now. I want to free her and not have to hide her away. I want her to be able to hold her head up and not cringe in the darkness, afraid he'll come to take her back, and this time, it'll be worse.

"Even with all that, you know what I want the most? I want for no one to ever have to watch his mother be raped and murdered again, and for no one to ever be raped by Abhar or his men or 'customers' ever again. And I definitely don't want anyone to have to watch that like I've had to. That's what I want. You think Scorpion will do that? Because I believe her when she says she won't. I believe her when she says to my face that she wants to close the brothels and the pits and focus on smuggling things, not people. Keep thievery down and get people to stop targeting those who can't afford it. She's better than Abhar, and I know it, and after meeting her, you should know it, too."

She covered her hand with her mouth, a well of sympathy brimming in her belly. "I'm sorry."

"I don't want your pity."

"I hid when they came to our house. They didn't know I was there, and I listened to them rape and murder my sister, and kill her baby." When he said nothing, she held out her hand. "Sit with me, Tahjis. Please. I don't like being alone."

He shrugged. "I'm not clean enough for that bed."

"I don't care." She watched him take a deep breath, rub his eyes with a finger and thumb, and pull the wrap from his head to reveal his shaggy hair.

"I came here to get Al-Kabar so we could kill Abhar. He deserves death ten times over for what he's done, not just to me and mine. Will you come with me? I need your help."

She had no idea what Korval would do if he found out she left. If he never knew, nothing would happen. "If I do, will you come back here with me?"

He grabbed the back of his neck while his feet twitched. "Is that what you want? Because we could go to Scorpion instead. She'd take us in and let us work for her as trusted lieutenants."

"The caliph wants me to work with the Fire Dancers. He said I should learn to use the power granted to me."

Tahjis stopped fidgeting and moved to the edge of the bed. "There's only one reason he would want that, and it's not devotion to the

Fires. You're a weapon, Fakhira. He wants to hone you and use you. When he leaves with his army, he'll be laying the foundation for you to come through and sweep the land clear."

"But—"

"But nothing. He keeps the Fire Dancers locked up here because they have power and he uses it, everyone knows that. He thinks you're like them, but you're not. You're something else, and he's too blind to see it. Fakhira, he doesn't care about you. He makes you feel like he cares, but he only wants more power. The Waters chose you to do something special, something no one else can. Stand up and do it."

He pulled her sword out of his pack and tossed it onto the bed, the hilt landing near her hand. "Take it. Use it. You have it for a reason, and it isn't to be a pampered cat in a palace, fed milk and honey until you bloat. You're a desert flower, yes, but the kind with thorns. He thinks you're a weapon. Show him that he's right, and also that he can't control you."

When she didn't move, he grabbed her hand and shoved it onto the hilt. The metal warmed her fingers and it felt like picking up something she forgot she needed. Her memories played in her mind, of Korval grabbing her neck, of how she woke up, of being told she couldn't leave. The Fire Dancers had truly been kind to her, but how much was real and how much faked?

Gripping the sword, she ran a finger along the curves of the blade, light enough not to cut herself, firm enough to feel it. Tahjis said she had a purpose, and the sword proved it. Why else would she stumble across such a thing if the Waters intended her to sit on feather beds and wear silk and eat little balls of fruit? "Show me my path," she murmured.

"It's with me." Tahjis sat on the edge of the bed and she made out a small smile on his face. "You fell into my home for a reason."

"Just like I fell into the Waters." She answered his smile with one of her own. "It's so hard to think when someone is feeding you incredible food and rubbing your feet."

"That's why the rich are soft. They never can think through the luxury. Come with me, please, and help me with Abhar. After that, I'll do whatever you want."

"Anything at all?"

"I look bad in a dress, so almost anything."

She managed to laugh and slid to the edge of the bed. "I'm not wearing anything."

He gave her a wave. "Bah. I've seen it all before." His voice cracked.

Her cheeks burned. "Maybe, but you have my clothes. I'll need them to leave."

"Oh! Right. Sorry." He pulled the sand-yellow clothes and stuffed sock from folds in his own clothing and set it all on the bed.

Since he *had* seen her nude before, and the darkness hid her well enough, she let go of the fur. Setting her feet on the floor, she had to step close to pick up the clothes. The heat radiating from him warmed her, and she wondered what he could see of her.

He touched her hip again, in the same place as the last time, and it scalded her skin. Light and tentative, he left it there for only a moment, then pulled it away. As before, he turned to scoot away.

Not sure why she did it, she grabbed his hand and didn't let him go. "It's alright. I don't mind."

"We don't—" His voice cracked again and he cleared it. "There's no time for this now. We need to meet Scorpion's men soon."

Shivering, she let go of him and he turned away. "After, then. We'll talk more after."

"Yes. After."

Chapter 16

Tahjis led her through the streets of the city, the soft glow of the nearly full moon providing ample light. Every time she tried to ask about the plan, he shushed her, and after the fourth time, she realized he must not want to be overheard talking about it. Despite the late hour, people still moved about on foot, on horseback, and in carts and carriages. In Aitrae Oasis, people went out in the early morning, stayed inside or under shade through the middle of the day to avoid the worst heat, then came out again near dusk as the day's searing heat faded. They slept through the coldest parts of the night, though, unlike these people.

Since Fakhira had dressed as Al-Kabar and carried her sword again, her mind felt clearer and sharper. The actions of the Fire Dancers made sense to her, though she still didn't fully understand everything Korval told her. It seemed his argument came down to not trying because he knew he'd fail. This seemed foolish.

She followed Tahjis down an alley, thinking nothing of it until he grabbed her arm and thumped her against the wall beside him. "This is the place." He pointed at the building opposite them, a place she didn't notice before he called her attention to it. "He's coming here tonight, to inspect it in operation."

Blinking in confusion, she asked, "How do you know that?"

"Scorpion told me."

"How does she know?"

"People like your bean seller."

"But how—"

Tahjis slashed a hand through the air, irritation showing in a mild scowl. "We don't have time for this right now. We're going to break in, find him, and kill him, along with anyone else who decides they don't like that plan. I'm hoping we can sneak well enough to keep that number low. But, like Scorpion said, however many of Abhar's men we kill now makes fewer we have to deal with later."

Fakhira took a deep breath and gripped the hilt of her sword. He'd gotten her this far and deserved her trust. "Is there more to the plan than that?"

"Not really. I usually improvise. It keeps my options open." He tapped her arm and led her down the alley to the back of the building. Stopping at the corner, he peered around, then ducked back with a tiny huff. He gripped her shoulder, pointed at her, then pointed at the ground.

She had no idea what that meant. When he slipped around the corner, she followed him. Two men flanked a door in the back wall, each standing with his hands clasped together. Their poses spoke of casual attention, bored indifference. Aside from them, the side alley had neatly stacked crates and barrels against the opposite wall. In front of her, Tahjis had dart-ed to where they gave him cover.

His gestures suddenly made sense when one of the two men noticed her. "What do you want?"

Caught unprepared, Fakhira put her hands up and shook her head. "Nothing."

"Then keep moving."

Tahjis covered his forehead in exasperation and flicked a hand for her to go away.

"What's that?" The guard noticed Tahjis's hand and pulled his curved sword from his belt. Lunging for the spot, he caught Tahjis by the shirt before he could jump clear.

Fakhira gulped and hesitated while the second man took a step to put his body in front of the door.

"Oh, look, it's Tahjis the Rat!" The guard held his sword to Tahjis's neck. "Didn't expect to see you here. Did you come to pay up? It's a little late, but Abhar might be in a generous mood. You never know." He looked Fakhira over, from sword to toe. "Is this your new boyfriend?"

Gasping and grasping the guard's arm, he shook his head. "I don't know him."

She blinked, confused by the lie. Too late, she realized why he said that.

"You're a lousy liar, Tahjis. Come on, boy," the guard said to Fakhi-ra, "come with us or Tahjis loses his head and we take his debt out of your hide." He held the sword closer to Tahjis's neck, cutting his flesh enough to get a tiny bit of blood.

Staring at him, she knew she couldn't let him get hurt, not because she did or didn't do something. She nodded and followed as the man hauled Tahjis through the door. The back room had stacked crates and a desk. It took Fakhira two steps in before she realized the crates held people. With a closer look, she saw these people were children, each of them lying limp on the floor of their crate, but still breathing. Most seemed asleep.

They moved through the room too quickly for her to register much of this. A set of creaking stairs took them up to a long hallway. The guard dragged Tahjis to a door near the middle, flanked by two guards, where he knocked and waited for a voice from inside it to invite them. This room featured emerald green and dark blue fabric draped over the walls and a mound of cushions in both colors. On this mound, a large, burly man in all black knelt with his back to them.

The man adjusted his pants and smacked something in front of him. When he stood, Fakhira saw a woman's naked body, which explained why the slap sounded like it hit flesh. She curled up, scuttling away from the big man.

"I'm not through with you." His voice rumbled in the room, dark and ominous. He turned and Fakhira thought his meaty face matched his voice. A thick mustache shaded his mouth, and his swarthy skin glistened with a sheen of sweat. "Tahjis, this is a pleasant surprise. Come to grovel and pay? Who's this?"

The guard shoved him at the floor, hard enough that he stumbled and fell. Landing on his side, he grunted and got to his hands and knees, then sat up on his feet. "It's nice to see you again too, Black Abhar. How's the family?"

Abhar sneered down at him. "Better than yours."

"No doubt."

"Hand it over." He reached out a beefy hand.

Tahjis took a deep breath and rolled to a crouch. "Funny thing. I didn't come here to pay."

Fakhira's eyes went wide. She pulled her sword, wishing he'd found a way to tell her before this idea came to mind. The guard in front of her reacted by pulling his sword out.

Abhar barked out a laugh. "You think you're going to challenge me? Let's see you try."

Tahjis sprang at him, pulling a knife. Abhar shoved a foot out, kicking him in the side and knocking him away. He reached over and grabbed a thick, fat blade and lunged with it at Tahjis. Fakhira took a step, intent on helping. A guard hopped into her way. She swung her blade and metal clanged as the guard's sword blocked hers. The impact reverberated up her arm to her shoulder, making her grunt with the pain.

Behind her, the door slammed open again and she snapped her head around to see the two guards from the hallway charging in, swords drawn. Spinning around, she avoided three different arcs, each of which could have taken her head. Panic pulsed in her veins as she realized she had to defend against three men at once again and still had no idea how to manage it. One wrong step, she knew, and she'd never recover.

Slipping to the side, she put the wall to her back. If she couldn't escape the room, at least she could keep them from surrounding her. Jerking her head to the side, she felt splinters fly when a sword plunged into the wall beside her.

"Feh. Stupid whelp. If you just paid up, you wouldn't be in this position." Abhar spat on Tahjis, who struggled to get out from under the large foot pressing down on his chest. His knife lay on the ground, out of his reach.

Distracted by his situation, one of the guards managed to hit her sword and scrape his blade down it. With no crosspiece, his blade would slide right down to cut her hand. She let go of it rather than risk such injury. The moment the sword left her hand, her body stopped being guided by an unknown force. Only then did she realize the sword could control her.

"Don't kill him." Abhar's words interrupted a strike aimed for her gut. "I have ideas for these two."

The guard managed to turn the blow aside, choosing to slam his shoulder into Fakhira, then punch her in the belly. She crumpled to the floor and endured another kick, then a heavy blow on the back of her head. The situation felt too familiar. At least this time, she didn't lose consciousness. The world swam and she couldn't crawl if she wanted to, yet she saw and heard everything happening around her.

"Turns out I'm done with you, after all," Abhar spat at the girl cowering in the corner. "Get back to work." He waved at Tahjis and Fakhira for his guards. "Tie these two up and have them taken to Kettery Row. I'll be there later with a special surprise."

Fakhira saw the naked girl scramble out of the cushions and to her feet without a glance for either her or Tahjis. One guard grabbed Fakhira's hands and wound a cheap linen scarf around her wrists, then her ankles. Another gave Tahjis the same treatment. When she found herself hefted up and thrown over on man's shoulder, her stomach rebelled and she managed to pull her scarf aside before she vomited.

She saw little as the guard carried her out. They went back down the hall and the stairs. In that back room, the guard dropped her on the floor and she landed in a heap, moaning. Foul-smelling water splashed over her, then he stuffed her into a burlap sack. It smelled of sweat and fear, of urine and bile.

"Cry out and I'll hit the bag. Be silent and I'll let you out when we get there." He cinched the bag shut and tossed it. She hit the wall and groaned, cutting it off as quickly as she could. The other guard repeated the warning, probably for Tahjis, then a lump slammed into her and let out an unfocused grunt.

Too weak to try to escape, Fakhira focused on staying conscious and not throwing up again. In the time that passed, she forced herself to blink rapidly, to wiggle her fingers and toes, and to form silent words with her lips while she breathed through her mouth. Tahjis's breathing changed to that of sleep without him saying a word. Fakhira didn't hear any squeaking, and hoped Brumble hadn't been hurt badly.

The door opened and closed several times before someone came and heaved Tahjis's bag, then hers. She avoided struggling, afraid she'd be beaten for it, and kept quiet. Her bag sailed through the air, then she hit something hard and slid. Creaking and bouncing confused her until she recognized the clop of horse hooves and chatter of people on the street. They'd been loaded into a cart bound for Kettery Row.

Chapter 17

Unloaded and tossed again, Fakhira sucked in fresh air as soon as the guard opened her sack. This room had little in common with the previous one. It spoke of genuine opulence, with silks and patterned rugs. The most obvious sign of wealth came in the form of a blue marble fountain in the middle. No one wasted precious water in such a way unless they had so much money they could afford to do anything.

For this meeting with Abhar, they had an audience. He lounged in a large throne-like chair of gold covered with green cushions. It stood on a dais of the same marble as the fountain, two steps up from the rest of the room. Cushions and rugs lay scattered about, some with women wearing collars, others with men sitting and watching. Beside Abhar's throne, a lump covered by black cloth had a golden chain snaking out to a hook on the throne itself. Abhar's hand rested on the top lump, which Fakhira thought might be someone's head.

Scorpion learned from him, Fakhira thought, though she had less money and more humanity. Her men may have been debased to a certain degree, but not with collars. They even seemed to enjoy her treatment of them. Scanning the room, she saw no woman here who appeared to enjoy her situation. All had their collars clipped to rings in the floor with no slack, keeping their heads down.

The most important thing in the room, she noticed last: her sword. It leaned against the throne, tip on the floor and hilt resting against the leg. Abhar didn't touch it or seem to regard it as anything other than a curiosity or trophy. His intentions might include giving it back when he released them, though she doubted that.

"Welcome to my favorite place." As Abhar spoke, someone shook Fakhira out of her bag. She and Tahjis were dumped onto the floor between the dais and the fountain, putting them in a clear space where Abhar could look down on them with ease. "This is my palace beneath Kettery Row. Tahjis, why did I choose this place?"

The Rat shook his head, not truly awake yet. Fakhira could see him struggling to comprehend the situation and his position.

"Ah, this will be no fun if he's not sensible. Douse them with water." A man picked up a bucket from the wide pool at the base of the fountain and threw it at them.

Fakhira saw it coming and screwed her eyes shut, holding her breath. Beside her, Tahjis coughed and sputtered. When she opened her eyes again, she saw the moment he understood and felt the horror of the situation.

His head turned around slowly, eyes flicking from one girl to the next. When he'd checked them all, he zeroed in on the black cloth on the dais. He made a noise, his voice cracking and failing. After he coughed again, he spat out a gob of blood. "Let her go."

Abhar laughed, deep and hearty. "You have no leverage here, Tahjis. There's nothing you have that I want. But, I'm still a businessman, and I know a dead thief is worthless. You're good at what you do, and have done well for so long. I don't need to kill you for managing to find your balls and trying to kill me once. Such things cannot, of course, go unpunished, but you'll survive this time. Next time will be a different story."

He grabbed the black cloth and whipped it away to reveal a woman a year or two older than Fakhira, her eyes flat and resigned. She'd been gagged with a white silk cloth, and sat on her feet with her hands bound behind her back, wearing no other covering at all. If only she had a reason to smile, this woman would be beautiful.

Tahjis screamed in rage and scrabbled to get free of his bindings. At a flick of Abhar's hand, a man kicked Tahjis in the head. He slumped and panted. "Let her go." This time, it came out as a plea.

"I see you have a better attitude already. That won't save her. What's your name, Tahjis's foolish friend?"

Fakhira saw the men near at hand, ready to pursue more violence, and chose not to provoke them. "Al-Kabar."

"Well met, Al-Kabar. I don't truly blame you for any of this. I'm sure Tahjis had a convincing story and plan, and you only wanted to help out of some misguided sense of brotherhood. Alas, you helped him try to kill me, so you share his punishment anyway. Allow me to explain. This is Santrice. I see from your face that he explained about her. Good. This should serve for you as a warning of what I do to traitors and would-be assassins."

Fakhira gulped and nodded. Everything fell into place, and she understood exactly what she was about to witness. She wanted to beg for mercy, for both Santrice and Tahjis. Her voice failed.

"Hold him," Abhar commanded. "Keep his head up and make sure he has a good view."

Two men grabbed Tahjis, one of them taking a handful of his hair to crank his head high. For added incentive, the other put a knife to his throat. He leaned down and told Tahjis, "It'll be worse if you close your eyes."

She couldn't watch and also couldn't look away. When Abhar shoved Santrice into the same position as her brother, forcing her head to the floor so she had to turn and look at him, Fakhira flinched. They stared at each other in silence until Santrice gasped in pained surprise, her face gone taut with despair.

Fakhira saw Almiya, brutalized by strange men. She saw that woman whose name she'd never know. She felt the outrage in her womb. Men had no right to do this to women. All her life, her parents taught her that she could always say no. Even when he picked a husband for her, Father made it clear she could dismiss him for any reason. No man had the right to force himself on any woman, and the Waters cursed such men.

Rage filled her heart as it had in the club. It shivered down her arms. The scarf binding her wrists froze. No one noticed. Their attention remained focused on the spectacle of Abhar violating Santrice. Abhar, she saw, split his attention between his two victims. So intent on watching both of them suffer, he failed to notice when Fakhira twisted her body, shattered the scarf, and untied her ankles.

"Brumble!" She jumped to her feet and ran for her sword, leaping up the steps.

"Get him!" Abhar slapped Santrice, the crack of his hand hitting her flesh chased by Santrice's sharp cry of pain.

The two guards holding Tahjis shoved his face to the floor without cutting his throat and sprang after Fakhira. She felt the sword take control of her movements and didn't resist it. Her legs sprang, flinging her out of the way of the two charging men and up onto the throne's seat. She flung a hand out and covered the steps in a rime of frost. The two men slipped and crashed into each other, falling in a heap.

Abhar watched this, his eyes narrowing when she turned to glare at him. She leaped at him and he hurried backward, grabbing and holding out his sword in time to deflect her strike. Behind her, Santrice scurried under the throne. Tahjis struggled on the floor, rocking around to get himself free.

Intent on Abhar, Fakhira whirled and flashed her sword, her hand chilling as she swung. He parried her blows, but took another step back with every clash of their blades. As they moved down the dais, the fountain exploded in a spray of ice shards. She reached a hand out and called. Water engulfed her arm and spread down her blade, swirling with blue light.

Abhar's eyes widened and he stumbled toward Tahjis. "Who are you," he growled at her.

151

Enraged and not expecting the question, Fakhira said the first thing that came to mind. "Al-Kabar."

Brumble ran away from Tahjis, a chewed scarf clutched in her mouth. Hands now free but feet still tied together, Tahjis roared his anger and surged up. He managed only to trip Abhar, who fell into the empty fountain. Guards converged on Fakhira and Tahjis, swords drawn and ready to throw their lives between threats and Abhar.

Forced to defend Tahjis while he untied his feet, Fakhira had to forget about Abhar for now. She stood over the Rat and begged the water to cover her whole body. Too many guards crowded in for her to block them all, so she swung the blade around to fend them off. They ducked and tried to keep clear of it, fear flickering on their faces.

"Don't get surrounded," Tahjis grunted. "I need a weapon." Now freed, he clearly wanted to chase after Abhar. Instead, he stayed low and stuck close.

Fakhira looked for the weakest link and lunged at him. She stabbed through his belly and kept going, shoving him out of the way. Tahjis followed her through the hole and grabbed the blade out of the falling man's hand.

"Get Santrice," she grunted. Jerking her sword out of the one guard, she flung it back to sweep off the leg of the nearest guard. It sliced through his knee, dropping him to the floor.

Tahjis ran for the throne. Fakhira slid into his wake, cutting off the guards from following him. Putting her back to him, she gave her attention to keeping anyone from getting past her. The guards fell back when a wide arc of her blade sent chunks of ice spraying out, hitting two men and making them groan.

Uncertain how she did that, Fakhira struggled to hide how much effort it took her to keep the water cold and on her blade. For a few moments, the thugs stayed far enough away that she could take a moment to pant, then Abhar ran up and threw a bucket of sand through them and at her. Stunned, Fakhira stood and blinked and lost control of the water. It splashed to the floor in a gritty mess.

Abhar sneered from behind a wall of his men. "It's just a stupid trick. Never mind lessons and all that. They're too much work. Kill them. All three."

"Time to go," Tahjis said. Brumble squeaked. He and Santrice, now freed from the throne, ran to the side.

Snapped out of a panic before it could build, Fakhira followed them with her sword still up. Within moments, she had to fend off new attacks as the guards closed in. Santrice led the way, running through a curtain hung to conceal a door. On the other side, they hurried up a spiral stair, boots clomping on the stone.

The sword took someone's hand, sending it flopping down the steps, and they kept going. Something cut Fakhira's leg as she turned and ran for it at the top stair. It hurt. It didn't stop her. They burst out through a door, and Tahjis yanked his shirt off, throwing it over Santrice's head as they dashed into an alley and kept going.

Two blocks away, Fakhira had to stop, leaning against a wall. Blood stained her pants around a slice where she must have taken a hit from the tip of a blade. The moment she saw it, the wound hurt worse, adding a wheeze to her panting. Santrice fell onto Tahjis, hugging him and crying and knocking him over as he gasped for breath through his own tears.

"We can't stay here." Fakhira pulled her pant leg up and winced at the wound, still bleeding and probably the source of her current light-headedness. "And we need food and water. Not only that, but someone will notice I've gone missing unless I'm at the palace in the morning."

Tahjis nodded. "We'll go back there and clean up, and then..." He held his sister. "We have to kill Abhar. Now he won't stop looking for us, and he'll kill us for sure."

"How? We just tried, and there were too many of them, not to mention he's not a weakling."

"I'm not sure." Tahjis kissed Santrice's head. "We can ask Scorpion."

"If we're going to do that, we should keep moving. It's not safe here."

"Don't leave me, Tahjis." Santrice sobbed into his chest.

He squeezed her. "Let's get you somewhere safe. Then we'll talk. We're still too close to Abhar's place, and he'll have his men out by now. We need to get out of here."

Santrice needed no further encouragement to get on her feet. Tahjis held an arm around her as they walked, and Fakhira kept her sword out. People on the street gave them a wide berth. As the early glow of dawn brightened the sky, they slipped into one of Scorpion's tunnels.

Chapter 18

"Not only is Abhar not dead, but now you have a damaged sister who needs help and he wants all three of you dead. Tahjis, you led me to believe the pair of you are competent." Scorpion glared down at them all from her perch.

Fakhira had a thought that although Scorpion might be better than Abhar, she would still need to be dealt with at some point. "It was bad luck more than anything else. Several of his men are dead now. He'll have fewer on hand for a short time."

"Yes, there's that, I suppose. You'll have to try again, now. I already received word he's retreated to one of his 'safe' houses. If you're lucky, he's only taking that one precaution, because he doesn't think highly of either of you. You can leave Santrice with my healer, who will help with your injuries, too, and then get out and go kill him. Do it right this time." She snapped her hand out in irritation, dismissing them.

"We won't fail again." Tahjis gathered Santrice and half-carried her out.

"See that you don't, or I'll have my guards show you how we treat traitors."

Fakhira scowled under the scarf hiding the bottom half of her face. Yes, she would definitely want to deal with Scorpion at some point. Not now. Although the caliph was wrong about Abhar, he wasn't wrong about the power vacuum his death would create. Scorpion's would cause the same, and having both at once would only result in utter chaos in Kamrik's underbelly.

The healer sat up and clucked her tongue at the three of them. "I see you've gotten into more trouble. Come here, let me have a look." She patted the cushions beside herself.

Tahjis sat with his sister, keeping his arms around her. "Scorpion said you would take care of her. Can you?"

Sitting down on his other side, Fakhira put her leg up, pulling her pants away from the cut.

The healer shifted and touched Santrice's knee, who flinched and buried her face in Tahjis's neck, letting out a small sob. "Oh, you poor dear." She closed her eyes and took a deep breath. "I can fix bodies, boy, but not minds. Magic doesn't do that. Only time and love can. But I can watch over her, if that's what you need." She turned to the cut on Fakhira's leg, poking and prodding it.

Fakhira hissed in pain. "Are you sure that's what you want, Tahjis?"

"No, but what else can I do? We can't bring her along."

A cool breeze swirled down Fakhira's leg to the gash, hurting as much as it helped. She gritted her teeth and waited for the strange agony to end. Tahjis was right, they had nowhere else to stash Santrice safely. Who knew if Abhar could find Tahjis's bolt hole, and what other choice did they have? Her eyes settled on Santrice's hair, the same shade and length as her own. It fell with the same waves, too. In fact, from behind, if they wore the same loose clothes, they could easily be mistaken for each other.

With a huff of effort, the healer let go. "I see you're keeping a secret, Al-Kabar. I trust you have a good reason, and can even imagine what it might be. As such, I'll keep it for you."

Fakhira paled and nodded. "Thank you. I appreciate that." She took a deep breath and waited while the healer tended to Tahjis.

"Santrice," Tahjis murmured, "I have to go. You heard Scorpion."

"No, I'll come with you. I just got you back, you can't leave me here."

"I don't want to." He hugged her close, stroking her hair.

Watching him, Fakhira had a wild idea. "Bring her with us. I know what to do." She held up a hand to keep Tahjis from arguing. "Trust me. I've watched your back and kept you alive so far. I don't want to explain down here though."

"A wise decision," the healer nodded. "Here, let me give you some clothes, dear." She produced a simple linen dress and helped Santrice change into it. Tahjis put his shirt back on. "Fires watch over you, children."

They took their leave with thanks, both of them coaxing Santrice to put one foot in front of the other, then to climb the ladder up and out. Tahjis chose a shadow in the early morning light and they hunkered down in it, Santrice between them.

"What's your plan?"

Fakhira took a deep breath. "She's going to pretend to be me at the caliph's palace. They barely know me, and we look similar enough. If we can get her there soon enough, no one will even realize I've been gone."

Tahjis frowned and shook his head. "I'm not taking her out of one viper den to put her into another."

"It's better than Scorpion's lair." She reached over Santrice to put a hand on his leg. "At the palace, they'll treat her like me, not knowing she's connected to you. They don't even know who you are. I told them about a pretend lover to try to get him to free Santrice, and said nothing about what you look like, or who you are. Just a man with a sister in Abhar's grip."

He scratched at the stubble on his face, thinking. "Santrice, can you pretend to a different name?"

"Who do you want me to be?" It came out flat and dull.

Tahjis clenched his jaws. "Not like that."

Santrice wiped her face and looked at Fakhira. "Why would anyone mistake me for you? I don't look like a man."

"Al-Kabar is a fake name. My real name is Fakhira. All you need to do is lie in bed, eat the meals they bring, say you feel ill, and not cause any trouble. Can you do that?"

Reaching out, Santrice tugged the scarf from Fakhira's face and pulled it away to reveal her mouth and nose and chin. "Oh, my. I had no idea."

She smiled and took Santrice's hand in hers. "Do you think you can manage to pretend to be me? We have the same hair, and I don't think anyone will notice. I've only been there for a day or so, and hardly saw anyone. Hide behind your hair. We're going to kill Black Abhar so he can never hurt you again, or anyone else. Then we're going to go stop other men who do the same things. I need someone to keep the caliph from knowing I was gone."

"You need my help?"

"Yes. Will you help me, please?"

Santrice squeezed her hand and more tears slid down her cheeks. "Don't forget about me."

Tahjis kissed her temple. "I won't, not ever. I'll come back for you, I promise."

"So will I."

"Then yes, I can do that." Santrice nodded.

They crept through the tunnels and into Fakhira's room through a swiveling pane of glass. The room appeared untouched, though Amil must have come in already. Fakhira took Santrice's hand and led her to the bed. "Climb in. The servant's name is Amil. If he asks where you were, say you got up and couldn't sleep, so you went for a walk in the halls. When you got back, you climbed into bed and fell asleep. Ask for breakfast and eat as much of it as you like when he's out of the room."

The other girl nodded and climbed under the fur. "I'll do my best."

"You'll be fine." Tahjis pulled the fur up to her chin and kissed her forehead. "I love you."

"I love you, too." She hugged the pillow and froze when someone turned the handle of the outer door.

Fakhira went pale and her heart stopped. Tahjis grabbed her and dashed them both into the bathing chamber. He pushed her against the wall, a hand over her mouth.

They heard someone moving through the chamber. "Are you awake?" Amil whispered.

"Yes." Santrice's voice sounded muffled, like she'd covered her head with a pillow.

"Where did you go? I didn't see you leave or come back."

Fakhira wondered if Amil slept outside her door. He seemed so certain he couldn't have missed her. The poor boy must have little time to himself, and she couldn't imagine how Korval got someone to do such things.

While she listened to them, Tahjis held her close in the corner of the bathing chamber. She felt the heat of his body against hers through their clothes. Their eyes met, and she found herself struggling to breathe.

"I walked in the halls for a while. You must have just missed me."

"Yes, I guess so. I'm sorry I wasn't here to help you. Would you like breakfast? Or can I bring you your robe?"

"Breakfast, please. I'm not feeling well, so I'll stay close to bed today."

"I'm sorry. I'll have them send some ginger tea and make sure you're not disturbed."

"Thank you, that would be good."

Tahjis stared at Fakhira's eyes, then seemed to notice his hand had landed on her hip. His other arm held her shoulder against the wall. Like before, he turned away. She raised a hand and touched his cheek, pushing to make him look at her again.

"I'll bring it right away. Is there anything else I can do for you until then?"

"No, thank you. I'm very tired."

Tahjis breathed in and closed his eyes, his body pressing against hers. She thought he meant to kiss her, and knew she wanted that. To help him, she tugged the scarf away from her face. It fluttered aside.

"He's gone."

Santrice's voice, pained and wavering, made Tahjis freeze with his lips an inch from Fakhira's. He snapped his hands away, backing off from her. "Alright. We should go before he comes back." He fled the room.

Fakhira fell away from the wall, stumbling without him there to hold her. She slid to the floor and covered her face, not knowing if what she felt was real or imagined. Did it come from being close to him, from the way he cared for his sister, or the way he needed and took her help? Cyric made her feel this way too, at first. Then it all went wrong. And after that, he protected her. Had she arrived in Kamrik with him, would she have fallen into his arms and stayed there, content to marry him as their fathers had intended?

"Al-Kabar," Tahjis hissed from the other room. "We need to get out of here."

Shaky and confused, she stood and tucked the scarf back into place.

She nodded to Santrice, still in bed, then followed Tahjis out the window. Having done it a few times now, she dared to take quicker steps in his wake and slipped. Sparks of panic shot from her heart to her fingers and toes, and she caught herself on the ledge by one hand.

Dangling thirty feet up, she swung to try to get a grip with her other hand, and only succeeded in loosening the hold she already had. Her focus narrowed to her fingers, to keeping them clamped on that narrow ledge.

Tahjis grabbed her arm and said nothing as he hoisted her up. Though he did much of the work, she noticed he only did as much as she needed him to. He helped her steady herself, held out an arm to keep her from falling again, and continued on as soon as she had solid footing. Panting, she followed him again, this time taking more care with her steps.

In her mind, the incident played again, this time with Cyric rescuing her. He'd do everything, pulling her up and standing her on her feet, then holding her hand the rest of the way. When they reached the roof, he'd put his hands on her waist and lift her. Tahjis left her to take that step without his intervention. Cyric would do everything for her, whether she asked or not. Tahjis would help only when she needed it.

Behind the scarf, she smiled, knowing which she preferred.

Chapter 19

They stood in the shadows of predawn, waiting for a pair of patrolling city guards to pass by. The caliph's men watched over this neighborhood too well. She thought about Korval's refusal to order Abhar's execution. Coupled with her encountering him in one of Abhar's clubs and his behavior, she wondered how much business the two men did.

Abhar could have some hold over Korval, but she suspected now that they merely had an arrangement along the lines of the caliph's appetites being satisfied in return for Abhar's illegal activities being ignored. She also realized that his approach to retribution against Trimar would only hurt the people of Trimar's caliphate, not Trimar himself. The two caliphs would kill regular people and destroy their goods to pursue an escalating war of slights against each other. Neither would ever feel the strain or pain of it themselves.

Only one course of action made sense: after they killed Abhar, she had to keep Korval from murdering all those people and making more orphans like herself. After that, she had to do something to stop him in the future. She hoped the Waters had a plan, because she didn't.

The two guards passed out of sight. She and Tahjis ran across the street and slid to a stop against the wall of the building he said Abhar could be found inside tonight, licking his wounds. About this, she had asked no further questions; she trusted him to be sure or to say he wasn't. Tahjis pulled a ring of keys out and used one on the lock. It clicked open and they slid inside. Hurrying in the dark, they listened at every door.

Tahjis held up a hand at a door with light spilling out on the floor. She heard faint noises that could come from anywhere or be anything. With his ear near the bottom, he obviously heard more. Holding up two fingers, he pointed inside. Although they hadn't discussed signals, she guessed he meant two people inside. His face crinkled up in confusion as he listened, then he shook his head. He held up four fingers, then curled one down. When he curled the second down and put his other hand on the doorknob, she got the idea.

Two. One. He yanked the handle down and threw the door open. Tahjis pulled a knife from behind his back and Fakhira lifted her sword. They found an office with two men, one on each side of a desk. Abhar sat behind the desk, cradling his arm and sneering. It surprised her to recognize the other man. The caliph's older servant, Zavin, sat in the other chair with his hand curled around a staff. At the tip of the staff, a yellow crystal glowed with a weak light.

Tahjis snarled and jumped at Abhar with his dagger. Fakhira surrendered to the sword, letting it carry her to Zavin before he could react. She punched him in the face with her empty hand and kicked him in the

164

gut. Zavin stumbled back and tripped over the chair. He fell and landed hard enough to jar the staff out of his grip. Behind the desk, Tahjis plunged his knife into Abhar's chest to the hilt.

Abhar screamed out his rage and pain, loud enough to carry deep into the building. They had little time. Fakhira shoved her foot onto Zavin's neck and pressed down. If he died here, there would be no witness to this attack. But with scarves covering her face and Tahjis's, he knew nothing. The caliph would leave in the morning, so she only needed to stall him. Killing him might even cause her problems. Without a witness to report something, Korval might turn the city upside down in his search for the assassins.

"Al-Kabar," Tahjis gasped.

Despite a dagger stuck deep in his chest, Abhar held Tahjis by the neck with his feet dangling half a foot off the floor. Tahjis gripped the thick, muscular arm, trying to make it stop as he struggled to breathe.

"Stupid boy," Abhar growled. "I should've killed you when I killed your father."

Incensed, Fakhira ignored Zavin's weakening attempts to grab and dislodge her foot. She leaped over the desk and plunged her sword into the large man's belly. The blade kept going, slicing through the meat with ease, and flowed out of his side. She followed it with a kick to send him back and to the floor then spun, swishing the blade over Tahjis's head to slice through Abhar's neck.

Sucking great lungfuls of air, Zavin scrabbled for his staff. Fakhira pivoted and jumped into his way, carrying the movement through with a kick to the man's jaw. His head snapped to the side and he groaned.

Tahjis rubbed his neck and caught his breath. "Who's that?"

"He works for the caliph."

"I heard him trying to negotiate for Abhar to release any women he held with the name Santrice. Abhar wasn't receptive."

Fakhira crouched beside Zavin and waved for Tahjis not to say more on that subject. They'd gone to some trouble to preserve her identity for Korval and needed to not throw all that away. "Can you hear me?" She gripped his jaw tightly.

"Yes." His eyes fluttered to show he had little sense.

"Where is the caliph going?"

"To march his army to Grev-Nol. They'll burn it to the ground, just like Aitrae Oasis."

She let him go and thumped his skull, knowing what she needed to do next. Zavin slumped, his chest rising and falling with the even rhythm of unconsciousness.

"Scorpion will take care of that." Tahjis yanked the knife out of the headless corpse and wiped it on Abhar's pants. Reaching over, he picked up the severed head by the hair. Clumps of goo and gobs of blood fell from the neck, splattering on the floor. "Where did you learn to fight like that?"

She turned away, bile threatening to surge up. "I didn't." Noise in the hallway made her spin and crouch with her sword ready. "They're coming. We have to keep them from sounding an alarm before morning." Her stomach hardened to steel in anticipation.

"Then we have to kill them." Tahjis took a deep breath. "If you can keep doing what you just did, I guess we'll be able to do that. Get into the hallway and block them away from the door."

She nodded and slid out of the office. Calmer than she had a right to be, she walked deeper into the building, sword held ready. The first of the men rounded a corner and ran into her blade. She carried it through to the next man, cutting both in half. The next man had time to see his fate before her blade severed his head. Behind him, another man blocked her new thrust with the curved sword he managed to raise against her. Her foot lashed out, sweeping his legs out from underneath him. She ripped her blade up his belly as he fell to the floor.

Several paces behind these four, she locked eyes with a fifth man. He took in the scene and dropped his sword, falling to his knees with his hands raised in supplication. "Don't kill me. I'll serve you if you let me live."

Narrowing her eyes, she looked him over and could only guess how many people he'd threatened and stolen from, how many he'd killed, raped, maimed, or orphaned. All because Abhar or some other master told him to. "I need no servants. You may have the same mercy you've shown your victims."

His eyes went wide with terror and he scrambled back from her. She followed him into a side room and recoiled when someone in the shadows punched the side of her head. Part of her mind remembered this needed to be a surprise in the morning, when the caliph had already left. She had to be careful. Raising the blade, she called the Waters to sheathe it in blue light and slashed at the man to the side. He squealed and fell in two gory pieces.

"Wait, please!" Cowering among the corpses of his comrades, the last man standing held his hands up and shuddered, scuttling away from her. "I'll do anything you say! I swear it on my mother's grave."

Panting from the fight, she held the blade aloft and looked him over in the light. The man had muscles and a groomed beard. He wore clean clothes and had no signs of sickness. Whatever he may have done, she saw a flicker of something worthwhile in him. He could atone for his sins under her guidance. "I am Al-Kabar. If you swear your life to me, you may keep it."

"I swear it, I swear it. My life is yours, Al-Kabar!" He pushed his open palm at her, and she had no idea what to do with it. "What would you have me do?" As he knelt there, eyes wide with entreaty, she noticed a burn scar on his palm and guessed he thought she would mark him some-how, as Abhar must have done.

With her free hand, she grasped his and willed the Waters to take the scar away and replace it with something else. Water enveloped her hand and sparkled with brilliant white light. The guard closed his eyes and turned away, though he gripped her hand fiercely. Fakhira saw herself on that ridge again, pointing down at the city with the sword. Tahjis squatted beside her, drawing lines in the sand with his dagger. This man stood to his right, eating a red fruit and peering down at Tahjis's handiwork. Someone else came with them, as she saw part of a man's boot.

Heat seared her hand and the guard groaned, the sound confused between pleasure and pain. The water swirled up her arm, picking up the tiny spots of blood and gore. It passed over her from head to toe and fell to the floor with a tiny splash.

Flinging his hand away, she gasped with the shock of what just happened. On his knees, the guard panted and held up his hand. His eyes wide, he showed his palm and she recognized the teardrop shape and jagged lines from the stone in the pommel of her blade. She held it up for him to see and nodded to him.

He threw himself at her feet. "What do you command of your loyal servant Behrouz?"

Slipping her sword into her sash, she took a moment to catch her breath. "We leave Kamrik in two hours. Get what supplies you can and meet us on the north side, near the waterhole that dried up a few days ago. Expect to travel through the desert on foot. We'll have no way to keep beasts."

"Yes. I will. Thank you. Fires and Waters bless you and keep you." Behrouz sat up and gazed at her in awe.

"Is there anyone else in this place?"

"Eight guards, Abhar, and his guest. No one else, I swear it."

She nodded and squeezed his shoulder. Where did her orders come from? Somehow, in those moments while her hand seared that symbol into his, a plan crystallized in her mind. With her new minion, she would march to stop the caliph from slaughtering innocent peasants, then rally his army away from him to attack Trimar's palace. Korval could either swear his fealty to her or fall under her wrath.

"If you know anyone else you trust who has skill with fighting, bring him."

"As you command, Al-Kabar." He covered his heart with his marked hand and bowed his head.

"Two hours." She left Behrouz there to find Tahjis patting down the dead guards left in her wake.

Tahjis slipped something into his pocket and noticed her. "Are they all dead?"

"All but one. I recruited him."

"What?"

"I'll explain later. We're going to need help to kill Trimar."

He broke into a grin and nodded. "What should we do with the head?"

She shrugged. "Set it up however you want, so long as it stays in here."

"Yes, Al-Kabar." He patted her shoulder on his way past her. Ducking into Abhar's office, he fussed for a few minutes, then emerged again. "I left a message for Scorpion, to make sure she remembers the deal she made with me." Returning to the back door, he cracked it open again, and peered out. They slipped outside and darted across the street, then plunged into the alleyways and dark places of Kamrik.

"Where are we going?" Tahjis fed Brumble a cracker from his pocket.

"North." Fakhira inspected her own hand, expecting to see the symbol she'd burned into Behrouz's palm. Instead, she found callouses she'd never had before, in the places her father and Shahan once had. The

Waters had toughened her hand to use the sword. "It's time to deal with Trimar and Korval."

He chuckled. "You're so different without that sword. Never leave it behind again."

Her hand went to the hilt, gripping it and feeling its familiarity and warmth. "No. I won't. Never again." It changed her, made her something she couldn't be without it. The world needed this version of her right now. Al-Kabar had a place and duty. He commanded men and dealt death. Fakhira only had pain and power she didn't understand and couldn't handle.

It seemed ridiculous--her decision amounted to letting a persona take her over. People sometimes whispered about madmen who had two minds inside. Yet she needed that mask between herself and the world. Al-Kabar could stand in the sun while Fakhira healed in the dark. No one would respect a woman commanding men anyway. To do what needed to be done, she saw no other option.

Fakhira closed her eyes and took a deep breath. Tahjis had taught her everything she needed to know to be a man. She could walk like a man, talk like a man, and act like a man. For this to work, she'd have to go to the length of even *thinking* like a man, and thinking of herself as one. No, *himself*. Al-Kabar was a man, and Al-Kabar would stalk the sands in her stead. One day, Fakhira would be ready to take the mantle for herself, but not today.

Al-Kabar opened his eyes and set his jaw. He had a lot of work to do.

Part 2:

Al-Kabar

Chapter 20

The sun beat down by the time Al-Kabar and Tahjis reached the water hole Fakhira had inadvertently drained a few days ago. Had it been such a short time? So much had happened. Al-Kabar's new servant sat in the shade of a date palm already withering from the lack of water, another man beside him. Al-Kabar smiled at that, though he knew he'd have to watch them until they allowed him to bind them.

"Who's this?" He approached with Tahjis one step behind and to his right.

Behrouz scrambled to one knee, bowing his head in fealty. "This is my brother, Radwan. He also worked for Abhar, and he also all worries that our lives might be forfeit when Scorpion sweeps through the town."

Radwan and Behrouz had been made from the same guardsman mold: tall, broad, muscular, and thick-necked. Radwan had a longer, wilder beard and stood an inch or two shorter. A thin scar puckered the flesh on his left hand.

"We're going to Grev-Nol," Al-Kabar said. "Once we get there, we're going to find a way to stop Caliph Korval from burning it to the ground."

"Why?" Radwan's brow furrowed and he stopped in the act of taking a bite from the half-eaten fig in his hand. "Who cares about Grev-Nol?"

"I do. If you wish my protection from Scorpion, this is the task I demand. There's more, too. I will tolerate no rape or other harassment of women or children. Our goal is to protect people, not harm them."

"What?" Radwan scowled. "What if I wish the company of women?"

Al-Kabar would have spat in disgust but for the scarf covering his face. "Earn it, like a man. Until then, you have two hands."

Tahjis grinned and stuck his nose into the conversation. "You know who I am?"

"The Rat," Radwan nodded. "Abhar wanted you dead. He spread the word far and wide before his death."

"Then you listen to me." Tahjis crouched down in front of both men, and Al-Kabar marveled at how he'd left behind the cowardice he'd had when they first met. "I saw Al-Kabar cut Abhar's head off as the killing blow. He's blessed by the Fires and the Waters, and I give him my loyalty. You don't have to do that, you only have to do what you're told. But if you cross him with so much as a toenail, I'll slit your throat myself so he doesn't have to waste his time dealing with you." Poking her nose out of the collar of his shirt, Brumble squeaked her agreement.

Radwan narrowed his eyes. "You're not scary, not even with that thing on your shoulder."

"I'm not trying to be scary." Tahjis shrugged and stood up. "Only telling you how it is."

Al-Kabar snorted. "You can run back home if you'd rather face Scorpion. Otherwise, we're going to Grev-Nol. The caliph left to gather his army early this morning, so we should be able to beat him there."

Radwan's eyes went wide and his brow jumped up. "You want to beat an army to Grev-Nol in the daytime? Are you crazy?"

"No," Al-Kabar said with a grin. "Clever and resourceful. This way." He turned and found the hole that had drained the small lake. Lowering himself down into it, he braced against the sides and walked down. It had been a torture to get up. Going down, on the other hand, proved easy. As he reached the bottom, he saw Tahjis coming down and stepped out of the way. The two brothers and their friend remained at the surface.

"Behrouz, this is crazy." Radwan hissed, probably unaware Al-Kabar could still hear him.

"You should've seen him: burning bright, a beacon of glory. He freed us. We were prisoners as much as any of Abhar's girls. He spared me and I pledged my life to him. You don't have to. You can go back if you want, but I'm doing this."

"You didn't say anything about following a madman and the Rat."

"The problem you're having," Al-Kabar called up, "is that you've never been on the right side before. You don't know how to do it. Don't worry. It's easy. You treat everyone else as your equal and all life as worthy and sacred. After you do it for a while, it'll feel natural."

Beside him, Tahjis hid a grin and a chuckle behind a hand. "You're better at this than I thought you'd be," he muttered.

Al-Kabar smirked. "I'm going to start walking. Come along or stay behind, but this is the last time I'll offer the choice. From here, I expect you to follow orders and do your part. It'd be *nice* if you could plan to do it without complaint, but I'm not foolish enough to expect that." He turned and crouched to jog down the gently sloped tunnel. Behind him, Tahjis followed, and boots sliding on rock announced the other two men joining them.

The Waters reached out to him in this place, calling him and bringing him along faster than he could have gone with only his two feet. It seemed like hardly any time had passed when the world righted itself and he slowed to normal speed in the large cavern with the underwater lake.

With the guidance of the Waters through the tunnel, he hadn't noticed the darkness. Now, he summoned water to his hand, creating a swirling, sparkling blue light that made the rock walls and ceiling glisten. Behind him, he heard a swift intake of breath.

"Take a short break and fill your bellies with the water if you wish. Do not soil this water with your waste." Al-Kabar walked to the water's edge and waded in to his waist. Cool and welcoming, he took a deep breath and let its embrace wash over him. He pulled his scarf away long enough to drink then tucked it in again.

He watched the light play on the surface of the pool and wished it would tell him how he should accomplish the insane task he'd set for himself. Korval wouldn't be dissuaded from attacking the town by mere words. Trimar wouldn't be killed by a man walking to the front gate and asking to see him. They needed a plan, one that would work.

Breathing in the damp, he closed his eyes and quieted his mind. The Waters would provide. So long as he placed his trust in them, they placed their trust in him. With these three men, he could save Grev-Nol and the next town on Korval's list. They could prevent a war that served no one and gained nothing.

"Al-Kabar." The voice behind him spoke with awe.

He opened his eyes and saw droplets dancing around him, each a tiny spark of white light. The Waters chose to put on a show for Radwan. Al-Kabar swished an arm through the spray to make it stop. Though he'd gained no insight into his problems, he felt as ready to tackle them as he could be.

Wading out, he called the water to both leave his clothes and come with him. His form swelled, bulked by the extra water that made muscles where he had none. "That tunnel will take us near to Grev-Nol." A thin stream flowed down the center of the tunnel he pointed at.

Radwan reached out to touch Al-Kabar but pulled his hand away without doing so. "You're dry."

"Of course I'm dry. What did you expect?" Al-Kabar raised an eyebrow at the man, waiting for an answer.

"My boots are wet from standing in the pool." Radwan pointed down and furrowed his brow.

Behrouz lifted his foot and tapped the bottom of his boot. "Mine aren't. Al-Kabar's binding is also a blessing."

"Don't worry, Behrouz," Al-Kabar said with a chuckle. "You'll still be able to bathe."

Tahjis laughed. "Or maybe it's a curse. Do you have a plan, Al-Kabar?"

Al-Kabar rolled his shoulders. "Enough of one to begin with. It'll become clearer when we reach Grev-Nol. " Turning to the new tunnel, he stepped into it and broke into a jog again. His dip in the lake had refreshed him enough to keep this up for hours. As soon as the others fell in behind him, the Waters rose and pushed them along the tunnel again.

What felt like a few hours later, he came out at the mouth of a small cave, discovering the tunnel served as overflow for a spring-fed pool at its mouth. Avoiding the pool, he hopped out of the cave and into a grotto. Boulders formed a screen around this tiny oasis, letting in enough filtered light to allow greenery to thrive here. Ferns and palms, jasmine and honeysuckle, even clover covered every surface aside from the pool itself.

"Bless the Waters," Behrouz said with awe.

Radwan said nothing, dropping down to sit. He alone panted and needed to rest.

"It seems the Waters can tell what's in a man's heart," Tahjis mused. "Is this a subtle message to leave him behind?"

Al-Kabar barked a laugh. "Something like that. The Waters don't think much of you, Radwan. What do you say to that?"

Instead of answering, he wheezed. Behrouz cupped his hands in the water and threw it at his brother with a grin. "This is what happens when you don't believe me."

Radwan waved everyone off, sputtering from the dousing and still trying to catch his breath. "I believe you now," he gasped.

"But will you trust me when it matters?" Al-Kabar shrugged, not expecting or wanting an answer. "Grev-Nol isn't far from here. I wouldn't expect the caliph to march his army through the middle of the day, so they'll likely arrive tomorrow night."

"Then why did we just rush here?" Radwan asked.

Tahjis tsked. "Because we'll need time to convince the villagers to hide, among other things."

Al-Kabar smirked. "Rest time is over. Let's go." He didn't care that Radwan still needed to recover and they'd all rather revel in the lush greenery. They didn't have enough time to waste it in luxury here. Easing through the narrow cleft separating the grotto from the rest of the world, he took a last few breaths of cool, damp air. The harsh, baking heat of midday hit him when he stepped out of the crack and into the sunshine.

Behind him, each of the men grunted with the forceful impact of the environment. Like him, they settled into it within a few steps, remembering something they'd known all their lives. In the name of self-preservation, Al-Kabar kept their pace to an easy walk, and he reminded them to drink whenever he felt his mouth going dry.

Chapter 21

Grev-Nol sat as a white and green jewel among low dunes of yellow-brown. Palms grew high enough to be seen over the tall stone wall, a barrier against the blowing sands. No one sane would be wandering about or manning the gate now, or for the next few hours.

"Tahjis, what do you think of that gate?"

"I think I can probably get it open if no one answers our hail."

Radwan doubled over with his hands on his knees and gasped out, "How?"

Behrouz slapped him on the back and laughed. "He's a rat! How do you think he'll do it?"

Shaking his head in amusement, Al-Kabar led them to the tall leather and metal gate. Invaders could easily punch through it with any blade and walk through. It hadn't been erected to keep out people, only sand. He walked up and looked the gate over, then grabbed a large metal ring and slapped it against the metal plate it rested against. The resulting clank should rouse anyone nearby. For good measure, he repeated the act twice.

Radwan and Behrouz leaned against the wall, enjoying the small shadow it cast. Al-Kabar stood in the open, where he'd be seen by anyone answering the knock. Tahjis crouched beside him, helping Brumble drink from his water skin. They waited long enough that anyone nearby should have come. At that point, Tahjis sighed and looked up at the twelve foot high gate.

"Did anyone bring a ladder?"

"Just a moment," Al-Kabar said. "I have one in my pocket."

Radwan and Behrouz chuckled. Tahjis rolled his eyes. "Behrouz, boost me up." He set Brumble on the ground, and she trundled to the hinges where the gate didn't quite meet the stone.

"Boost you up?" Shading his eyes, Behrouz peered up. "You're not tall enough to reach that high."

Tahjis rolled his eyes. "That's why I need the boost. What's the matter, you don't think you can lift a scrawny rat like me that high? And here I thought Abhar only got the biggest and best."

Behrouz raised an eyebrow as he heaved himself away from the wall to form a basket with his hands. "You have the mouth of an impudent woman."

"Better than the mouth of an ass." Tahjis grinned and set his foot into Behrouz's hands. "On the count of three, lift as hard as you can."

Al-Kabar watched with his arms crossed as Tahjis counted down from three. Behrouz flung him upward and Tahjis jumped. The Rat caught the top edge of the gate with both hands, a feat Al-Kabar found impressive.

Tahjis found a foothold and hauled himself up and over the edge. The gate shook and rattled as he swarmed down it. They heard a light thump as the Rat landed on the ground.

They waited through more rattling and clunking and through squeaking and muttering. After a minute or two of all this, he said, "It's open now, you can push it in."

Al-Kabar waved for the men to help as he shoved. Radwan held the other two back, watching Al-Kabar struggle alone against the weight. The doors had been balanced to swing shut, and he didn't have the strength to oppose that. "If you're trying to prove something, you fail. I already know I'm not the strongest man here. Come help, or we'll never get inside."

Behrouz pushed past Radwan and lent his strength to the task. Between the two of them, they heaved the gate open far enough to get inside before it fell shut again. Radwan took his time walking past them, and Al-Kabar resisted the urge to trip him.

The gate clanged shut and Behrouz shoved his brother's shoulder. "If you're not going to help, at least don't hinder."

Radwan sneered. "You may be content to serve him as a slave. I'm not. He's impressive, yes, and the Waters favor him. That doesn't make him perfect."

Al-Kabar ignored them. Brothers needed to argue and he had more important things to do. Striding away, he noted Tahjis falling in behind him and the two brothers bickering from several paces behind. After all his displays of the Waters' Grace, he had no idea what would sway Radwan to his side. Time would tell. Until then, the former guard needed to be watched lest a knife be lodged in Al-Kabar's back.

"I hate to ask, but is there a plan?"

Glancing at Tahjis, Al-Kabar nodded. He'd put some thought into it, and his conclusions felt right, if dangerous. "We're going to evacuate the town and prepare it to repel the army. Or, if they won't leave, we'll recruit them to defend it. When the army arrives, we'll make an effort to convince them the Fires and the Waters favor this town. If we succeed, that should reduce the numbers we have to repel by a good amount."

"So we'll be fighting Korval's men," Behrouz said.

"Yes. I think that's unavoidable."

Behrouz's face drew down. "I'm not sure I'm ready to die for strangers."

"We're planning to not die here."

Tahjis chuckled. "An important part of any plan. There's the town bell. I'll go ring it." Despite the heat, he hurried forward to a metal pole with a bell suspended from the top and a rope hanging from it.

"He isn't bound to you," Behrouz said.

Al-Kabar shook his head. "No."

"He's a thief and a liar. Are you sure you can trust him?"

Watching the Rat scurry into the market square, Al-Kabar crossed his arms. Though Fakhira had had reservations when they first met, their foray to kill Black Abhar had erased them. "I trust him with my life. What do you think of the wall? The gate's flimsy and pathetic, but the wall seems solid."

"I agree. We'll have to shore up the gate."

The bell's clanging cut them off. Al-Kabar crossed his arms and waited, hoping to present an impressive figure despite his small stature. Tahjis rang the bell five times and let the rope go. It pealed twice more before it stopped swaying. Doors opened and people flooded to the small square. Grev-Nol boasted too many residents for them to all be called by the single bell. They'd have to convince these people to get the rest roused.

"People of Grev-Nol, your town is in danger!" Al-Kabar waited for the murmuring of the mob to die away. "As I speak, the army of Caliph Korval approaches. Caliph Trimar has sent us to help you evacuate."

"Why not send his army to fight?" a man in the crowd asked.

Al-Kabar restrained himself from trying to find the speaker. "I don't claim to know the mind of the caliph. The force coming will overwhelm Grev-Nol and burn it to the ground. If you leave now, your lives can be saved."

One man wearing the maroon and brown of Trimar's army pushed to the front and stared Al-Kabar down. A puckered scar marred his middle-aged jawline and muscles rippled across his shoulders. "If Korval comes here to take our town, we'll defend it. He won't destroy it without a fight."

Murmurs ran through the crowd, agreeing with him. Al-Kabar frowned and wrapped his hand around the hilt of his sword. He could keep himself and his men safe enough, he thought. Having others here would complicate his plans. Worse, his rage burned to tear this man into pieces for what his kind had done to Aitrae Oasis and Fakhira's family.

When he looked back at the guardsman's eyes, he wanted to see soulless globs of evil. Instead, he saw a man whose honor fiercely demanded he protect his family and home. It grated to think of him as a person. The enemy should be the enemy, not a man with thoughts and feelings and wants and needs. Those dogs who brutally murdered Almiya needed to be put down, not understood.

Al-Kabar ground his teeth, grateful for the scarf hiding it. "If you insist upon staying to fight, then I insist that the women and children be sent away with an escort. Unless you have an underground cavern to hide them all in, they'll be at risk. Even if we hold Korval's men off, arrows, fires, and flung stones may still find them. If we don't..."

The guardsman's hands formed a fist and gave Al-Kabar a curt nod. "I agree. How long do we have?"

"Until morning at the least. This is not a time to worry about possessions."

The guardsman nodded again. "Grev-Nol faces imminent attack," he told the crowd, his deep voice carrying better than Al-Kabar's had. "All women and children will leave at dusk. Ten men will volunteer to escort them to Tymars. Every adult will carry one bottle of water to be shared. Take one keepsake only. Choose things to keep the children calm. Dress for the night's chill. Ten volunteers to me."

Al-Kabar nodded his approval, though he tensed when Trimar's men crowded around them. The guardsman counted off his volunteers and sent them to rouse the rest of the town. Around them, townsfolk dispersed to follow his orders.

"I'm Rahim," the guardsman said, offering his hand to shake.

"Al-Kabar." he shook the hand, matching Rahim's firm grip. "I sense that your people will listen to you. Mine will listen to me."

"We know our town. When they breach the gate, that knowledge may be important."

"Agreed. I want to brace the gate. What do you have that we can set up to fling things at them?"

Rahim grinned and his eyes gleamed. "Let me show you what we can do."

Chapter 22

"Is this wise?" Rahim handed crude brushes to his men so they could paint the walls with pitch.

"Probably not." Al-Kabar grinned. "It would just be foolish for us to stay here and wait. Trimar didn't send us to stand toe-to-toe with Korval's army. We're here because we could arrive before the attackers, and because we can cripple the army before it gets here. While we might be able to stop them completely, I doubt it, so it's best to be prepared."

"I fought in the last war, near a decade ago now. Five men can make a difference on a line like this. Remember that." Rahim nodded and walked away.

Al-Kabar wondered if this man had gotten his scar from Fakhira's father. Tahjis fell in beside him and the other two followed to the wall. One by one, they climbed a ladder to the top and slid down the other side. Tahjis pointed them in the direction the army should come from and they set off, running across the desert with the Waters' help.

Ten minutes away from Grev-Nol, Tahjis asked, "Are you sure you want to go up against the army to save a bunch of Trimar's men? With the women and children gone, we could walk away and count this a victory."

Having had thoughts along the same lines already, Al-Kabar sighed. "I'd be lying if I didn't admit that's an attractive option. It won't help me get close to Trimar, though. To earn the chance to get close to him, we'll have to make ourselves into heroes for his people. Having Korval hate me personally can only help."

"Behrouz," Radwan grumbled, "you've brought me on a mad quest, following a lunatic."

Al-Kabar rolled his eyes. "You had your chance to back out and didn't take it. Which of us is less sane?"

Behrouz chuckled. "I'd like to have my name feared in Kamrik. Behrouz the Mad, known associate of the infamous demon Al-Kabar—it has a nice ring to it."

Tahjis clapped Behrouz on the shoulder. "That Al-Kabar is truly a monster to be feared. He walks on a carpet of rats, their mouths foaming with madness. His blue scarf hides his twisted, hideous mouth that can suck out your soul if you lay eyes on it. And his sword! It burns with the heat of a thousand fires, so hot it's cold. No mere man stands a chance against him. So eat your vegetables, little Behrouz. If you don't, Al-Kabar will come in the night and burn your heart until it freezes in your chest!"

They laughed together and Al-Kabar smirked. He saw Radwan grudgingly join in the mirth.

"I heard Behrouz the Mad once sliced a boy in half for staying up past his bedtime," Al-Kabar said.

"And the Rat," Behrouz said. "Pick up your toys or he'll send his horde of minions to steal them!" He nudged his brother in the ribs.

"Oh, alright," Radwan groused. "Treat your mama with respect or Radwan...the Feral...will send his mama to...eat your eyes."

For a moment, they all stared at him. Then Behrouz burst into laughter and the others laughed harder. Radwan joined in. Al-Kabar smiled, pleased his men had found a slice of joy in the middle of this grim task. Soon, they fell into a companionable silence. With the setting of the sun, they reached a spring too small to support a settlement and took a break.

Al-Kabar squatted in the struggling grass at the edge and dipped his hands into the muddy water. The moment they touched the liquid, a vision flashed into his mind. Hundreds of men marched under the stars, headed this way. They would stop in a few hours. Images and whispers gave him ideas for how to sabotage them without killing too many.

He pulled his scarf away long enough to splash his face and drink, then tucked it into place again and straightened. "We'll see the army in about an hour. I want the four of you to sneak into their camp. Your goal is to cause damage without being noticed. Slit some throats if you must, but focus more on supplies. Make leaks in their water barrels, toss their food in the sand, cut their saddles, break their wagons. If you can make it useless without being seen or heard, do it."

Radwan raised an eyebrow. "What will you be doing?"

With a crooked grin they couldn't see, Al-Kabar said, "I'm going to introduce them to Al-Kabar." He turned away and, with the night's cool breeze to keep them all fresh, broke into a jog.

"Al-Kabar is mad," Radwan muttered.

"As a jackal," Tahjis said.

They had to work to keep up with him and spared no more effort for chatter. The run took them along ridge after ridge until they heard the steady hum of hundreds of conversations bubbling over the edge. Al-Kabar ducked at the verge and peered into the gorge. Fires flickered among dark shapes where there should be none.

Al-Kabar glanced aside as his men thumped against the dune, panting and wheezing. "Each man take a different route. Work until you hear a signal or alarm, then retreat. If you're seen, kill the witness if you can. Otherwise, run and circle back to this point. We need to leave before dawn so they don't see you. Understood?"

"The Fires and the Waters watch over us all," Behrouz intoned. The rest murmured their agreement.

Watching them skulk down the dune, Al-Kabar took a deep breath and waited. When the last of them reached the valley floor, he began his own slow descent. At the bottom, he took a deep breath and resolved to trust in the Waters. They had a plan. He would follow it.

Making no attempt to hide himself, Al-Kabar strode toward the encampment. Chattering remained a steady buzz, punctuated by the nearby crackling of dung-burning fires and snorting of restive horses. Sentries walked in pairs, alert and armed with torches. He hoped the others found easy places to slip in.

"Identify yourself," the taller of the two sentries barked.

He'd reached twenty paces away before being challenged. "Al-Kabar." He stopped and held his empty hands up. "I bring a scouting report from Grev-Nol."

"Scouting report?" The shorter one raised his torch and peered at Al-Kabar. "No scouts were sent out."

Al-Kabar shrugged. "That you know of. Seems the caliph didn't see fit to personally inform every sentry about it. How shocking."

The taller one scowled. "They didn't set up a password. Name someone in the camp."

The test seemed stupid given the size of the army. Al-Kabar played along anyway. "I trained with Cyric of Aitrae Oasis. He lost his home and family there, as did I." He touched his forehead. "Waters bless their souls."

Both sentries echoed his gesture and intoned the same words. They let him pass. He patted the shorter sentry on the shoulder as he walked into the camp. These men had probably been chosen for the duty by volunteering, not for some particular skill or virtue. Given that, he expected the others would have no trouble going unnoticed.

Small tents stood in imprecise rows. Scattered among them, small fires burned in contained rings. Men sat around these fires, some roasting food on knives or skewers. Most had cups or canteens. One large tent perched in the center of the camp with lanterns hanging from hooks and two men standing guard at the entrance. Fresh smoke and stale sweat filled the air.

Al-Kabar found a place near a group of men and stooped behind a tent. "I've heard Al-Kabar guards Grev-Nol," he whispered. He slipped up the row and stopped to mutter for anther group of men, "Scouts reported there's a demon in Grev-Nol." Another few tents along, he said, "I heard a scout tell Korval about Al-Kabar in Grev-Nol. They know we're coming." One more time, he ducked to plant another rumor. "Did you hear them talking about Al-Kabar? He's a jackal in man-shape."

He flitted about the camp to say all the same things several times over, staying away from Korval's big tent. Around one corner, he encountered Tahjis as he sawed away at some ropes. Tahjis jumped and hid his knife only to grin at Al-Kabar.

"Did you hear what they're saying?" Al-Kabar asked.

Tahjis raised an eyebrow at him, then shrugged. "No, what?"

"Grev-Nol is prepared for the assault. Trimar sent a jackal shapeshifter called Al-Kabar to defend it, and he can fight with the strength of a thousand men. He has demon powers and his eyes burn with hate for the living."

For two beats, Tahjis stared at him, face blank. He cracked half a grin and played his part. "I don't want to fight something like that. Facing Al-Kabar would be madness."

Al-Kabar smiled and nodded. They clasped hands and parted. The lingering feel of his hand made Al-Kabar shiver as he recalled Tahjis's touch on Fakhira's hip. Distracted by trying to set that aside to get this job done, Al-Kabar rounded a corner and found himself face to face with a weary man, one he recognized.

Cyric rubbed his temple with two fingers and grunted. He frowned at Al-Kabar's boots then at his eyes. Brow furrowing, he grabbed Al-

Kabar's wrist. "Who are you? No one covers his face here."

His touch brought other memories to the surface. Fakhira chose Tahjis, yet Cyric remained her rescuer. When he could have saved himself, he came for her. She remembered the feel of his touch, how it thrilled her at first, then became awkward and strange. Anticipation and expectation colored everything that afternoon and evening. He'd fumbled. She'd stumbled.

Cyric reached out to snatch at the blue scarf. The movement shook Al-Kabar out of Fakhira's confused meanderings. He yanked his arm away and grabbed the front of Cyric's shirt, pulling him close enough to smell his warm breath. He hadn't been drinking. After everything the man had been though, this seemed a minor miracle.

"I'm here to deliver a warning," Al-Kabar growled. "Run to your master and tell him that Al-Kabar has claimed Grev-Nol in Trimar's name. If he moves against it, Al-Kabar will lay waste to his army. Tonight is a warning and a threat. No one else needs to die out here."

"No one *else*?" Cyric shoved Al-Kabar away and drew his curved sword. "Who *are* you?"

"I have no wish to harm you." Al-Kabar drew his own straight blade and held it out. "But I will defend myself."

"You came here to deliver a threat to kill us all, but you don't want to harm me?" Cyric barked a laugh. "Excuse me if I don't believe you."

The Waters hadn't prepared him for this encounter, and Al-Kabar faltered, knowing Fakhira would mourn if he killed this particular man. He backed away, sword held up to ward the other man off. "Fakhira would see your life spared."

Shock plain on his face, Cyric stared for a beat then rushed Al-Kabar and slammed into him. They crashed to the ground and rolled over a tent, knocking it down. Al-Kabar found him easy to overpower as he failed to show the spirit and determination he'd shown in Aitrae Oasis. He wound up straddling the larger man, sword raised and ready to plunge into Cyric's throat.

Drooping in defeat, Cyric dropped his sword. "Kill me swiftly, that I might sooner find her in the next life."

Al-Kabar raised an eyebrow. "She lives."

Muttering nearby caught his attention and he noticed the group of men watching. The scuffle had attracted attention and knocking the tent down had eliminated the only barrier between them and a campfire. Bared swords glinted in the flickering light.

"How?" Cyric's voice came out as a strangled whisper.

Launching himself off the man's chest, he called the Waters. They surged from his skin and encased his body in a shield, flaring with blue light. Swords swung around him, scraping water away without touching his flesh. Each strike flung drops away from him to soak the sand underfoot. His body shield sloshed together, filling the gaps with a thinner barrier.

Darting between the tents, he heard men shouting in his wake. The others would take that as an alarm and retreat, so he had no need to come up with a signal. He rounded a corner and tripped into a fire, rolling over it and dousing it in a puff of steam. To his surprise, he landed on his feet and kept going. Someone punched him in the shoulder as he hurtled through the camp. Stumbling into a tent, he realized that though the water protected him, its light marked him as the threat.

He dove past another tent and ground his teeth, forcing the water to fling itself up and freeze at the same time. In his wake, it slammed into the sand, tents, and pursuit as jagged shards of ice. Ducking across to the next line of tents, he stopped running and tucked his sword away. A horn blared into the night and he followed the lead of other men who turned toward the center tent.

In the distance, a shout rang out. It came from too far away to be understood and Al-Kabar slipped inside a tent to wait while the men scrambled to figure out the message and react to it. He noticed a canteen near the flap and drank from it. When he'd had enough, he dumped the rest out onto his palm and watched it dance until it sank into his flesh. All around him, voices rose in panic and despair.

"Saboteur in the camp!"

"Al-Kabar's wrath is already on us."

"Goudarz is dead, his throat slit in his sleep."

"This campaign is cursed. We should turn back before Al-Kabar gets us all."

"I won't fight a demon!"

Al-Kabar afforded himself a grim smile and waited for those men to move on. When he peered out through the flap, he found the area clear and slipped to the edge of the camp unchallenged. This night had been fruitful so far.

199

Chapter 23

"What happened?" Behrouz jogged behind Tahjis with a sack slung over his shoulder. "I thought we'd have more time."

Al-Kabar wanted to ignore the question. For the sake of Radwan's tenuous loyalty, he couldn't afford to. "I spooked a man before I intended to."

"The rumors seemed effective to me," Tahjis said with a shrug. "I overheard two men talking about Al-Kabar the jackal demon, expecting him to shoot everyone with fiery death rays, or something like that."

"That's what you spent your time doing?" In the rear, Radwan huffed and puffed to keep up with the group. "Why did we bother causing all that damage?"

Al-Kabar smirked. "To give them real acts to attribute to Al-Kabar. Rumors without slit throats and damaged gear wouldn't make them fear him, only chatter about the rumors. Adding the rumors gave them something scary to attribute all the damage to, instead of the obvious answer of a team of men causing trouble. Now they fear a demon jackal that can sweep into their camp in the darkness and kill them in their sleep."

"Where did you get such a mad idea?" Behrouz asked with reverence.

"The Waters." He felt them buoying his feet, making the run swifter and less taxing than it should be. "We need to reach Grev-Nol before dawn. Less talking and more running." Picking up the pace to push them harder in the chill of the night, he let the exertion dull his thoughts. Meeting Cyric had raised too many uncomfortable questions and he didn't want to dither over anything that distracted from the goal.

They reached Grev-Nol before dawn and Rahim let them inside to help continue the preparations. Al-Kabar's men needed to rest. So did he, but he chose instead to walk around the town and familiarize himself with it.

Though the women and children had been sent away already, he came upon a group of women sharpening stakes and the tips of sticks to be used as makeshift arrows. They worked together, humming and singing songs he'd never heard before. Stopping to watch earned him grim smiles of acknowledgment.

"Are you surprised to see women here, Al-Kabar?" The speaker reminded him of Almiya. She had the same shade of copper skin and wore her dark hair the same length, and she held herself in the same no-nonsense way.

He nodded. "I must admit that I am, yes."

"Grev-Nol has been targeted before. It's a beautiful place that grows food for other parts of the caliphate, making it attractive to other caliphs as a target. When my mother was a child, a caliph brought an army here and tried to take it. The men stood on the walls while the women cowered inside. As our men fell, someone called for the teenage boys to help hold shields and fire arrows. My grandmother stood and said, 'I'll go so my son can live.'

"Other women also stood, leaving their children behind to survive while they went to die in honor on the walls, defending our town. Most of the adults died, but they turned that caliph away, keeping the town mostly intact. Since then, any girl who wishes to learn is taught how to fight." She patted the scabbard leaning against her chair.

"I wonder why the Fire Dancers all claim women shouldn't fight," Al-Kabar mused.

The woman shrugged. "Perhaps it's to save their own necks. If women could fight, then the Fire Dancers would be on the front lines."

He thought back to Korval's Dancers. They'd all been soft and manipulative. Trimar had sent his Dancers to torch Aitrae Oasis, but they may have only gone to places already deemed safe by the army. "Perhaps." No one questioned the will of the Fires as delivered by the Dancers. Since they worked in groups of five or more, everyone assumed them above reproach by virtue of having to agree with each other.

"Will this be a problem, Al-Kabar?" She fixed him with a pointed stare.

As he looked around, he noticed the rest of the women also demanding an answer. "No. The Waters guide me and they have no issue with women taking up arms. I have no idea why the Fires are affronted by it. May I know your name?"

The woman smiled at him. "Jannat." Her mouth curled with interest and invitation. "I'm not married."

Al-Kabar had never taken the time to appreciate a woman's body before and let his eyes dance over Jannat's. She wore close-fitting linens that would offer little protection in battle. The tiny flicker of interest at her curves confused him, and he nodded at her to distract himself. "Well met, Jannat. Waters watch over you."

"I'll see you again after." Jannat lifted her delicate hand and waved as he walked away.

Behind him, he heard the women break into giggles. If they knew what they'd find under his clothes... Fakhira wanted to go back and reveal herself. She longed for their acceptance as a fellow woman warrior. More than that, she wanted to understand how they made her feel.

Around the next corner, he found Tahjis squatting against a wall, holding Brumble out to a local rat. The rats sniffed each other's faces and rubbed whiskers.

"Gathering new minions?"

Tahjis grinned. "This is Trava. She's going to help us."

Al-Kabar crossed his arms, torn between bemusement and curiosity. "In return for what?"

"Truce between the town and the local rats."

"That seems like asking a lot for one rat's help."

Tahjis's grin turned smug. "Trava is promising the help of the entire rat population."

"Ah. That's quite reasonable, then."

"I think so." Tahjis rubbed Trava's head, the two rats squeaked, then Trava ran off and disappeared through a hole in the wall. "I thought we might need extra help, especially if we're going to hold up your demon thing."

"Good thinking. You're supposed to be resting, though. The sun is rising already."

"And your excuse is?" Standing, Tahjis faced Al-Kabar with his chin up.

"I'm Al-Kabar." He smirked and looked away, growing uncomfortable with Fakhira's interest in the Rat.

Tahjis burst into laughter. Brumble squeaked from his shoulder. "I'm glad you're developing an ego big enough to rival a caliph."

Al-Kabar shrugged. "I'm not tired, and there are things that still need to be done. Have you seen the catapults?"

Giving him a sidelong glance, Tahjis nodded. "I walked past them. Didn't expect to see that kind of thing in a place like this."

"Korval won't expect that either. These people are more ready for an attack than they seemed on first blush."

Nodding again, Tahjis leaned out to check around the corner of the building. Whatever he saw satisfied him. "You haven't blushed since we left Kamrik."

The change of topic took Al-Kabar by surprise. He blinked and couldn't think of a response. After several long seconds of him opening and closing his mouth like an idiot, he finally said, "Is that somehow a bad thing?"

"Just something I noticed." Tahjis shrugged and stepped close enough to take Al-Kabar's hand. He lowered his voice. "Not always sure who I'm talking to."

"You're talking to Al-Kabar." He shifted, trying to make Fakhira and her complications go away.

"Is that how you want this to work? I know you made that decision on your own, but your idea came from wanting to join the army. We're clearly not joining the army, since we went and wreaked havoc in their camp. Do you need to be a man to be Al-Kabar?"

"Do you think Radwan would follow a woman? How about Behrouz?"

Tahjis put his back to the wall. "I'm following you."

"You're fulfilling your part of our bargain."

Frowning, Tahjis pressed his lips together. He said nothing and refused to look at Al-Kabar.

Fakhira wanted to put her arms around Tahjis and hold him close. She longed to show him that she knew he stayed for something else. Al-Kabar wasn't so sure. Despite his connection with rats, Tahjis's honor had put him in the position of feeling a debt between them for Santrice's rescue. It bothered Al-Kabar to have him here for that. It bothered Fakhira that this debt might be the only reason he stayed.

"You can go if you want. You've done enough to pay me back for killing Abhar already."

"Maybe." Tahjis lifted his hand like he meant to touch Al-Kabar,

206

but stopped himself and formed a fist at his side instead. "We'll talk more after." He sounded sour as he stalked away.

"Yes. After. For now, get some rest."

Tahjis waved irritably without looking back.

Chapter 24

"Wake up, Al-Kabar." Jannat shook his shoulder.

Bright sunshine blinded him. He'd fallen asleep in a corner of the room where his men bedded down and found himself now in an empty space. He sucked in a breath and rubbed his eyes. "What is it?"

"We can see something coming. Rahim thinks it's Korval's army." Her hand felt heavy and hot on his shoulder.

"I should get to the wall, then. Thank you."

She smiled and pointed to a tray on the floor beside them. "I saved you some lunch."

The tray held cut fruit and a biscuit with a clay pitcher of water and a cup. "Thank you, I appreciate that."

"Can I..." Jannat bit her lip and picked up a slice of lime. "If you're still tired, I can help you eat."

The offer reminded Fakhira of the Fire Dancers and their pampering. As good as that had felt, Al-Kabar needed to be sharp and able to handle himself. "No, thank you." Taking the lime, he tried to think of the kindest way to ask her to leave so he could eat without letting her see his face.

"Is it bad?" She reached out and brushed her fingers over the scarf.

Al-Kabar caught her hand. "Yes." He hadn't come up with the reason for the scarf yet. Hideous wounds seemed a perfect fit. "I...would rather not let anyone see it. Some men take pride in their scars. I'm not one of them."

She nodded and leaned in, confusing him. Her lips pressed to his through the scarf, giving him a chaste kiss. When she opened her eyes again, she grinned. "It works fine, at least."

"I...ah..." Not sure how to explain the flutter in his belly, Al-Kabar shifted his gaze to the tray. "Thank you," he repeated.

"You poor thing." Jannat backed off and stood. "You were hurt badly, I think. When the battle's over and Korval's forces routed, maybe you'll tell me about it."

"Maybe." He shifted and squirmed, only relaxing when she left the room. Turning to the corner, he pulled his scarf away and ate. What he didn't drink any of the water, he took into his flesh. Aware he could hold more, he left the tray behind and hurried to the nearest well.

The sun hung high overhead, baking him. Korval had to be possessed by some madness to drive his men across the desert in the middle of the day. They had to be on rations, and that would make them willing to take risks to assault a place with plenty of water. It still seemed stupid to push them through the day when they could easily have stopped out of sight and waited until evening.

He crouched beside a circle of bricks surrounding a full spring and dipped his fingers into the cool water. Staring at the rippling pool, he wondered if he had the power to contain it from a distance. The water surged up his arm to encase him. Rested and refreshed, and facing the prospect of a major battle, he decided this would be a good time to push his limits.

As he walked, people stopped and stared. Some bowed, others dropped to the ground in awe. Radwan and Behrouz watched him with their weapons ready by the gate. Tahjis sat at the top of the wall, handing out arrows in groups of ten. Al-Kabar climbed a ladder to reach him and peered over the edge. In the distance, he saw a dark ripple that must be the approaching army.

Beside him, Rahim sucked in a breath. "By the Waters, Al-Kabar! How?"

"By the Waters is how." Al-Kabar held out his hand, calling the water there in a large mass. It formed a ball about four feet across. "How far away do you think they are?"

Rahim blinked and coughed and pointed at the army. "Three miles, maybe. In this heat, it'll take them at least another hour to reach catapult range."

"So we have some time." Al-Kabar stared at the water, thinking about how best to utilize himself. Once the battle began, he'd wait with the other swordsmen for the gate to buckle under pressure. Until then, he could probably find a way to make himself useful. "I need more water."

Rahim's brow went up. "What for?"

"To taunt them."

211

Behind him, Tahjis frowned. "Is that the best plan?"

"Men driven mad by thirst will be sloppy and easier to defeat."

Rahim stroked his dark beard. "I'm not sure we can spare water for that."

Al-Kabar shrugged. "It'll be returned when I'm done with it."

"Ah. In that case, we can do it." Rahim shouted down, "Bring buckets of water!" At the base of the wall, men scrambled into action.

Tahjis bunched the last ten arrows together and handed them to the last archer. He glanced at Al-Kabar and opened his mouth. Instead of speaking, he shut it again and scurried down the ladder to go find the catapults. The Rat wouldn't fight hand-to-hand if he could avoid it.

Watching him, Al-Kabar imagined he'd intended to disparage the plan. Something happened in the camp, he thought, and it shook the Rat's confidence. Whether it was his confidence in the mission or in Al-Kabar, he had no idea. He wouldn't let it affect his own certainty. The Waters chose him for a reason.

Six men brought two buckets each, setting them down at the base of the wall. Al-Kabar took a deep breath and pointed at the first, willing the Waters to bring it up to him. The surface of the closest bucket swirled and formed a peak, spinning upward in a thin stream. Beside it, the next bucket did the same, the two streams joining. By the time the first finger of water reached him, all six buckets flowed up to his hand.

Along with the ball he already had, a thick layer of water encased him. "I'll be back soon." He jumped off the wall, the water cushioning his landing enough that he landed gently on his feet. His water suit kept him cool as he ran toward the army. Closing the distance, he made out the front rank of riders. The horses plodded with their heads down and their riders held blankets over their bodies. Behind them, the foot soldiers slogged through the sand, packs weighing them down.

Al-Kabar doubted anyone would see him until he did something. Those people focused on putting one foot in front of the other and not falling into a sinkhole. He stopped and called the water off his body. Instead of forming a ball, he sent it in rivulets to form a wide pool, one only a finger's breadth deep. Though he would have liked to make the pool far away from himself, he couldn't keep control over it unless he touched it. He dropped to one knee to make himself harder to notice and watched.

The horses noticed it first, grunting and lifting their noses. Their attention forced their riders to notice. One horse moved ahead of the others, straining to reach the pool. When it dipped its head down, Al-Kabar pulled it far and fast enough to cause the beast to grab a mouthful of sand. It backed away and sneezed and shook its head, rousing its rider from torpor.

"Witchery!"

"There's a person!"

"It must be Al-Kabar."

The wave of panic that rolled over the army seemed palpable. Al-Kabar stood up straight, the water flowing up to his hand. His rumors had worked, and he had no fear of them. These stupid, tired, weary men—

Unexpected things flew through the air at him. Until an arrow sank into his leg, he had no idea what to make of the strange shapes. The next hit his belly, a third pierced his neck, and four more grazed his arms and legs. More arrows plunged into the sand around him. Bright, burning sparks of pain lanced his body. He stumbled several steps to the side and ripped the arrow out of his neck. Blinking, he fought to think through the agony.

The water swarmed around his body, encasing him without him ordering it to. He lost his balance and fell, buoyed by the water. Ahead, he saw the riders smack their swords on their horses' flanks, goading them into a gallop. Bearing down on him, he turned to scramble out of their way. Blades flashed in the light at him, hacking at the water without cutting through it to him.

He struggled to his feet, feeling the water's chill, and pulled the arrow out of his leg. Though the footmen had started a charge in his direction, the front rank slowed when he dropped the arrow. Behind him, the horses circled until he was surrounded. Heedless of them all, he yanked another arrow out and, feeling his strength returning, threw it down.

"I am Al-Kabar," he growled. The Waters somehow granted him a measure of healing, or at least kept him from bleeding to death. "Stand against me and you will die."

The footmen stopped and stared from a dozen paces away. "He's a demon," someone breathed.

For several beats, no one moved while Al-Kabar removed three more arrows and threw them to the ground. Suddenly, someone shouted, "He can't take us all at once!" It might have been Cyric.

Al-Kabar froze and saw himself torn apart by hundreds of hands.

He turned and ran for the wall, hoping the sun's intense heat would make it possible to outdistance them. Two riders charged their horses at him, swords out and ready to slice him in half. Fakhira remembered another mounted soldier doing the same, a lifetime ago. Cyric wouldn't step in this time.

His injured leg burning in pain with every step, Al-Kabar charged the riders. He cried out to force his body to keep going. Those blades would cut the water, not him. Several feet away, his leg buckled, sending him tumbling to the sand. The riders both pushed their mounts to trample him.

Rolling to his side, he raised to his hands and knees and waited. Taking these blows might help convince these men to flee. He shifted the water to take the strikes in his stead and gritted his teeth. One horse plowed into him while the other rider swept his blade at Al-Kabar's legs. The horse hit him with enough force to send them both into the sand. Its rider pitched onto his face while the beast screamed and flopped to its side.

Al-Kabar felt a sting on his thigh where the second rider's blade must have sliced through the water, on the same leg that had been shot. He swallowed a groan. Showing weakness would only encourage the soldiers. Rising to one knee, he surveyed the situation. Again, the soldiers stood, watching him uncertainly. The downed rider scrabbled to his hands and knees, shaking his head and spitting sand.

His foot firmly planted, he stood and drew his sword. Holding it out to offer the threat of violence, he watched the soldiers. The front ranks shifted uneasily, the points of their swords faltering. "I am Al-Kabar! Stand

215

against me and you will die!" With that, he turned his back on them and put all his effort into walking without a limp.

Several steps away, he heard murmuring. In case they planned to charge him anyway, he shifted the waters to cover his legs more and flow along the sand. It made him move faster than he could run and seemed a superior way to travel. When he reached the walls, he paused for a moment, trying to figure out how to scale it from the outside. Rahim would lower a rope the moment he stopped gaping. Rather than waiting, Al-Kabar shifted the water again and made it lift him up to the top.

He called the water with him and threw enough inside to refill the six buckets still standing in a row at the base of the wall. Clumps of material from the catapults flew overhead to rain down on the army. Those on the wall beside Al-Kabar stared at him. He gritted his teeth and used the remaining water to help him stand upright.

"Al-Kabar...ah," Rahim gulped and stared. "There's...an arrow sticking out of your shoulder."

Too many sharp aches across his body made it hard to single any one out. He reached up and groped for the missed shaft. "I can't reach it. Pull it out for me."

Rahim gulped again and touched the arrow with a finger. "Shouldn't we get you some araq to numb the wound first?"

Al-Kabar took a deep breath, wrenched his arm around, grabbed the arrow, and yanked it out. It hurt more now than it had with Korval's army crowded around him. "I'll be fine." He noticed those around him staring and pointed irritably at the soldiers rushing across the sands. "We have an army to repel!"

The archers turned their attention to the onrushing mass of men and fired. More loads from the catapults sailed past. Al-Kabar pulled the water around to encase his body again, needing its support to stay standing. He watched men fall under the hail of arrows and barrage of what appeared to be large rocks and broken blades.

Fakhira held her breath, hoping Cyric stayed near the back. He'd served as a guard in a small town, though, and had no particular special skills. He had to be on the front line. Korval had no reason to value his life. She had no reason to value his life either. Cyric served as a reminder of the past.

Al-Kabar growled to push Fakhira's confusion away. He had more pressing problems to deal with. "Call it out when they're close to breaching the walls." When Rahim nodded, Al-Kabar climbed down the ladder and pushed himself to lope through the town. Every step jarred his wounds. Teeth clenched together, he sought the well he'd drawn from earlier and found it half-empty. What remained wouldn't be enough. Following the call of the Waters, he stumbled and grunted to the next well.

It held enough water. He let himself fall in and made no splash.

Chapter 25

The Waters pushed at his mouth and he opened wide for them. Liquid poured into his throat and lungs and belly, filling him with calm and soothing his pain. Cool pressure surrounded him. His wounds itched as they healed.

Floating in chilled bliss, Fakhira wanted to stay forever. The ragged holes in her flesh matched the gaping holes in her heart. Her family should have had someone like Al-Kabar to protect them. Instead, they'd had only Fakhira. She let those men torture and kill Almiya, whose screams and whimpers echoed in her mind as fresh as the moment they happened.

The water became that basket, a place to hide while others suffered. Why did Grev-Nol get Al-Kabar when Aitrae Oasis hadn't? Nothing made these people more worthy than her family. Worse, they supported the men who'd come to destroy her home by supporting Trimar. Al-Kabar ought to kill them all for that transgression, not save them. He should have joined the army after all and supported Korval in delivering his justice.

"Is that what you really think? Rahim deserves to die because he works for Trimar?"

Fakhira's brow furrowed. Thinking about him confused her. He wore the colors of those despicable men yet he wanted only to defend his home. His duties made him no different from Cyric.

"What about his young wife? Should his Almiya suffer and die because yours did?"

Again she listened to Almiya's final minutes, bringing tears to her eyes. No one deserved that and she knew it. These people bore no more blame for Trimar's attack on Aitrae Oasis than she did for Korval's attack on Grev-Nol. Shame burned her cheeks for her moment of weakness.

"We are here for you, Al-Kabar. To remind you, to hold you close, to help you mourn. Your flesh is nearly finished healing. Remember that you are neither immortal nor invulnerable. We can protect and heal, but only with enough water to surround you fully. More water gives us more power. Go, Al-Kabar. Go protect the innocent."

Propelled upward, Al-Kabar lurched out of the well and hung over the side. He heard shouting and the clang of metal on metal and saw a drop of water fall in front of his face to land on the dirt. No more wasting time or water, and no more indulging base desires for revenge. Trimar needed to die. Korval's behavior marked him as the same man with a different face. He might also need to die.

He called the water as he pulled himself out of the well and felt the liquid sink into his flesh again. His feet touched the ground where the droplet had fallen and pulled it up to join the rest. Dry on the outside, he took a deep breath and ran for the front gate.

Chapter 26

As Al-Kabar turned the corner of the last house, the gate blew inward. The wood and metal braces flew apart, crashing into the men who'd been holding them. Blades hacked into the leather, chopping it open, and he saw Radwan among those jabbing spears at the first rank of men trying to pour through the holes.

He'd returned too late to save the archers littering the ground, stuck with enemy arrows, and too late to save the defenders now pinned under debris from the gate. His healing must have taken longer than he thought. Calling the water from his body forward, he flung it between the defenders and the gate, covering the holes. The defenders fell back as a group and let out a ragged cheer of his name.

"It won't hold for long," Al-Kabar growled. "Bring braces and shore up the gate. Any archers still alive, come down now!" Though he wanted to take the water from those six buckets still lined up at the base of the wall, he found he couldn't do two things at once.

Archers rushed down the ladders, Rahim among them. The guard had the good sense to line them up on the ground and get them to fire high enough to send the arrows over the wall. When their hail rained down outside the gate, men screamed and grunted.

Al-Kabar hurried to the gate to stand in front of the defenders and saw a return volley of arrows from the outside in time to slide his water up and knock most of the shafts away from people. In doing that, he left the gate unprotected and Korval's men crashed through the holes. Al-Kabar called all the water to himself and drew his sword.

Metal clanged on metal. Men shouted and cried out. Blood danced through the air to hit the sand and sink in. Al-Kabar whirled in the center of the chaos, his sword flashing. His water armor glowed with the brilliance of the sun. Somehow, his sword could tell friend from foe without hesitation. He cut down so many that the defenders pushed forward to make the gate's holes death for any coming through.

Another rain of arrows fell in on the defenders. Al-Kabar spared the effort to block them, earning a slash to his side. Hands grabbed him and pushed him away from the gate. He looked up to see Tahjis hack a grasping hand off an enemy wrist as he hauled Al-Kabar out of the fighting.

"You're being stupid," Tahjis said, "going up in that."

Sitting on his shoulder, Brumble let out a long, high screech that reminded Al-Kabar of a war cry. A blanket of rats overran the battle. He watched in surprise as the tiny creatures flowed through the fight and somehow knew which men to ignore. One man shrieked as rats swarmed up his body and enveloped him. They brought him to the ground and left a half-chewed corpse in their wake.

"Where else should I be?" He hissed with pain as he pressed on his wound.

"Blocking the gate and protecting against their archers. From behind the fight where you don't have to worry about getting stabbed."

Al-Kabar gritted his teeth and scowled, not wanting to admit the Rat had a point. He shifted the water to block the gate, trapping a handful of men inside with the remaining defenders and a throng of rats. They died quickly.

"Korval's not stupid," Tahjis continued. "He won't keep pressing when it's obvious he can't gain anything." Crouching beside him, Tahjis poked at the gash. "This is pretty bad. How did you heal the rest?"

"Dunked myself in the well."

Tahjis shrugged. "Can't do that right now. They need you."

Behrouz withdrew to join them, panting and cradling his arm. "I'm not much good like this," he gasped out. "Not too many injuries up there, though. So that's good. They outnumber us by so many it's scary, but we're holding our own thanks to these walls. Praise to the Fires and the Waters for them, and for the sands not piling up to give them ladders."

"We need to do something to make Korval give up," Al-Kabar said. "He needs to see this as futile."

Tahjis squinted into the distance as the defenders took a moment to breathe in the respite provided by Al-Kabar's water. "Go taunt him from the wall."

"I can't block the gate and protect myself at the same time." Al-

223

Kabar winced. "And I can't keep myself going if I can't use the water to hold my wounds shut."

"Taunt him the old-fashioned way," Behrouz said. "Shout something and duck so the archers can't hit you. Cut a few arrows out of the air with your sword while you're at it. That's always impressive."

"Agreed." Tahjis pulled the wrapping off his head, exposing his shaggy hair, and wrapped it around Al-Kabar's torso to bind the wound. "This'll keep you from bleeding to death while you handle that." He patted Al-Kabar's shoulder. "Go on, save us all. That's what you do."

With their help, he stood. Behrouz draped Al-Kabar's arm over his shoulder and helped him hobble to the nearest ladder. From there, he had to do all the work himself. Agony seared across him, pushing him to go faster so it would stop sooner. Halfway up, he had to pause to shift the water, deflecting another volley of arrows and allowing another dozen men in through the holes before he could cover them again. Every time he did that, he noticed, some water hit the ground and sank in.

At the top, he grunted and hauled himself onto the ledge. "Korval!" He bit back all his pain to rise to his feet, sword out and ready to defend himself. Below him, men with swords and spears covered the land in every direction as far as he could see in the harsh sunlight. "Your arrows do nothing against us, and your men push in to their doom. We can keep this up for days."

The men closest to the wall looked up and pointed. Scanning the army, he noted a banner near the back and guessed the caliph would never hear him. Instead, he had to speak to the men who could.

"What do you think is happening to the men who manage to get inside? Every time you press forward, you send another dozen men to their deaths. The arrows fall on the water, harming no one." His sword jerked his arm forward to chop at an arrow heading for his heart. It cut the shaft in half, sending both pieces tumbling down the wall.

"I am Al-Kabar, and Grev-Nol is under my protection! To stand against me and my men is to die. Turn back now and we will not pursue you." He watched the men, noticing how they mulled this over as a group. Discussions broke out. When another volley of arrows required him to shift the water, no one pushed through the gate.

The blare of a horn in the distance made the men shift and mutter. Al-Kabar didn't know what it meant, though he could guess.

"Listen to that. He doesn't care about your fate. Charge forward to murder these people, that's what he wants. The people of Grev-Nol have done nothing to you! They didn't order Trimar to attack and none of his soldiers live here. Attacking this town is not justice, it's vengeance against the wrong people."

A small group pushed through the army, shoving men aside. Someone in that group shouted. Al-Kabar couldn't make out the words. From the way his arms made sharp, angry gestures, he guessed the man at the center wanted the soldiers to fight and had no idea why they refused to. When that group reached the front, another volley of arrows flew in.

Al-Kabar deflected his attention long enough to shift the water. Men shouted and metal clashed. When he slammed the water back into place, a horn blasted from that small group near the gate, in a different pattern. The army pulled back, receding from the walls and gate in a rush. Two more arrows flew at Al-Kabar, and his sword managed to deflect one. The other hit him in the chest with enough force to knock him off the wall.

The water cushioned his fall. Without it blocking the gate, the defenders of Grev-Nol rushed to block it only to find no one attacking. Al-Kabar groaned and sat up. Behrouz rushed to his side and eased him up to sit against the wall. "Al-Kabar, you did it! They're retreating."

He pushed Behrouz away and grabbed the arrow. "Time will tell if they decide to set up a siege or not."

"Bring araq for Al-Kabar!"

"Don't bother." He gritted his teeth and wrenched the arrow out. With the water now supporting him, his pain lessened. Bracing against the wall and taking Behrouz's help, he stood.

His hand touched Al-Kabar's chest and he gave him a queer look. Al-Kabar ignored it and lurched away, letting the water take most of his weight. Joining Rahim at the gate, he stared out, watching the army continue to retreat.

"That last group took some of our people," Rahim said. "Instead of running through, they reached inside and pulled six of ours out, then your waters slammed down and they ran off."

Al-Kabar flushed, fresh anger and shame boiling in his veins. "Who did they take?"

"I'm not sure. We were rotating everyone to keep us all fresh."

"Account for everyone. Now. Tahjis!" When the Rat raised Brumble up over the heads of the others, he wished he had the ability to find humor in it. "Get ours together, apart from the locals."

Brumble squeaked and the Rat lowered her out of sight in the crowd. Al-Kabar staggered to the nearest solid wall and leaned against it to wait. Within a few minutes, Tahjis and Behrouz joined him.

Tahjis wore a scowl so tight he resembled his namesake. "Radwan is missing."

Chapter 27

"One of ours and five of theirs," Al-Kabar spat. Part of him wanted to leave Radwan to his fate. The rest of him disagreed. He knew about the caches and tunnels. Behrouz wouldn't accept leaving his brother to Korval. Radwan deserved better from him.

Rahim approached with a fierce scowl. "They took four of our men and one woman."

Al-Kabar could well imagine what Korval's men would do to the woman. His eyes narrowed and his hand clenched into a fist. "Their names?"

"Farzin, Kaveh, Shahin, Markat, and Jannat."

The last name made Al-Kabar pause. Although he cared about the four men, he knew well what happened to women in the clutches of an enemy army, and this particular one had left an impression on him. "We'll get them back. I need to heal these wounds. Tahjis and Behrouz, get whatever you need to infiltrate the camp and pull out six people who might be injured." He pushed off the wall.

"We'll need enough people to carry them," Tahjis said.

"That's not one of the options." Al-Kabar stalked away to find the well again.

To his annoyance, both Tahjis and Behrouz followed him. "We can't sneak six incapacitated people out of an enemy camp without at least seven people. It's not possible."

"Then hope they aren't incapacitated!"

Behrouz gulped. "Al-Kabar, I trust you, but, ah, is it possible your...*emotions* are clouding your judgment?"

Al-Kabar froze and rounded on him with a growl. "Ask that again."

Tahjis covered his eyes with a sigh. "One of them was bound to notice eventually."

"I'm sorry, Al-Kabar. I felt—when I helped you up—" Behrouz raised his hands in surrender. "I'm not your enemy. I won't tell anyone if you don't want me to."

Fakhira ripped the scarf away from her face and stared him down with Al-Kabar's hard eyes. "Do you think anyone would follow me if they knew?"

"*I'm* still following you," Tahjis said.

Fakhira rolled her eyes and waved to dismiss the Rat. "Besides him."

"I..." Behrouz gulped. "Probably not?"

"Exactly." She tucked the scarf into place again and stormed away as Al-Kabar.

"I'll still follow you," Behrouz pleaded. "You spared my life and I gave you my oath."

Al-Kabar ignored him and jumped into the well. He floated while the Waters healed his wounds, imagining Tahjis and Behrouz grumbling to each other in his absence. He doubted they carried out his orders and assumed they'd argue more when he emerged again. Simmering about it kept him occupied until his flesh knitted together.

When he broke the surface, he found both men gone. Either they miraculously went to do as he told them, or they'd chosen to abandon him to his madness. Despite their words, the second seemed more likely. He heaved himself up to sit on the rock wall and think about how to free those people. He couldn't get to them before they noticed Jannat's gender, so he had to accept she might be lost already.

The thought made him burn with rage. She'd get all the same treatment as Santrice and Almiya and that unnamed woman. Fakhira remembered hearing her father tell her brothers how to treat women. He used the words "respect" and "equal," telling them how only women could be trusted to handle food properly.

"Honor your mother," he told them with an unusually serious cast to his face. "Through her, the Fires and Waters gave you life. One day, your wives will do the same for your children. Always remember they are the chosen vessels of rebirth, not us. We defend them and cherish them and provide for them. They take care of us. This is a fair trade, and if you uphold your end, you'll live to old age as a happy man. If you don't, you'll find rat poison in your food and scorpions in your bed."

Until the day Aitrae Oasis fell, she'd thought all men felt this way. Her rude awakening grew more vulgar every day.

Al-Kabar stood and called the water into his skin with a sigh. He needed a way to track the army without being seen. Without knowing where Korval withdrew to, he had no idea how to accomplish that. Even the Waters had no idea which way to go, leaving him more in the dark. His best option—following the army in daylight—seemed to also be the worst.

With no other ideas, he hurried to the front gate. Rahim led a group of men in repairing the gate while others tended to wounded. The dead had already been removed. Pausing to watch, he noticed Tahjis step up beside him, peeling a lime with a small knife. His head wrapping remained wrapped around Al-Kabar's torso.

"Running off to martyr yourself? Oh, no, of course not. Al-Kabar is invincible."

"If you have something to say, say it."

"You asked Behrouz and I to prepare for this mission. I didn't realize the purpose was to get us out of the way so you could go off on your own and suck up all that glory."

Al-Kabar's hand clenched into a fist. "I'm not here for that."

"I know. You want that vengeance thing you keep saying is wrong."

His fist connected with Tahjis's jaw, snapping the Rat's head to the side and making him stumble. The half-peeled lime bounced once and rolled away. "You ran the show in Kamrik. Not here."

Tahjis rubbed his jaw. "Is that how your mother taught you to fix problems?"

He wanted to hit the Rat again. "Are you a problem?"

"I don't know. Am I?" Tahjis noticed he'd cut his thumb and sucked on the tiny wound. He stumbled around the corner, where he leaned against a wall in the shade.

Determined to understand why the Rat had turned against him, Al-Kabar followed him. He grabbed the front of Tahjis's shirt and thumped him against the wall. "It seems like you are."

Blinking in a daze, Tahjis grabbed his wrists. "I don't know who you are anymore, Al-Kabar. A few days ago, I sat on your bed, wanting to share it with you. You've become something I wouldn't touch if you paid me to."

Fakhira stared, stunned. She noticed how only a few inches and a thin piece of cloth separated his lips from hers. She noticed the metallic taint of blood on his breath. She noticed the beaded sweat on his cinnamon skin. Letting go of his shirt, she pressed close and kissed him. The scarf got in the way and she broke off long enough to tug it aside.

Though he hadn't reacted to her initial advance, Tahjis returned this second kiss. His hands wrapped around to her back, pressing her close. She needed this, needed to know something good waited for her. Everything else had been taken away, and she needed this to remind her she had something to live for.

"Oh. Uh." Behrouz cleared his throat. "I guess that's why he stays."

Startled by his voice, Fakhira let go and covered her mouth, turning her back on both men.

Tahjis cleared his throat. "Are you ready to go, then?"

Fakhira's cheeks burned. She rubbed her face and tucked her scarf into place.

"Yes, I think so." Behrouz coughed. "If you'd rather do this without me—"

"No." Fakhira let Al-Kabar take over, knowing she needed the distance to get this done. "This is important, and I need your help. Both of you."

"Thank you for admitting that," Tahjis murmured.

Al-Kabar turned to face both men and nodded. "Do either of you have anything better for a plan than following the army before they leave sight of the town?" When both shook their heads, he gave them another nod. "Then we should go."

Chapter 28

As the sun set several hours later, Al-Kabar lay on the ridge of a sand dune, overlooking Korval's new encampment. They'd set up their tents in tighter rows with four times the guards and the horses picketed along the outer edge closest to Grev-Nol.

"They're taking you seriously as a threat," Tahjis said from beside Al-Kabar.

Behrouz lay on his other side. "Of course they are. We just routed an army at the flimsy gate of a tiny town that should've been a pushover. Korval may be arrogant, but he's not stupid."

"Did he take prisoners to get information or to provoke me?" Al-Kabar sighed. "I guess I know the answer already."

"Both," Tahjis agreed. "We'll have a much harder time sneaking into the camp separately now. We'll need to move together and take down guards without making noise, then hide the bodies somehow."

"I have a bad idea." Behrouz grimaced. "Al-Kabar could walk in openly, and the Rat and I use that as a distraction to find and free the prisoners."

"You're right," Tahjis said. "That *is* a bad idea."

"It's not the worst idea I've ever heard." Al-Kabar stared down at the sentries, each pair patrolling in sight of four others.

Tahjis raised an eyebrow. "Yes, it is. You just haven't thought it through yet. What do you think Korval is going to do to you? He's a caliph. He didn't get the job by being nice. It wasn't handed to him on a platter. He schemed and backstabbed and plotted and grew an ego bigger than this camp. Behrouz said it already, but let me put it another way. You stopped him from getting something he wanted."

Al-Kabar frowned, wondering how far Korval would go. If he discovered Fakhira, what would he do? "I don't see how we'll all sneak into the camp without being noticed. They're too tense and alert."

"We could spook the horses," Behrouz said.

"They'll expect that." Tahjis shrugged. "I don't see a way to do this tonight. Maybe they'll get sloppy tomorrow."

Al-Kabar looked away from the camp, scanning the ridges. "Jannat may not live that long. If she does, she may not want to."

Tahjis rubbed his eyes. "I still say it's not going to turn out well for you, Al-Kabar. We won't be able to fight our way in to you. If it comes down to a fight, we'll have to run for it, and there's nowhere to hide without you."

Al-Kabar shrugged. "Run for Grev-Nol. They'll help you."

"That's a long run with pursuit."

"Steal horses."

Behrouz turned away. "I'm sorry I brought it up."

"It's the only way." Al-Kabar nodded with certainty. He imagined the nightmare that could easily become Fakhira's life if this went sour and knew he had to risk it for Radwan, Jannat, and the other four men. "One for six. It's a good trade."

Tahjis's mouth twitched, his fingers flexed, his shoulders shifted, his eyes flicked from spot to spot. He took a deep breath and closed his eyes. "Not if it doesn't work."

"It'll work. You'll make it work." Al-Kabar shifted a hand to touch Tahjis, then thought better of it. "Go, circle around. I'll wait a little while before I go in."

"We can come up with something else," Tahjis said. It sounded halfway between whining and begging.

Fakhira pulled the scarf away and touched his face. "Before Korval decides they're no longer useful?"

He took her hand and squeezed it. "How long will it take him to decide you're no longer useful?"

"When they came for my sister, I ran and hid. When they brutalized a woman I didn't know, I ran and hid. In Abhar's lair, I didn't run and hide. It felt right. The Waters chose me for this, and I can't turn away. Not after saving Santrice. Make this sacrifice count, Tahjis. For her and for me. Free them and take them to the Waters. Keep them safe. That's your part in this."

He kissed her palm. She noticed wetness on his cheeks, invisible in the waning light. "He'll torture you and he'll kill you."

237

She smiled at him, hoping it would make this easier to bear. "Not if I can help it. Spill a barrel of water for me."

Nodding, he pressed her hand between both of his. "I will."

"So will I," Behrouz said.

"Then I'll be fine."

Tahjis covered his mouth and made a strangled noise. He nodded again and scurried down the ridge to circle around the camp.

"Good luck, Al-Kabar." Behrouz bowed his head and followed Tahjis.

Al-Kabar replaced his scarf and watched them until they disappeared around a dune. Now he had to wait and hope this plan didn't send him to his doom.

Chapter 29

Al-Kabar walked through the camp under his own power. For a moment, he thought the sentries meant to fight him, then they both gulped and chose instead to escort him, at his request, to Korval. They brought him to the large tent in the center and asked him politely to wait while they informed Korval of his presence.

Inside the tent, Al-Kabar noted the faded rugs covering the sand, an old, worn bench, and a simple cot. Two small trunks sat on one side and thin wisps of smoke curled upward from a large brass brazier in the center. Korval stood at the cot, tugging his blue vest on over his white shirt.

"Good evening, Caliph Korval." Al-Kabar gave him a shallow bow.

"Is it?" Korval fussed with the leather bracers on his forearms. His mouth curled up in one corner as if he smelled something unpleasant.

"I warned you to stay away from Grev-Nol."

Korval's nostrils flared and his jaw clenched tight. "You killed my men."

It irritated Al-Kabar that he had to admit he'd begun the killing, though he hadn't personally harmed anyone until he reached the point of escaping the camp. He had to deflect that point. "You put them in harm's way by bringing them here with the intent to flatten Grev-Nol."

"I might have been turned aside from that goal by other means."

"Really?" Al-Kabar's brow jumped up. "Had I walked openly into your camp instead of sneaking into it, you would have taken a meeting with me and listened to what I had to say?"

Silence answered him while Korval's entire face puckered in distaste. "Perhaps."

Al-Kabar snorted. "Let's dispense with this. I've come to ensure you have no further plans to attack the ordinary people of Grev-Nol."

"I intend to move on to attack Hegrides."

"Then I'll oppose you there instead."

"Why?"

The question took Al-Kabar off guard and he paused to collect his thoughts before answering. "Because it's a town of ordinary people. Avenging Aitrae Oasis by murdering common folk and destroying their resources is cruel and stupid. If you want to hurt Trimar, you need to go after Trimar."

"Ah ha." Korval's expression cleared. "So you don't work for Trimar."

Al-Kabar frowned. He might have said too much. "I serve the Waters."

"Clearly, I can't stand against the Waters." Korval crossed his arms and set a wide stance. Everything about him suggested triumph to Al-

Kabar, though he couldn't say why. "It would be foolish to try. Had I understood what I faced three days ago, I wouldn't have even left Kamrik. I could be sleeping in my own bed and handling Black Abhar's death personally."

Al-Kabar echoed Korval's stance. He had no idea how the caliph learned about that already, nor could he imagine where this conversation would go. He shifted, trying to hide growing unease and the feeling he'd already somehow failed. "Your personal comfort doesn't concern the Waters."

"That doesn't surprise me." Korval paced across the rugs, his eyes flicking to Al-Kabar several times as he covered the space and returned. "It's interesting, though, that the Waters waited for me to leave. Had I discovered Abhar's death before I left, I would've stayed, at least long enough to guide the aftermath. It's as if the Waters preferred for me to be elsewhere, outside the ability to interfere."

"I can't speak to such things, Caliph. I serve the Waters, they don't serve me."

"But you did kill him. And then, despite leaving after my army, you reached Grev-Nol before me, prepared it for assault, and found me to wreak havoc in my camp. You're truly an amazing individual, Al-Kabar."

Wary of a trick, Al-Kabar tensed and gripped the hilt of his sword. Its cool reassurance convinced him to stay and listen. "What do you want?"

Korval waved in annoyance. "Oh, please. Relax. I've seen what you can do. I doubt my men can do you much harm. I want the same thing you seem to want, which is to safeguard my people. Trimar destroyed one of my holdings, which weakens my ability to protect the rest. I came here because I need to respond somehow or he'll press further." He bared his teeth. "Many more innocent people will die. If we work together, you can help me stop Trimar from killing more with as little bloodshed as possible."

His words surprised Al-Kabar. He'd expected to hear from the same Korval who told Fakhira she needed to accept injustice as a thing that must exist. This other Korval, the one inside the tent with him now, he could work with. It seemed he would join the army after all. "I'm listening."

"With your power, you could kill Trimar. His death will not only prevent him from targeting any more innocents, it'll send a message to oth-er caliphs that the Waters won't tolerate open warfare of this kind."

"Including you."

"Including me." Korval nodded. "I admit I never thought about it before. If it matters to the Waters, then it matters to me."

A guard burst into the tent. "Caliph, we've caught two men trying to free one of the prisoners."

"Really." Korval gave Al-Kabar a bemused smirk. "Yours?"

Al-Kabar tensed, readying to defend himself. "Yes."

Chuckling, Korval waved in dismissal. "An opportunity to show my good will laid at my feet. Have the prisoners and the would-be rescuers released into Al-Kabar's custody."

His brow shooting upward, Al-Kabar pondered whether this cemented Korval's sincerity or proved his willingness to do anything to get what he wanted. "Are they confined to the camp?"

"No, of course not. Your men are free to go if they wish." Korval waited for the guard to bow and leave. "How would you best use my army to achieve the goal of killing Trimar?"

"Ah...send them home? I don't need an army."

Korval barked out a laugh. "Don't be foolish. Trimar has an army. You can't defeat an army without an army of your own."

"I don't need to defeat an army. I only need to defeat Trimar."

Korval cocked his head to one side. "Do you intend to walk up and stab him in the eye? Even with all your power, if you want to get close to Trimar, you'll need to draw him out and distract him. More than that, you'll need to cripple his command structure so his military doesn't seize control in his stead. He'll have advisors too, and they share his views. This isn't a matter of killing one man that you've embarked upon, Al-Kabar. You want to topple his regime, and that takes a great deal of effort. And blood."

Al-Kabar sighed and rubbed his eyes. This task grew in complexity with every word out of Korval's mouth. Part of him wanted to stab Korval to make him stop pointing out how hard his job was. The rest of him saw a leader unused to doing the right thing instead of the easy thing, but willing to change that for the Waters. "I see."

"When the issue is murdering a common man for sleeping with your wife, it's simple. You stab him while he's in the act. When that man instead has power, there are other concerns."

Though he disliked the comparison, Al-Kabar nodded. "What do you suggest I do?"

Korval's new smile seemed stifled. "Let me find a military target for us to strike. Something to draw Trimar out. If he leaves to lead his army, you take his palace. If not, you find a way to kill him with all his soldiers gone. When he's dead, I'll help you find them and root them out. Together, we can find a steward for Trimar's caliphate until a replacement who meets your standards can be installed."

"That seems a major effort. Can't we just install you? So long as you intend to uphold the Waters' goals, I see no reason to find someone else. After all, you have a great deal of experience with the job."

"That I do, Al-Kabar. That I do."

Chapter 30

Al-Kabar left the caliph's tent feeling he'd missed something. The guards escorted him to another tent where he found his own men, the four from Grev-Nol, and Jannat waiting for him. Jannat lay curled up on a cot while the other sat or stood on the sand. All the men showed signs of fighting: bruises and fresh blood.

Jannat no longer wore her leather armor and her pants had been ripped enough to see flesh. She faced away from the tent flap, her shoulders shaking. Tahjis sat at the foot of her cot and Behrouz perched between it and the flap as a stalwart defender. Al-Kabar raised an eyebrow and looked to Tahjis.

The Rat glanced at Jannat then gave Al-Kabar a hard stare. "Some of Korval's men were giving her personal attention."

"Why did they release us?" Behrouz asked.

Radwan grunted. "*Did* they release us?"

Al-Kabar edged between Jannat's cot and the tent wall to crouch beside her. Tears flowed down her face. He touched her shoulder, then pulled his hand away when she flinched. "You're safe here." When she opened her eyes, he put his arm around her and stroked her hair.

"It was four of them," Tahjis said. "We got there just as they were getting started."

Behrouz nodded. "We were going to be stealthy, but burst in as soon as we realized what they were doing and injured two of them. More men came right away and overpowered us before we could kill any."

"I see." Al-Kabar brushed Jannat's cheek. He thought he understood why she reacted this way. Even if they hadn't managed to have their way with her, she'd been at their mercy and only the unlikely intervention of two men prevented the worst. Putting his mouth close to her ear, he whispered, "They won't touch you again. I'm going to take care of this, then I'll be back for you."

Clutching his shirt, she pulled with unexpected strength until she could stare into his eyes. "Promise," she demanded.

"I promise they'll be punished, and I promise I'll return directly after."

Seemingly satisfied, she let go and curled up tighter. He kissed her forehead through the scarf and straightened. "You four," he gestured to the Grev-Nol men, "can leave if you wish. Ask the guard for supplies to get back home if you need them. The town is safe from Korval. I've made a deal with him that means he won't attack."

"What of Jannat?" one man asked.

"I'll see to her."

The four men nodded, giving Jannat one last look before leaving.

246

When they'd gone, Tahjis shook his head. "What did you trade away to Korval? Your soul?"

"Trimar is Black Abhar and Korval is Scorpion."

Behrouz and Radwan stared at him. Tahjis opened his mouth. "I suppose. That make sense, in a way. With you at his side, he won't be able to get away with half the things he does now. Why pick him over Trimar, though?"

"The viper we know," Behrouz said.

"Yes, that's what I thought." Al-Kabar drew his sword to go deal with Jannat's tormentors. "Introduce me to these guards."

Radwan scowled at Jannat. "Women shouldn't be in battle anyway. They're the things we fight to protect or conquer."

Al-Kabar noted Behrouz's frown and Tahjis's flat scowl at this statement. "Women aren't things."

Radwan grunted. "I meant they're not soldiers."

"I know what you *meant*." Al-Kabar ground his teeth together to keep from hitting Radwan in the face. "A woman can be a soldier if she's taught how. Jannat wanted to protect her home and family. She learned how. She's a soldier. That makes her our sister. Tahjis, let's go."

Following the Rat, Al-Kabar stalked through the camp, head high and showing his anger for any who dared to meet his gaze. Men snapped to attention, watched with curiosity, or jumped out of his way. Radwan trailed behind him, probably wanting to prove his loyalty, or maybe wanting to escape from Jannat's discomfort.

They reached a campfire. Eight men sat around it, nursing drinks, foul moods, and minor injuries. When one noticed Tahjis, he jumped to his feet. "Escaped prisoner!"

"Shut up," Tahjis spat. He pointed. "Those four are the ones."

"What about us?" The one soldier's appearance marked him as no different from the rest, though the others appeared to consider him their better. At the least, they let him speak for them.

Giving this man a cool stare, Al-Kabar said, "I understand you were put in charge of the female prisoner."

"That's right." He bared his teeth in a scowl. "Couldn't believe my luck when I noticed she was a girl. Then this skinny rat and his big friend come barreling in and spoil everything. Who in the name of the Fires are you, and why is this runty twitch walking free?"

Seeing nothing but the men who defiled and murdered Almiya, Al-Kabar's hand flew in a blur, backhanding the soldier so hard he staggered to the side. "I am Al-Kabar." He spat into the fire. "The Waters curse your soul." He raised his sword and watched the soldier's eyes go hard.

"I remember that name," the soldier snarled. "You murdered my brother in his sleep." He drew his own curved blade and raised it, keeping the fire between them.

"And you tried to rape my woman." The words came out of his mouth intending to mean the same as "my soldier," but he realized that claiming Jannat for himself would keep others away from her more effectively than any threat. Despite that, this lesson needed to be harsh and swift, and this man's desire for revenge would only cause problems later. On top of that, he felt no remorse and seemed the type not to understand why he should.

Al-Kabar stepped into the fire, its heat held at bay by his water, and slashed his sword to cut the surprised man's head off. Stooping, he grabbed the grisly trophy by its wrapping and held it up. "The rest of you, remember and spread the word. There will be no more rape by soldiers in this army. Any other who dares to commit this grave crime against the Fires and Waters will be cursed and executed, his body left to rot in the sand."

When he turned, he saw Radwan staring with his mouth hanging open. Tahjis blinked stupidly. Al-Kabar stormed out of the fire and back to the tent. He strode inside and held up the head for Jannat. "Is this enough justice, or do you demand more blood?"

Jannat wiped her face and forced her tears away as she turned to look. "Did he suffer?"

"No, but I cursed him in the name of the Waters. His next life will be torture. I've commanded that his body be left to the desert and not burned."

"Good." She turned away with a satisfied nod.

"Behrouz, find her some clean clothes to wear and have this thrown away." Al-Kabar passed the head over and settled on the edge of Jannat's cot. Tahjis poked his head into the tent, then backed out.

The moment Al-Kabar returned to her side, Jannat lurched into his arms and clung to him. "Thank you."

Concerned about revealing his secret and not sure how best to comfort her, he held her awkwardly. "I tried to come soon enough to prevent that entirely. I'm sorry I failed you."

"No one else would've come at all."

"No one else would've *succeeded*. They would've died trying. I'm no better than anyone else, just more powerful."

Her head leaning on his shoulder, she gazed up at him. "You're wrong. You're something special. The Waters chose you for who you are, not by chance."

Flustered by the naked adoration in her eyes, he looked away. "Perhaps. I'll have someone take you home as soon as you're fit to walk."

"Don't send me away."

He froze as she pressed a kiss on him through the scarf. Pushing gently on her shoulders, he pried her away. "Jannat, after what you've just been through, I don't think this is a good idea."

"Whatever keeps you from showing—" Tears and fire both in her eyes, she grabbed the scarf and pulled it away from his face. She stared, blinking in shock. "You're...but...I don't..."

Fakhira sighed and pushed Jannat away. Worried about the men barging in, she fixed the scarf. "What you do openly, I do in secret."

Stunned, Jannat reached up to touch her mouth. "I kissed you."

"Through the scarf." Al-Kabar stood, saddened by her reaction. "You can go whenever you're ready, I only ask that you keep my secret safe."

"Go?" Jannat rubbed her face and shook her head. "No. I'm not going anywhere. If you can fight, so can I."

"What they just did to you—" Al-Kabar goggled at her. "How can you not need time to recover?"

"I'm a warrior." Jannat's lower lip trembled as she held up a fist. "No man will put me down with violence, no matter what kind."

"Aren't you hurt?"

Jannat gave a hollow laugh. "I ache, yes. I hurt. He hit me and groped me. I'll heal. He's dead. I fear nothing."

Though Fakhira admired her strength and determination, Al-Kabar crossed his arms, wanting to find a reason why Jannat shouldn't come with him. So long as she fought by his side, she risked being treated the same or worse. No matter how much faith she placed in him, he couldn't *always* protect her. "I intend to work with Caliph Korval."

She sucked in a breath. "To attack Grev-Nol?"

"No, to kill Trimar."

"Oh." She looked down at her hands. "If you think he needs to die, then I'll find a way to help."

The tent shook as someone threw the flap open. Tahjis pushed against Caliph Korval, trying and failing to restrain him. "How dare you execute one of my men!"

Al-Kabar flung a hand at the caliph, using water to throw him to his knees and hold him outside the tent. "When your men behave like dogs, they'll be treated like it. Be glad I let the rest live! And you, for that matter, for condoning it."

Korval struggled against the water, shaking from the effort. "Release me," he snarled.

Al-Kabar moved to shield Jannat, wanting to keep Korval's rage focused on himself. It would also help if she didn't spoil what he decided to say next. "Your men nearly raped my woman."

"What?" Korval's rage disappeared. He leaned his head as far as Al-Kabar let him to try to peer around at Jannat. "There was a woman taken?"

Fakhira wanted to slap him for daring to be offended by this. Al-Kabar soothed her with his pragmatism. "Yes. *My* woman. She's a warrior in her own right and if anyone else lays so much as a finger on her, they'll be treated much more harshly than a simple beheading. Further, if any of your men are discovered to be treating any other women this way, a river of blood will flow."

Korval opened his mouth, studied Al-Kabar's face, and shut it. He frowned at the sand for a long time, then cleared his throat. "You're right." The words came out slowly. "We...have some *barbaric* rules left over from darker times." He paused again and wriggled again. "I'll let my men know that this practice ends tonight."

Easing the waters around Korval, Al-Kabar nodded. "I'll believe it when I see it."

Standing, Korval gave a curt nod without looking at Al-Kabar. "In the future, I hope you'll bring an incident like this to my attention personally."

Al-Kabar chose not to promise anything, though he echoed the nod. "I'll meet with you again in the morning to make plans."

Korval's mouth twitched as he inclined his head in a gesture of confused respect, then he walked away. Tahjis held the flap open for Al-Kabar's men to file in. Behrouz had returned during that display and now offered Jannat both clothes and a blanket to hide behind while she changed. Al-

Kabar noted how all of his men regarded him with open awe—even Tahjis, who crouched to help Brumble drink from his waterskin.

Uncomfortable with their reverence, or maybe only Tahjis's, he looked away. "We should all get some sleep."

"Jannat is staying?" Behrouz sounded uncertain. "Or are we taking her home in the morning?"

"She's staying for as long as she wants to." He sat on the rugs covering the sand and wished he could have privacy for a while.

"Share my cot, Al-Kabar. Please." Jannat's pleading eyes tugged at his heart.

"If you wish it."

"Is she really your woman?" Behrouz asked.

"Yes." Jannat bobbed her head. "I am."

Tahjis frowned. "Can I speak with you privately, Al-Kabar?"

Noticing Behrouz seemed highly confused, Al-Kabar sighed. "If it's about Jannat staying, no. Otherwise, yes."

"I have no issue with Jannat staying."

Grateful for small favors, Al-Kabar followed him out and through the camp. They passed the sentries on the edge and kept going until they could speak without fear of being overheard. Tahjis stared out into the darkness lit only by the stars.

"What are you doing?"

"Playing the part. She knows. She'll play the part too."

"What's my part?"

Fakhira tugged her scarf away and hoped the darkness hid enough

253

from the sentries. "Keeping me together."

He glanced at her and shook his head. "Do I need to worry about how you humiliated Korval?"

"I humiliated him?"

Tahjis snorted. "It's easy to forget how naïve you are. You showed how weak he is compared to you. You disciplined his men and physically dominated him, making it clear who has the power. His men will question who runs the army and the caliphate, and they'll start to look to you. That's why he was so mad. You're making him look irrelevant. Like a puppet."

She furrowed her brow. "I hadn't thought of that."

Facing her, he gripped her biceps, sending warmth coursing through her. "These men will follow you. You're doing something they all dream of. Standing up to a caliph is madness. No one in his right mind would do that, but you did it. You're doing it. You're showing them that these men in power are just that—men. Not gods, not saints, not heroes. You're a hero, a real one, and they can see it."

The awful weight of duty pressed down on her shoulders. For one minute, she wanted to be held and protected and allowed to be Fakhira. Cyric, who she could find somewhere in the camp if she looked, would do that for her whether she wanted him to or not. Tahjis wouldn't unless he had to. "I can't run a country."

"Nobody cares." He squeezed her arms and she thought—or maybe just hoped—he wanted to kiss her. "Let Korval be your puppet. But watch him. He thinks you're a threat and he's the type of man who seeks to eliminate threats."

"Will you watch him for me?"

He looked away and sighed. "Is that my part?"

As much as she wanted to keep him by her side, she nodded. "You're a thief. That's a spy with a special taste for shiny things." Glancing to the side, she could make out the movement of the sentries in the flickering firelight. Out here, they shouldn't see anything, but she couldn't take the chance.

"You're good at being Al-Kabar." He walked away, returning to the camp.

She watched him go, unsure if he meant that as a compliment or an insult.

Chapter 31

Al-Kabar woke to the blare of a horn. Jannat, draped over him like a lover, jumped to her feet at the sound, ready to hit someone. With no threat present, she relaxed and dropped to the cot beside him. Leaning over, she brushed her lips against his scarf in a chaste kiss.

Part of him wanted to take her in his arms and tell her everything would be alright. Fakhira knew that for the lie it was and refused to allow it. He held Jannat's hand and watched her wince as she stood without the rush of panic to cover her aches. Swinging his boots onto the rug, he tentatively touched her hip and looked up at her.

"Will you be alright to walk," Al-Kabar asked, "or should I kill someone and take their horse for you?"

Jannat gave him a pained grin. "I think walking would be better than riding for me today."

"As you wish." For no reason he could name, he leaned in and kissed her belly through his scarf and her pants.

She hesitated for a moment, then hugged him to her. "I might

257

want to ride tomorrow, so take your time today and pick out a good horse to steal for me."

"I'll steal the caliph's horse for you, out from under his nose." He stood and brushed her cheek. "For today, I'll see if I can get you a spot in a wagon."

"Ugh, get your own tent, Al-Kabar." Radwan rolled his eyes and left.

"Watch yourself," Tahjis muttered as he stalked out.

Brow furrowed, Behrouz opened his mouth and failed to say anything. He waved them both off and followed his brother.

"Alone at last," Jannat said with a grin. She lowered her voice to a whisper. "You're a better man than any real ones I've met."

Al-Kabar felt his cheeks warm. "Thank you. We should leave. They'll want to take the tent down." He took her hand when she reached for his scarf and pushed her toward the tent flap. "Later. Not now."

She smirked and pulled him out with her into a buzzing hive of activity. The moment he stepped clear of the tent, two men yanked the stakes and ropes to pack it. He wanted to know where the army would march today, but as he led Jannat through the camp, he found that Korval's tent already taken down with the caliph nowhere in sight. They stopped past the edge of the camp to watch its dismantling with Tahjis, Behrouz, and Radwan.

The soldiers moved quickly, scooping up empty tents and piling them into wagons. Al-Kabar led Jannat to the lead wagon and helped her up to the driver's bench. Though several men moved to stop them, Al-

Kabar glared, Radwan clenched a fist, Tahjis cleaned under his fingernails with his dagger, and Behrouz crossed his arms. Objections faded away without being voiced.

"Please stop intimidating my men," Korval said with a sigh from behind them.

Al-Kabar turned to find the caliph approaching with two unexpected companions: Cyric and Zavin. He clamped down on Fakhira's stunned reaction and crossed his arms, waiting to hear what Korval had to say. At least he now knew how Korval had learned about Black Abhar. His men fell back, giving him space. Cyric gave Al-Kabar a hard stare. Zavin stopped several feet away and planted his staff in the hard-packed sand, watching everything.

"I see you gentlemen are acquainted," Korval said. "I've taken the liberty of assigning Cyric to you as an assistant. His purpose in your company is to advise you on accomplishing our goals. I've made sure he understands your demands of men who serve you." He brought Cyric closer and gestured for Al-Kabar to walk with them, away from eager ears. "My army will march deeper into Trimar's territory for the next few days.

"Your goal should be to get your men into Trimar's palace in Jashtel to wreak as much havoc as you can. Obviously, we want Trimar dead, and that falls on your shoulders. Eliminating his circle of advisors is also important, though you can feel free to spare any man willing to lend his local expertise to us."

Though Korval referred to Cyric as an "advisor," Al-Kabar heard "babysitter and spy." He chose to be grateful for the scarf that kept Korval from seeing his scowl. "I don't need an advisor."

Korval rubbed his temple. "Then consider him my representative, sent along so I know you aren't intending to invade my own palace while I'm out."

Crossing his arms, Al-Kabar wished he stood tall enough to glare directly into Korval's eyes. "And what guarantee do you offer me that your intentions don't include destroying small towns full of innocent people?"

For a moment, he thought Korval might storm away in a huff. Whether it came from offense or annoyance at guessing his true intentions, Al-Kabar couldn't say. Korval drew himself up and offered his hand to shake. "I swear on my life that my army will not attack any place without certainty that the target holds no innocents. We won't attack women or children, or men who offer no resistance."

"You swear this to the Waters?"

Korval took a deep breath and nodded. "I so swear this to the Waters."

Al-Kabar shook his hand and hoped the oath held all the gravity it appeared to. "Good fortune to you." He turned his back on them and walked away. Behind him, Cyric and Korval had a short whispered conversation, then he heard Cyric hurrying to catch up with him.

"Where's Fakhira?" When Al-Kabar said nothing, Cyric grabbed his shoulder. "Please, just tell me where she is. I need to know she's safe."

Stopping to face him, Al-Kabar raised an eyebrow. "Why do you care?"

Cyric sighed and shook his head. "When she went lost in that sandstorm..." Raw and wretched grief flashed across his face, chased by fierce hope. "Is she safe?"

"Yes." Al-Kabar shrugged away from him and continued on. Fakhira struggled to accept that Cyric had mourned her. His heart broke when the Waters claimed her. She'd assumed he moved on, lumping her together with all those lost at Aitrae Oasis. Instead, he held her up as some great lost love.

Al-Kabar caught Tahjis's eye and nodded to Cyric, following a few paces behind him. "This is Cyric. He's coming with us, at Korval's request." This news made his men shift into their intimidation stances again.

Cyric held up both hands in surrender. "My instructions are to slip away and alert Korval's guards if you return to Kamrik. Otherwise, I'm here to help."

"We'll see." Al-Kabar's eyes flicked to Jannat. "For now, we'll walk with the army. Later today, we'll split off and take our own path to Jashtel. If any of you want to stay with the army, you'll be free to."

Jannat quirked an eyebrow. "I'm not a delicate flower."

"I never said you were."

"Yet you treat me like one."

"Is it so wrong to wish for your safety?"

One corner of her mouth tugging into a grin, Jannat crossed her arms and stuck her nose in the air. "Yes. I demand that you make amends."

Though he could tell she teased him, Al-Kabar refused to behave like a love-struck fool. "Women," he grunted in dismay. With a shake of his head, he caught Tahjis rolling his eyes, Behrouz taking a sudden interest in his boots, and Radwan sniggering. Cyric stood back and watched, which Al-Kabar figured came from not knowing how to fit into the group yet.

Al-Kabar took Jannat's hand and kissed it through the scarf. "I apologize to my warrior princess. How dare I think, for even a moment, that you might want to relax in pampered luxury instead of suffering in the sand and hot sun with all of us unwashed dogs."

"I like your apologies." Jannat threw him an inviting glance.

His cheeks burned as he considered the shape of her body and the feel of her skin. It shouldn't entice him. With Tahjis on one side and Cyric on the other, Fakhira already had too much to handle. Jannat's inclusion in that group confused both Fakhira and Al-Kabar, and neither knew what to do beyond keeping the pretense intact for as long as possible.

Thankfully, the driver of the wagon climbed onto the bench, giving Al-Kabar an excuse not to respond. The army moved out soon after and set a hard pace in the early morning light. The Waters kept Al-Kabar and his men—but not Cyric—fresh, though they still had to walk. Hours later, the sun blazed overhead and Korval slowed the army's pace. When Al-Kabar saw the rocky outcropping of his hidden grotto looming in the distance, he waved to it for his men and helped Jannat jump off the moving wagon.

Cyric trailed behind as the small band jogged across the sand to the rocks. Al-Kabar led Jannat through the crack in the rocks so he could see her reaction to the grotto. Halfway through, when he could taste the humidity in the air, he saw her eyes light up. When she stepped through and found herself in the tiny paradise, she gasped in surprise.

"How did you know this is here?"

"Al-Kabar serves the Waters," Tahjis said, his tone scolding her for being stupid.

Rolling his eyes, Al-Kabar escorted Jannat to the spring-fed pool in the center. "How long do you think it'll take Cyric to catch up?"

"Long enough for us to leave him behind if we want to," Radwan said.

Al-Kabar laughed. "In his place, I might stay here rather than trudge out to find the army again and report on us." He watched Jannat wade into the pool and cup water in her hands to splash her face and hair. The sight made his belly flutter.

"The hole to the tunnels is too obvious," Behrouz said with a frown. "He'll find it and wind up in the cache. The longer we keep an eye on him at this point, the longer it'll be until Korval knows about the tunnels. That matters, doesn't it?"

"Yes." Tahjis pulled the wrapping off his head and followed Jannat's example.

Radwan plucked a shiny red fruit from a tree and sat to peel it. "We could just kill him. Leave his body in the desert. It's not like Korval will miss him anytime soon."

Fakhira recoiled from the thought of turning on her one-time savior. "No," Al-Kabar said. "Let's at least pretend we have some honor. Besides, if he can be swayed away from Korval, then we'll have another man to work with. Getting into Trimar's palace might take the work of many hands."

"This seems as good a time to plan as any other." Jannat sat at the edge of the pool, her bare feet remaining in the water. "How are we going to get at Trimar?"

Al-Kabar stooped and slipped his hands into the pool, seeking guidance from the Waters. He saw that image again, of himself standing on a ridge overlooking a city with Tahjis by his side. This time, it also showed Radwan, Behrouz, and Jannat. The moment had been frozen, and he thought it tried to say something through their positions and stances.

On Al-Kabar's right, Tahjis squatted with his fingers in the sand. Next to the Rat, Behrouz peered down at the sand, caught in the act of eating an orange fruit. Radwan stood on his other side, hands on his hips and annoyance plain on his face. To Al-Kabar's left, Jannat watched him with a wistful smile, her hand on his shoulder. Cyric stroked his beard thoughtfully beside her, eyes on Jannat's neck.

As interesting as the vision seemed, it told him nothing of how to get at the caliph. "I expect Trimar's palace is similar to Korval's. A rat can find a way inside a building, I'm sure. If that doesn't work, we also have a pretty face and plenty of muscle." He pulled water through his arms to settle under his skin. "Most importantly, we have time. We'll reach Jashtel well ahead of Korval finding anything worth attacking."

"I doubt I can find a hidden way in," Tahjis said. His damp hair dripped onto his shoulders. "I've never been to Jashtel before. No contacts there. I know what to look for, but we're going in blind."

"Do we need to sneak in?" Radwan pointed to Al-Kabar. "Can't you just push all the guards out of the way?"

Finding it a fair question, Al-Kabar gave it some thought. "Every time I use the water to do something, I lose a small amount. In some cases, I lose a lot of it. Unless there's more nearby, we're all better off if I save it for the worst situations. The more I have, the more of us I can protect. Sneaking in would be best, or crafting an assault at a weak point during their guard rotation."

"How long do you think we'll have before Korval can distract him?" Behrouz asked.

"No idea." Al-Kabar shrugged. "It all depends on what he winds up doing. If he goes to Jashtel and sets up a siege, that would make things very different than if he, say, finds Trimar's military training site and razes it."

Huffing and puffing interrupted them as Cyric stumbled into the grotto. He dropped to his knees in the soft grass and gasped for breath. Everyone else went quiet and turned to eating fruit and drinking water. Al-Kabar sat across the pool from Tahjis and Jannat, watching the two people who confused Fakhira the most.

Though Al-Kabar preferred to sit and relax, Fakhira wanted to understand her feelings toward each of them. The Rat had done so much for her, and she knew she wanted him. His touch filled her with longing, and his words weighed heavily on her. When he scowled at her, she wanted to move the earth to make it stop. She'd always thought "love" meant a wife getting used to her husband and falling into a rhythm with him. That it could mean fighting side by side, pursuing the same hopes and dreams, and feeling so much desire came as a surprise.

With Jannat, she understood nothing about her feelings. She knew of men and women who preferred their own gender. It always seemed to her that no one ever had difficulty determining what attracted them. If a woman wanted women, she knew it. Fakhira had no idea. No woman had ever interested her before, yet here she stood, her eyes tracing Jannat's curves. Her stomach fluttered as she watched Jannat pull her dark hair aside to rub her neck with water.

If only she could find a way to have both without upsetting either. She suspected they might not be good at sharing with each other. Worse, she might not be good at sharing either of them.

Cyric shuffling to the edge of the pool interrupted her thoughts. He presented another set of problems. Fakhira knew he'd saved her life. For that, he deserved more from her than disdain. Watching him drop down and drink, she entertained a fleeting interest in his strong hands holding her and guiding her.

Pulling the wrapping off his head, Cyric dunked himself into the pool. Tahjis's hand flashed out with a knife. He met Fakhira's eyes and asked without words what she wanted.

Behrouz said, "Do it."

Al-Kabar shook his head. "We've already discussed that."

Tahjis looked away and tucked his knife out of sight as Cyric broke the surface again.

After drawing a few deep breaths, Cyric wiped the water from his eyes. "How did you do that? You all ran too fast for me to keep up."

Radwan grinned with malice. "Al-Kabar serves the Waters."

"I have no reason to make your job easier," Al-Kabar said.

Cyric sighed. "I didn't ask for this assignment. Korval thinks we'll become great friends because we both survived Aitrae Oasis."

"Obviously, we're going to bond over our losses." Al-Kabar snorted. "And here I thought he was a clever, complex man. Why are you telling us all this?"

Replacing his wrapping, Cyric shrugged. "Deception rubs me the wrong way. I was in the Guard. Korval seems to think that qualifies me to be a spy in your midst." He fished in a pocket and pulled out a blank silver coin. "He even gave me this token. It's magic. If I toss it into a fire, I can speak to him no matter the distance. I'm to discover your secrets and report them whenever I can."

His hand snapping out in a flash, Tahjis snatched the coin away and examined it.

"I'm not your enemy." Cyric sighed. "I joined the Guard to protect people. We broke up fights, punished criminals, and lived lives. Korval demanded that everyone in the Guard fold into his army, and when I lost Fakhira, I had nothing better to do with myself than throw my life away on a stupid war."

Al-Kabar noticed Tahjis's eyes narrow at the name. The Rat flipped the coin through his fingers and eyes Cyric. "Who's Fakhira?"

"I was going to marry her. She—"

Al-Kabar stood and slashed a hand through the air to cut him off. "We don't have time for this. Let's go."

Cyric hopped to his feet and grabbed Al-Kabar's arm. "You said she's safe. Where? Can I see her? I'll do anything you want if you take me to her."

Tahjis's brow shot up and his eyes flicked from Cyric to Al-Kabar and back several times. "You have another woman, Al-Kabar?"

Jannat perked up and Behrouz furrowed his brow. Radwan ignored them and gathered fruit for the trip.

Al-Kabar rolled his eyes. Fakhira thought Tahjis might really be asking if she had another man besides him. "No." He turned to Cyric again. "If you swear your loyalty to me over all but the Fires and the Waters, I'll bring you to Fakhira after Trimar is dead."

Without hesitation, Cyric stuck his hand out. "I swear it. She means more to me than Korval ever could."

Though the declaration surprised him, Al-Kabar shook his hand. He pressed the binding of the Waters onto Cyric, marking his palm with his sigil. "Then let's go. The sooner he's dead, the sooner you can see her."

Behrouz slapped him on the back then showed off his own palm. "Welcome to the team."

Gasping for breath, Cyric stared at the symbol. "Are you all marked?"

"No. It's voluntary for those I trust already." Unwilling to answer any more questions, Al-Kabar plunged into the tunnel. Jannat and his men would have to scramble to put their boots back on and catch up. He didn't care.

Chapter 32

The Waters carried them through the tunnels for hours. When Al-Kabar grew weary, he halted them in a small cavern with a pool in the center. He longed to strip and bathe properly. Instead, he waded in fully clothed, one hand casting blue light for everyone to see. In the center, the water reached his chest.

While the men shared their food and settled to rest, Jannat joined Al-Kabar in the pool. Stepping in front of him where he squatted to let the water reach his chin, she wrapped her arms around his neck and her legs around his waist. Al-Kabar held her waist, not sure if he dared to touch her more.

"Put out the light," Jannat purred into his ear.

He nodded to the men. "They're using it."

"They can suffer."

"Don't rub it in our faces," Tahjis grumbled.

"Put out the light," Jannat repeated, this time loud enough for everyone to hear. "Your woman demands it." When Al-Kabar tried to turn his head to make sure none of his men would need it in the near future, Jannat put her hands on his cheeks and held it in place. "No, don't look to them for approval. Put out the light."

He gave her a mild glare. She matched it. He doused the light.

"Now I'm going to make mad, passionate, noisy love to Al-Kabar," Jannat announced to the cavern.

Someone chuckled. Someone else groaned.

"No," Al-Kabar grunted. "You're not. We're drinking this water."

Jannat laughed, and the sound warmed him. She tugged away his scarf, exposing Fakhira to the darkness. Jannat's fingers explored Fakhira's face with a gentle touch. When she found and traced Fakhira's lips, Jannat leaned in and kissed her.

With so little experience to draw on and so much uncertainty, Fakhira froze. The thrill of excitement flushed her cheeks and filled her with fire. The dark let her forget whose lips caressed hers and she returned the kiss. Her hands pressed the warm body close and drew them both under the surface. She imagined Tahjis running his hands down her back and darting his tongue between her teeth. Fakhira's own hand caressed up her partner's side, then over the swell of—

She pulled away and stood in the pool, holding Jannat at arm's length. Replacing the scarf, Al-Kabar's gruff voice said, "Not now. I meant that." Before lighting up the water again, he pushed it away, drying himself.

In the first flicker of light, he saw Jannat's disquiet and thought she might only have wanted to try kissing a woman to see what it felt like. Jan-

270

nat shifted her expression for the benefit of the men, to a big-eyed pout. "Can you blame me for trying?"

Knowing he had to play the part for most of the men, Al-Kabar took her chin in his hand and brushed her cheek with his thumb. "Not here, with them listening. I won't share any part of you."

Jannat grinned at him, mischief in her eyes. "Yes, Al-Kabar." Her tone made his name into another word for "master." She brushed past him, dripping wet, and walked out of the pool to sit on the stones and pat the spot where she wanted him to sit.

Al-Kabar glanced at Tahjis and found him lying on the stone with his back to her. At that sight, Fakhira longed to reveal herself, if only so she could hold him. Turning away from him, Al-Kabar obeyed Jannat and settled himself behind her to sleep.

When he woke from strange dreams about rats, Al-Kabar flared his light. Behrouz, who had slept between Tahjis and Radwan, straightened. Something flashed in the light near him and he fumbled with his pockets. Shrugging it off as a trick of the light, Al-Kabar rubbed his eyes and yawned.

"Did you sleep?" he asked Behrouz.

"Yes. I think Cyric saying the name of his woman in his sleep a short time ago woke me."

Al-Kabar frowned. "Ah."

"Do you really know she's safe?"

"Yes."

"How?"

Rubbing his eyes again, Al-Kabar wanted the question to go away. "It's not important."

"Since his loyalty hinges on it, I'd say it is."

"It's not your concern," Al-Kabar snapped. His voice echoed louder than he'd intended. The others stirred.

Behrouz flinched and pursed his lips. Bending to the task of refilling his waterskin, he gave Al-Kabar a worried frown.

Fearing he'd been too harsh, Al-Kabar waved in Behrouz's direction. "Later."

With the others waking, neither said anything else, though Behrouz nodded his acceptance. Soon after, the group returned to speeding through the tunnels. Several hours later, they reached the mouth of a cave and emerged in the chill darkness of late night. They kept going until they reached the ridge Al-Kabar had seen in his visions. In the distance, they saw the blazing lights of Jashtel. The city lay in a wide strip along both sides of a dark ribbon Al-Kabar assumed to be water. It boded well for success.

"The Roken River," Cyric said. "Jashtel straddles it. Korval told me we should be able to walk in through the front gates without a problem if we approach in daylight. Near dawn, we can expect to see caravans and single travelers going in and out."

"That's not long from now," Radwan said.

Al-Kabar nodded. He wanted to know why the vision showed him this ridge and those poses. It had to be important. Peering down at Jashtel, he saw nothing special. "Does anything seem off about the city?"

For several seconds, no one spoke. Jannat put her hand on Al-

Kabar's shoulder. "It seems fine to me. Are the Waters telling you otherwise?"

Not wanting to reveal how little he truly knew, Al-Kabar nodded. "We'll split up inside the gates. All of you have useful skills. Ply them in whatever way you're best at and meet near the palace at midday. Search for those who have no love for Trimar and pick up whatever news you can about him and Korval."

"I'll stick with you, Al-Kabar." Jannat curled herself around his side and rested her head on his shoulder.

Though Fakhira knew what she wanted now, the press of Jannat's body still distracted her. For Al-Kabar to do his job, he needed a clear head. "I don't need an escort. Go with Behrouz and Radwan to keep them from bickering so much. Tahjis should go alone, he works best that way."

Radwan scowled. "We don't need a girl to babysit."

Jannat sneered. "And I don't need little boys to spank for their tantrums. But what Al-Kabar asks, I do." She pressed her mouth close to Al-Kabar's ear. "I'll show him that a woman can be more than a toy."

Wishing she'd chosen to object, Al-Kabar nodded his approval and gave Radwan a cool glare.

Behrouz frowned. "What about Cyric? Are you sure you trust him?"

Cyric shrugged. "If it'll make everyone feel better, I'll go with Al-Kabar so he can keep an eye on me."

Though Al-Kabar didn't want that, it seemed Behrouz thought it important. He knew better than to ignore the wisdom of others. "That's fine." He ignored Tahjis, who he assumed would be unhappy about it, and took one last look down the ridge and across the valley. Still seeing nothing of interest, he led the group down the slope. Perhaps the Waters only used the moment because all six of them stood together there. How they stood maybe meant more than where. Hopefully, it wasn't a warning, of danger in the city that would make this the last time they all met in one place.

Chapter 33

Jashtel's stench roiled out through the front gate, noxious enough to make Al-Kabar gag. He glanced aside to see Tahjis—who'd grown up in the worst parts of Kamrik—grimacing and covering his nose. Combined with the steady stream of braying mules and complaining children, the press of bodies sent more than one traveler scurrying to the side to empty their stomachs. Al-Kabar also noticed fresh piles of waste that he hoped had come from animals.

Four guards, all wearing heavy maroon scarves over their mouths and noses, waved people through without speaking or stopping anyone. Al-Kabar caught them eyeing his troupe, probably noticing how all but Tahjis wore swords openly. Suspecting they might give Jannat trouble, he held her close with her sword between them. Like this, anyone would assume Al-Kabar wore two blades and a woman.

As he'd ordered, they split up inside the gate. Cyric, who'd stripped away the blue parts of his uniform, fell in at Al-Kabar's left, matching his stride as he strode up the main road. People lined this packed dirt road with the waste channel in the center, shouting about this bar or that shop or an inn nearby. As they'd done in Kamrik, people gave Al-Kabar a wide berth.

Once they left the opening stretch of the road behind, the stench and crowd thinned, and stores sold goods for travelers: things to hold water, boots, clothes, camping gear, tools, parts for wagons, minor magical charms, and similar items. These merchants would be no help to them; they saw travelers, not residents, and probably benefited from Trimar's edicts and policies.

Al-Kabar glanced at Cyric. "How do you think you can help me get into the palace?"

Cyric shrugged. "I doubt I can. Korval had no advice for that and I've never been here before. Can I ask you something?"

Another sidelong look gave Al-Kabar no clues about what subject Cyric wanted to discuss. He assumed it would be about Fakhira. "If it's intended to dissuade me from my goal, no. Otherwise, feel free."

"Where did you find Jannat?"

Taken off guard by the question, Al-Kabar furrowed his brow. "Why do you ask?"

"I've pledged myself to Fakhira, and I intend to do right by her. But I must admit the thought of her holding a sword and fighting by my side..." He sighed and gazed off to the side. "We escaped Aitrae Oasis before the soldiers left and I had to defend her. She's sweet, but meek and easily frightened. The idea of a woman so bold and fearless is hard to resist."

Al-Kabar struggled to hold back his surprise. If he wanted Fakhira to be more like Jannat, did that mean he'd treat her more like Tahjis did? The implications sent Fakhira's mind whirling. She might have discounted him for no good reason. Their first meeting had been so awkward, then he'd given her the impression he wanted to be a protector.

"Ah." He pondered revealing himself to Cyric and rejected the idea. Right now, they all needed to be focused on the mission. "Jannat is from Grev-Nol. They seem to have different ideas about women there."

Cyric put a hand on his shoulder and stopped him. "Then you barely know her. I know you don't want to talk about Fakhira. Just tell me if it's because you're in love with her?"

The absurdity of his question made Al-Kabar bark in laughter. It took him several beats to recover. "Sorry. No, not at all. You may have to fight Tahjis for her, though." The admission slipped out before he realized what he'd said.

"Tahjis?" Cyric squinted at him. "Why would Fakhira ever want a thief?"

Al-Kabar shrugged and headed up the road again. Fakhira felt a need to defend her Rat. "Perhaps he's more than he seems. I find him a loyal ally and invaluable second opinion. There's no question I'd never achieve my goals without his help and input."

"Is he bound to you?"

"No. It's not necessary with him."

"Korval said you survived Aitrae Oasis. What did you do there?"

The abrupt change of subject confused him, and he had no answer.

277

Al-Kabar cast about for a believable profession and came up blank. "Nothing of consequence."

Cyric raised an eyebrow. "Really? Is that another way of saying you know me because I was a Guard? Is that why you hide your face? So no one will connect you with all the crimes you've committed?"

Though he had a thought to agree, Al-Kabar imagined news of him being a notorious criminal spreading and making everything more difficult. He also suspected Cyric would treat him differently. "No. I mean I was no one until the Waters chose me as their champion. Ordinary."

"Ah." Cyric nodded to a pair of patrolling guardsmen. "I don't know what I can get for you, but I can try to ask them questions. Maybe I can learn something useful."

"Sounds like a good idea." Al-Kabar allowed a shop window to distract him while Cyric continued on. He found a way to position himself so he could watch the encounter while pretending to examine the scarves on display. Fakhira noticed the fabrics had dull, muted colors where she remembered seeing bright colors in Kamrik. People walking on the streets here wore a lot of brown and tan with only faded colors for accents. Al-Kabar fit in here, though his blue scarf marked him as a curiosity. Cyric stuck out in his crisp white, obviously a foreigner.

The front door of the shop opened and an elderly woman hobbled out, a package under her arm. She turned her wrinkled face to Al-Kabar and reached for him. He obligingly offered a hand to help her down the steps.

"What a nice, bright color you wear." The woman touched his

278

scarf. "I miss the blue dyes."

"Thank you, grandmother. I noticed there's little of it here. Why is that?" He tried to keep one eye on Cyric's reflection.

The woman sighed. "We've been at war with one caliph or another almost constantly for, oh, about three years now. It seems like every time one war ends, another begins, and I don't know what any of them have accomplished. Prices go up, refugees come, soldiers leave. It takes most of what my children bring in just to feed us these days."

Al-Kabar frowned. Trimar had to be insane to start war after war when his people couldn't afford to support it. "I'm sorry to hear that, and I wish you well, grandmother."

"Good morrow, young man." The woman tottered away, clutching her package as if afraid it would be stolen out from under her arm.

Al-Kabar watched the woman until she turned the corner, then turned to see Cyric laughing with the two guards. He patted one on the arm and walked away while the two guards returned to their patrolling. By the time he reached Al-Kabar, his smile had turned to a disturbed frown.

"Those guards are too young for the job. They seem big enough, but they're only sixteen. They said the older men were all moved to the palace or sent to other towns to patrol them while the army is out at war. I think those two in particular are good boys. As for the rest of Trimar's guards, who knows? At that age, a young man might turn the power of enforcing the law into a chance to get away with crime."

Al-Kabar related what he'd learned. "With his people reeling from the last conflict, he sends his men to raze Aitrae Oasis. Why? They looted it and took some girls. He had to know Korval would retaliate, and those men couldn't have taken enough to pay for that."

"Speaking of those girls, I wonder where they are?"

Because Fakhira wanted to forget the things she'd seen and heard during the attack, Al-Kabar hadn't thought of them. "It's only been..." With a start, he realized he had no idea. So many of the days blended together. A few days here and a handful there made him shake his head. "Too long."

Cyric nodded. "The army probably still has them. If we're lucky, Korval will find and free them."

That seemed a foolish hope. Al-Kabar sighed and felt the weight of more duty heaped onto her shoulders. He'd have to be strong not to break before this ended. If this ever ended.

Chapter 34

Trimar's palace reminded Al-Kabar of Korval's with its grandiose opulence. Lush greenery billowed around the front of an apricot stone facade. The wide stone path leading from the road to the door could handle three carriages abreast. Guards in Trimar's maroon and brown stood at attention. Unlike the patrolling city guards, these men seemed experienced and capable.

The buildings surrounding his home held no spaces for the poor or unwashed. Al-Kabar and Cyric found themselves hustled from one corner to another until the guards warned them not to come back. Tahjis found them and held his tongue, not wanting to repeat himself. The three of them waited in uncomfortable silence two blocks away, in a bazaar closed for midday.

"Something must have happened to them," Cyric said when it seemed an hour had passed.

Tahjis shrugged. "I doubt anyone would attack them. They carried swords openly."

"Jannat is more at risk with a sword than without one," Cyric said.

Privately, Al-Kabar agreed with Cyric. No one paid any attention to a woman roaming the streets on her own. In Aitrae Oasis, they followed the edicts of the Fires closely. It meant only women could buy and sell food in the market, and they required no male escorts. He'd gotten the feeling that safety might be less assured in larger cities, yet Fakhira remembered seeing lone women on the streets of Kamrik.

As he opened his mouth to ask Tahjis where they might look for the pair, Jannat ran into view with Radwan following on her heels. No one chased or otherwise threatened them and neither glanced back. When Al-Kabar waved to her, she slowed and headed for him. She flopped her arms around his neck and gasped for breath.

"Where's Behrouz?"

Radwan stopped and doubled over to catch his breath. "Don't know. Separated."

Tahjis crouched and checked on Radwan. "How?"

Jannat took one last deep breath as she leaned against Al-Kabar. "We found the peasants' market. Since men aren't wanted there, they said they'd wait for me while I took a look around and maybe buy some food."

"I turned to talk to a shopkeeper," Radwan said as he shoved Tahjis away and straightened. "When I turned back, he was gone. If he said anything, I didn't hear it."

"When I came back out, we asked around for him, and no one remembered him or saw anything," Jannat said. "We looked everywhere around there before we gave up to come meet you."

Cyric held up his hand, showing Al-Kabar's sigil. "Can you find him through the binding?"

"I'm not sure." Al-Kabar let go of Jannat and closed his eyes. Uncertain how to ask for what he wanted, he called for the Waters and hoped they would look within him to interpret his request. For them, he pictured Behrouz and the symbol on his palm. They showed him on the ridge again, taking a bite of that fruit. He hadn't done that on the ridge.

With a grunt of annoyance, he focused on the symbol instead of the man. Then he got the idea of wanting to find it. With that shift in direction, the Waters flared in his heart. Cyric gasped and Al-Kabar opened his eyes to see Cyric clutching his hand to his chest, smothering blue light. Al-Kabar sensed Cyric's location, along with the second that had to be Behrouz. He turned to look in the direction they'd find him.

Everyone else followed his gaze to eye the palace.

"Is he on the other side?" asked Radwan.

"No." Al-Kabar crossed his arms. "He's inside. I'm certain of it."

"Maybe that's where they take people to be questioned," Radwan said, his expression clouded with anger.

"There's only one jail," Tahjis said. "It's on the other side of the river, as far away from the palace as a thing can get and still be in the city. The few people willing to talk to me said the palace only holds Trimar and his family, visiting guests, and his servants and guards. He has no contact with his people, prisoners or not, unless they're wealthy."

Every time he learned something new about Trimar, Al-Kabar found another reason to hate him. "What kind of people does he keep in his prison?"

Tahjis shrugged. "Most criminals go into his army. Korval does that too. They get sent on the worst missions, ones they're likely to get killed doing. Those men who rushed Grev-Nol first were probably all murderers. So you won't find anyone like that in the prison. It'll be people who broke small laws and couldn't afford to buy their way out when they got caught."

Al-Kabar smirked. "How did *you* never wind up in prison?"

"The only men who ever caught me were Abhar's goons." Tahjis smirked. "And that was never my own fault."

Though Fakhira wanted to stick out her tongue at him, Al-Kabar refused to let her. "Is there any chance that raiding his prison to free everyone there would get Trimar out of his palace?"

Radwan shrugged. "I doubt it. From what we heard, he rarely leaves and considers his personal safety of high importance."

Nodding his agreement, Tahjis added, "I don't think he's going to be drawn out by anything short of his palace catching fire."

"Then we should set his palace on fire," Cyric suggested with a grim smile. "He burned down my house, so why shouldn't I return the favor?"

Righteous anger surged in Al-Kabar's blood. "Yes," he growled. "Let's do it."

Tahjis frowned. "With Behrouz inside?"

"The Waters will protect me from fire." Al-Kabar held up a fist and water rushed out to encase it. "Once it's burning, I'll go in and bring him out."

"Alright, if that's how you want to do this." Tahjis produced Brumble from the folds of his clothes. "Go find the rats in the palace and see if you can find ways to start lots of small fires." Setting the rat down, he watched her scamper away. "She'll get things going inside. Outside is up to you."

Jannat dug dirt out from a fingernail and sounded hesitant as she said, "Al-Kabar, we don't really have anything to start a fire with."

"Then find something. Now. And use it." To his satisfaction, Jannat, Radwan, and Cyric all jumped to the task, spreading out and inspecting their surroundings.

Tahjis leaned against the wall they sheltered in the shade of and crossed his arms. "What're you going to do when Trimar is dead?"

"Install Korval as caliph here."

"And then?"

"And then what?"

Tahjis spread his hands. "That's what I'm asking. What happens when you win?"

Al-Kabar crossed his own arms and shrugged. "Go home."

"Where's that?"

"Aitrae—" No, Fakhira wouldn't go back to a charred husk of nothing. Al-Kabar scowled at the ground and wanted to throttle Tahjis for making him and Fakhira both think about things they preferred to leave alone. "I don't know. Maybe I'd be best off traveling to other caliphates to see if they need help."

"Ah." Tahjis left a long pause. "We could go back to Kamrik."

Al-Kabar thought of the life Tahjis had before Fakhira met him and knew he couldn't be satisfied with it. "And do what? Run errands for Scorpion?" Shaking his head, he looked away. "I was chosen for something bigger."

Before Tahjis managed to respond, Jannat returned with a clay jug. "This is full of the purest, most vile alcohol I could find."

Radwan rounded the corner behind her and produced flint and steel from his pocket. Cyric carried rushes. Combining all these things seemed promising.

"Tahjis, find us a place to start this." Al-Kabar flicked a hand and watched the Rat's mouth twitch irritably. He scurried away. The others followed Tahjis, trying not to attract attention. Al-Kabar stayed away, figuring his scarf marked him as too unusual to go unremarked.

Jannat returned first again, breathless and grinning. She jumped into Al-Kabar's arms and planted a kiss on his mouth. "I shouldn't be happy to torch my own caliph's palace, but doing it for you gives me a thrill. Besides, it's his own fault for having such incompetent guards."

The others returned before he could push her off. Knowing Fakhira wanted Tahjis—or maybe Cyric—and not Jannat made her attention more uncomfortable than before. He hugged her close anyway, to keep up appearances. "Is it done, then?"

Tahjis returned last. "It's lit up. No one saw us. Trimar only has men watching the obvious entry points. It's almost like he *wants* someone to break in." He scowled and crossed his arms."We've all done our parts. It's your turn now."

Al-Kabar nodded, not sure why the ease of the task made Tahjis unhappy. "If Trimar runs out, feel free to kill him. I don't need the honor reserved for me." He squeezed Jannat and left her behind. As he strode to the palace, he called water. It streamed out of cracks in the walls to surround him.

Walking to the front gate, he found the guards no challenge. They rushed him, he flung water out, they fell back, he kept going. Inside, he found no one. Flames licked the curtains and raged on the rugs and furniture, yet no one ran for the doors or panicked. He guessed the fires hadn't reached the second floor yet, and all the people might be up there.

The Waters showed him which way to go to reach Behrouz, and he tossed open a door in his path to find a room with the man inside. The small space, no larger than a closet, held a chamber pot, a lumpy mat with a thin blanket, and a small jug of water. Surprised to find him so easily and without any guards, he leaned out to check the hallway again. Finding it empty of anything but fire and stone, he shrugged.

"I knew you'd come, Al-Kabar. Thank the Waters you found me." Behrouz sat, unable to move far from his perch with his wrists locked inside metal cuffs welded to the wall.

"What happened?" He grabbed the cuffs and commanded the water to freeze around them.

"I waited on the edge of the market for Jannat—is she alright?"

"Yes. She and Radwan both said you disappeared." Frost formed on the metal.

"I thought I saw Tahjis and went to check with him. There's no sense in doubling our efforts, I thought. Someone hit me in the back of the head. I think the second time knocked me out. I didn't see who did it, though."

"Can you walk?" Al-Kabar grabbed the cuffs and smashed them against the stone wall. They shattered, flinging iron shards he caught with his water.

Behrouz rose to one knee and nodded. "They barely touched me and I haven't been here long."

"Good. Let's go." He went to check the door and found it no different from before. Behind him, Behrouz approached at a run, which seemed strange. When Al-Kabar turned to look, he caught sight of a length of white-hot metal in Behrouz's hands before it slammed into his side, sizzling and filling the air with steam. The impact threw Al-Kabar to the floor.

Before he had a chance to react, Behrouz hit him with the burning metal across the back, then on the back of his skull.

Chapter 35

"Ah, he's coming around. Keep a hold on him." The unfamiliar male voice confused Fakhira.

She lay face-down on a hot stone floor, something heavy holding her arms and pinning her down. Her feet burned with enough agony to make her whimper. Opening her eyes, she saw fire. By craning her neck, she discovered a woman in red sitting on her back and holding her hands. Another sat on her legs and held her ankles.

"Welcome to my palace, Al-Kabar. I have to say that you surprised Behrouz with how you chose to come for him."

One woman grabbed her head wrapping—no, Al-Kabar's head wrapping—and forced him to look up. Al-Kabar saw a man he didn't recognize in enough finery to mark him as Caliph Trimar, holding Al-Kabar's sword. Beside him stood Behrouz, a smug grin on his face. The woman forced his head around so he could see his men and Jannat lined up on their knees, hands bound behind their backs.

"They realized we'd set a trap before you did, apparently. My guards, more numerous and attentive than they pretended at, caught them rushing to warn you. You should take better care with your allies, Al-Kabar." Trimar waved a hand toward him. "Take that scarf off. I want to see who I'm talking to."

The fire kept him from sensing any water and the two women bound him too well to squirm loose. His captor ripped the scarf away, then his head wrapping. Fakhira's hair fell around her face. Through it she saw Trimar, Cyric, and Radwan all stare at her. Cyric blinked and mouthed her name.

"How unexpected. A shame you can't be used for anything, because it would be nice to have a matched set." Trimar grabbed Jannat by the hair and wrenched her head up. "You, of course, know what happens to women who take up the sword."

"Whatever you put in my mouth," Jannat growled, "I'll bite off."

Trimar laughed. "Don't worry. I won't touch your mouth. Take her to my play room and secure her there. Take special care with her face." He shoved her down and slapped her.

Fakhira flinched and struggled against her captors. This shouldn't be happening. "How? I bound you."

"Shut up." Behrouz sneered at her. Something in the expression seemed off, as if he didn't understand where it came from. He shook his head as if trying to clear it. "I did my part, Trimar. You know Korval's plans and you're free to act without Al-Kabar stopping you. It's time for you to pay me."

Radwan launched himself at the guards as they grabbed Jannat, to no avail. "If you harm a hair on her head—"

"What will you do?" Trimar laughed again. "Nip at my ankles?"

One guard kicked Radwan in the kidney. Another kneed Tahjis in the gut. The third punched Cyric in the face.

Fakhira saw no way out of this disaster. She never expected this from Behrouz. Radwan always seemed more likely, and she'd trusted him enough. Helpless to resist, she tried to block out Jannat's defiant shrieks. Unable to see the men once they slumped to the floor, she closed her eyes to try to gather her strength. Maybe if they believed she'd passed out again, they'd get sloppy.

"This is all very entertaining, Trimar," Behrouz said, his words strangely halting and awkward, "but I need to deliver Al-Kabar, or whatever her name really is, to Zavin."

"Zavin?" Fakhira regretted speaking, but hadn't been able to hide her surprise. Korval's trusted advisor had plotted against him? Nothing she had seen pointed to that. The man had struck her as loyal to the caliph.

"Fine," Trimar said. "Knock her unconscious and bundle her up for transport."

"What about these men?"

"They're obviously loyal to her. Hang them from the walls. That should be enough to quell the newest rebellion brewing here. I'll be in with the woman."

"Should we kill them first?"

"No." Trimar sneered. "Make sure they suffer as long as possible."

"The curse of a thousand tiny deaths upon you," Tahjis spat.

With one last burst of effort, Fakhira strained to throw her captors off. She failed with a growl. The woman on her back wrapped a wiry arm around her neck and squeezed. As her world went white, she saw a small shadow in the window.

Chapter 36

Fakhira had no idea how much time passed before she awoke again. This time, she sat on a red velvet cushion with her ankles and knees bound and her wrists tied to a hook in the ceiling. Only a thin shift covered her body and when she pulled her head up, her neck screamed in protest. Santrice sat beside her, given the same treatment. On her other side, Korval lay on the floor unconscious, his hands bound to his feet.

Beyond the ring of fire, the opulent chamber tugged at Fakhira's memories. With Santrice here, she knew it had to be the Fire Dancers' rooms at Korval's palace. Korval's condition, though, made no sense. She looked to Santrice, who jutted her chin at the room. Fakhira thought she understood the message: someone would overhear anything they said.

"What happened?" Fakhira thought this question safe enough. Anyone here should already know the answer.

Santrice took a deep breath. "The Fire Dancer came to see me. She knew I wasn't you before she saw me."

"I certainly did." Mahdis, the lead Fire Dancer, stepped into the flames with her hands on her hips. The fire writhed around her, licking at her red silk dress and ochre flesh without harming either. "This girl has no touch of the Waters at all. You, on the other hand, pulse with their power."

Two more shapes approached the burning ring: Behrouz and Zavin. They stayed outside the ring and watched. Fakhira needed to understand the situation to get out of it and somehow return to save Tahjis. At least Mahdis wanted her alive for some reason. She caught Behrouz's gaze and he looked away. Whether he did it for shame at his own actions or to avoid being drawn back under her spell, she couldn't say.

Fakhira gave her attention back to Mahdis and wished she knew what magic words to use. "Let Santrice go. It was my idea for her to pose as me, and she's been through enough already. She doesn't deserve to be used again."

Mahdis flicked her eyes to Santrice and back. "Well, you see, I have a problem that I think Santrice can help me with. I was perfectly content to let you and my husband run around Serescine, chasing after Trimar and his armies, razing whatever you wanted. But you had to go after Trimar personally. On his own, Korval would never be able to assassinate Trimar. You, on the other hand, have more than enough power to walk up, slit his throat, and leave without a scratch."

Fakhira furrowed her brow. "Why do you care about whether Trimar lives or dies?"

"I don't." Mahdis paced down the line of fire, her hand caressing individual flares as if they were favored pets. "I care about the timing and manner of his death. Korval's campaign would have rendered his people weak and angry. When they found out why Trimar keeps taking them to war, which they would have when they 'intercepted' the communiques I planted, the remnants of the country would have risen up to revolt against him. Korval would march into their cities as a righteous savior with promises of food and plumbing.

"But then you came onto the scene. You and your power threaten everything I've been working for all this time." Mahdis sighed and rubbed her forehead. "Of course, I realize now that I should have expected the Al-Kabar to appear when I set these plans in motion. You were inevitable once Trimar decided to be outraged that we wouldn't let his son molest our daughter."

Raising her brow, Fakhira blinked rapidly. Until now, she'd thought she faced nothing more than men who abused their power. "Why is Korval here? You could have just left him unaware, leading his army across the desert."

"You rendered him useless," Zavin said. "You stole through his camp, defying his ability to secure his men. You rallied a tiny town to defeat his army, proving him an ineffectual warrior. You walked into his camp and forced him to take you on as an ally, showing he had no backbone. You disciplined his men and laid down new rules, declaring him irrelevant. You personally defeated him with a flick of your wrist, making it quite clear who the better man is."

"In short," Mahdis said with a sigh, "he can't do his job anymore because his army doesn't respect him anymore. I'd have killed him already, but then my daughter would have no father. However ineffectual he is at his other duties, he's proven himself capable at that one. When he wakes up, I'll deal with him. Until then, keeping him inside the fire with you is the most secure way I can hold him."

She waved a hand to dismiss the subject and settled on a cushion. "Fakhira, I need to negotiate with Al-Kabar. May I?"

Wishing she could call the Waters through all this fire to at least gain their guidance, Fakhira nodded. "What do you want?"

"I'm a Fire Dancer, Al-Kabar. I want to dance with the Fires. From you, though, I want you not oppose me."

"So you manipulated one of my men into taking me prisoner? Why not ask for a meeting? Whatever means you used to contact Behrouz could easily have been employed to contact me instead."

Mahdis sighed. "You're so simple. In return for you leading Korval's army against Trimar and his people, I will let Santrice live. She'll be cared for so long as you do what I want and don't fail. Should you or your men go against my wishes, or if you fail at the goals I set, I'll curse her soul, slit her throat, and have her body left for jackals in the desert."

Santrice, who could have cowered and cried, spat at the fire. "You're no different from Abhar."

"On the contrary," Mahdis said as she raised her chin, "I'm nothing like Abhar. It's time for the Fire Dancers to take our rightful place as rulers of the desert sands. I'll do whatever it takes to make that happen."

"Including murdering an innocent woman," Al-Kabar said.

"One life more or less doesn't make much difference."

"Unless it's yours."

Mahdis laughed. "Yes, of course. But I'm a Fire Dancer. My life is worth more than a girl who happens to be your lover's sister. Or was that a lie too?" When Fakhira clamped her mouth shut and refused to answer, Mahdis held up Korval's token. "I'm also worth more than some chit who happened to survive the razing of Aitrae Oasis." She flung the token into the fire. "But if you cooperate, none of that matters and we can all be happy. So, what do you say, Al-Kabar? Struggle or be reasonable?"

Fakhira closed her eyes to block out Mahdis's smug face. If she rejected the offer, she and Santrice would both die. If she accepted the offer, they'd both become Mahdis's slaves. To her frustration, no third option offered itself. Behrouz wouldn't step in, Tahjis wouldn't climb in through a window, and Cyric wouldn't storm the palace. Radwan and Jannat could do nothing. Their fates rested on Fakhira's shoulders, not the other way around.

Fakhira sagged against her bindings, not knowing the right thing to do. One option cut off her head in the name of principle. The other cut off her options and betrayed her purpose. At least the second might give her another chance to succeed. "I accept your offer."

"You don't have to save me," Santrice said, her head falling forward in defeat.

"Nonsense." Mahdis rose and passed through the flames to untie Santrice. "She *does* have to save you. It's in her soul. That's why the Waters chose her in the first place."

Fakhira strained against her bindings for the first time but found the effort too difficult in the heat. "Now what?"

297

"Now? You're going to stay there for a while. I'll be back later." Mahdis dragged Santrice through the fire. Zavin took Santrice from her on the other side and they left the room.

Behrouz stayed behind, frowning at Fakhira. "Why did you pretend to be a man?"

Thinking back to her original plan, Fakhira sighed. So much had changed since that first plunge into the Waters. "Women don't take up the sword."

"Jannat did."

"And now, thanks to you, Jannat is Trimar's prisoner. Unless he's tired of her already and she's now hanging from the walls of his palace with everyone else I care about."

He rubbed the mark on his palm. "Some things are more important."

"Like what? Money?"

His brow furrowed. "I don't know." He turned and wandered away.

Chapter 37

"I think Zavin bespelled him."

Korval's hushed whisper startled Fakhira. "What?"

"Keep your voice down." The caliph wriggled onto his back. "Zavin is a mage. It's not his specialty, but he can cloud the minds of the weak-willed."

"I thought you were unconscious," she whispered.

"No, I woke up before you did and heard everything. I wish you'd told me you were Al-Kabar, but I'm fairly certain I understand why you didn't. The important thing now is to escape and stop my wife. I spend so little time with her outside of her official Fire Dancer capacity that I had no idea she'd turned into this...thing. What do you need to get free?"

"Water." Fakhira wanted to weep without knowing why, but had no tears to give. "I'm so dry I'm not even sweating anymore, and the flames are too high to call any over them."

"Now that you mention it, I've stopped sweating too." Korval sighed. "I suppose there isn't enough moisture in our breath?"

"No. The fire gets it too fast. Or I'm too weak to catch it." Fakhira looked down, knowing she would never see Tahjis or Cyric again. As much as she wanted to hope they'd survived somehow, she knew in her heart that both men must have been hung already.

He stared up at the ceiling in silence for several minutes. "There's something else here we could use."

Thinking he must have seen something, she looked up. The rope binding her wrists hung on a hook anchored in the ceiling. The second hook hung a few feet away. She saw nothing else on or in the smooth marble overhead. "Like what?"

"Blood."

"I'm not sure we have enough to work with."

"Could you use it?" He seemed so cool and calm while talking about something so gruesome.

Tiny jolts of something, maybe fear, shot to her fingers and toes, giving her the strength to lift her feet. The bindings made standing impossible, and she slumped again, unable to accomplish anything. She sighed. "I pulled the water out of alcohol, so I should be able to pull it out of blood. I can't imagine how you expect to spill any, though."

He wriggled and contorted his body. Though it had no effect on his restraining ropes, she saw something silver flash in the light. A small knife with no hilt fell to the floor. Korval relaxed, panting from the effort.

"If you have a knife, you can just cut the ropes."

"Doubtful. This blade is awkward and difficult to use effectively in the best circumstances. Like this, I'll never get a good grip on it. Besides, only the best for my household. I'd be surprised if these aren't the enchant-ed ropes, designed to foil such simple efforts."

Staring at him, Fakhira frowned. "Why would you have rope like that?"

Korval bared his teeth in a feral grin. "Why wouldn't I?" He curled around the knife and spent the next several minutes trying to pick it up with his fingers. The small, thin length of metal slipped and scraped on the marble floor, defying him until he used his tongue to stop it. With the knife between two fingers, he hissed and sucked on his tongue for a beat before stopping. "Fakhira." He took a deep breath. "I want you to know that I'm sorry. For not doing enough to protect Aitrae Oasis, for how we met, and for the things I'd hoped to convince you to do for me.

"Once, I was a young man and I had lofty ideals. I took the caliphate from my predecessor because I believed I could make things bet-ter. Then I got into the job and found there was only so much I could do or change without great effort and expense. I took the easy path instead of the hard one. Because of your actions, I now regret that. Maybe if I'd made some of those hard choices, my wife wouldn't have turned to my mage."

"Why are you telling me this?" Fakhira's belly felt leaden. She blinked at the man who'd tried to rape her in an illegal cesspit of debauch-ery that he allowed to operate. Since then, he'd proven himself not so depraved as he'd first seemed, but he hadn't struck her as a man who'd will-ingly sacrifice himself for anything.

"The only thing I've ever really wanted is for my people to have good lives. I know you don't think you can run a caliphate, but you're wrong. You can. You'll do it better than I ever could because you won't compromise your ideals in the face of pressure to let everything stay the same. Your very first idea was to educate people, and I have no doubt the rest of your ideas will be equally brilliant."

He took a deep breath again, this one girding. "Use my blood well, Fakhira. If you can manage it, I'd prefer to live. If not, know that I go to the Fires willingly to be cleansed. May the Waters send me back a better man."

Fakhira gasped as he slashed the blade across the easiest part of himself to reach—his neck. Rather than let his gift be wasted, she called his blood and pulled the water from it. Pink-streaked liquid streamed to her, snaking around her legs and torso to her arms. When it reached her arms, it seeped into the rope and froze, bursting the rope. She fell to the floor in a heap, her hands and arms numb.

Using the water in place of her fingers, she ripped away the ropes on her legs and staggered to her feet. As little as she wanted to hurt Korval, she couldn't save him if she stayed trapped inside the ring of fire. Resolute and focused on the fire, she urged more water out of Korval and used it to shield herself. His gasping gurgles filled her ears.

With a deep breath, she stepped through the fire. Behrouz sat with his back to her, his attention taken by a Fire Dancer. The rest of the Fire Dancers, aside from Mahdis, lounged on the couches and cushions. Fakhira couldn't see her sword, but she did see basins and pitchers full of water. Calling to it, she felt the sweet embrace of the Waters as more and more wrapped around her.

"She's free!" The shrill, feminine shriek sent Fire Dancers scrambling.

Behrouz rolled to his side, pushed the Fire Dancer off him and grabbing his pants. "Don't just sit there," he growled.

"Stay where you are," Fakhira said. She held up a hand, water swirling with blue light. "Tell me where to find Mahdis."

Behrouz stood, holding a curved blade with one hand and his pants with the other. "Don't tell her!" He paced toward Fakhira. "You're not getting out of this room alive."

Her arms tingling with a thousand pinpricks of pain, Fakhira grimaced and shook her head. "I don't want to hurt you, Behrouz. You pledged yourself to me. That binding means something to me even if it means nothing to you."

Instead of answering, Behrouz charged her. He led with his sword. She let him come, forming the water into a berm on the floor that reached up in time to trip him. Sprawling at her feet, his sword clattered to the stone and slid away. She covered him with water and held him there.

Fakhira squatted in front of him and touched his face. "Break the compulsion, Behrouz. Remember who you are and what matters to you. You serve Al-Kabar, not Mahdis or Zavin."

He thrashed with all his might. "Let me go, you sand whore!"

Whatever Zavin had done to him, mere words wouldn't break it. The six Fire Dancers in the room gathered together beyond him. To deal with them, she'd need all the water she could get and couldn't risk him getting free in the meantime. "I'm sorry," she whispered. "I'd save you if I could."

The water scooped up his sword and brought it to her hand, now able to curl around the grip. She wanted to save him, to tie him up and keep him safe until she could break the spell on him. There had to be a way. As she slashed down with the sword, she saw his eyes widen in fear. This man had served her, and she repaid his moment of weakness against a mage with death?

At the last moment, she turned the blade, sweeping it in an arc until the butt end of the hilt slammed into the back of his head. She couldn't prevent it from giving him a nasty slash across his shoulder, but he'd live. Though she wanted to weep for what Zavin had done to him, she turned away from his limp form and faced the Fire Dancers.

"If you fight me, I'll win. You know that. I don't want to kill you all. Tell me where Mahdis is and all of you can live."

The six women glanced between each other. One stepped forward, hands on her hips. "Mahdis is our sister. We won't let you harm her."

So many had to die today, all for the want of power. Fakhira thrust her water out at the line of women, knocking them off their feet. "The Fires and the Waters are supposed to be two sides of the same coin," she told them, unable to hold back tears. None of this had to happen. "Allies," she said between sobs, "not enemies."

She called her water back to encase her body as she ran to them. Jets of fire blasted past her, licking the edges of her liquid armor and sizzling tiny parts away. With the foreign sword, she slashed through the air. The Fire Dancers had little training for battle and the blade bit deeply into one woman's side. When she yanked it out, she noticed the metal growing hot and pulled water from the dying woman's blood to cool it.

Fire blasted around her, obscuring her sight. She spun the blade blindly, catching another Dancer and cutting her arm off. Even without her own sword, Fakhira still managed to cut down these women who trusted their fire to protect them. She whirled and ducked and thrust in a confusing storm of billowing flames until she threw the last Fire Dancer to the floor.

Panting from the fighting, Fakhira held her blade over the Dancer's neck. The woman, no older than Fakhira herself, stared up in terror, tears streaming down her face. "Please don't kill me."

"I don't want to." Fakhira took the Dancer's hand. "I also don't want to be stabbed when I turn my back on you."

The Dancer gulped. "Like you said, the Fires and the Waters should be allies, not enemies. My name is Omeed, and I can be your ally. You'll need Fire Dancers to be legitimate as the ruler of the caliphate. No one will accept you without at least one."

Knowing the truth of Omeed's words, Fakhira nodded. "Will you pledge to me on your life that you'll be loyal to the Fires and the people? That you'll raise objections with words instead of knives? That you'll never go behind my back?"

Taking a deep breath, Omeed nodded. She raised a hand and swiped her palm across the blade at her neck, then offered it to Fakhira. "I so swear with my life and my blood."

Fakhira pulled the blade away, wary of a trick. When Omeed remained still, Fakhira swiped her own hand against the knife and clasped

Omeed's. "As it should be. I swear my loyalty to the Waters and the people. As sisters, we'll guide them." She felt warm approval wash over her.

"As true sisters." Omeed sniffled. "These women were my sisters but they betrayed me."

Fakhira pulled Omeed up and hugged her. "I will not. Where will I find Mahdis?"

"She and Zavin were taking Santrice to your room. I don't know what for."

"Thank you." Fakhira pulled away and met Omeed's eyes. "Tie this man up, please. Zavin bespelled him. Also see to Korval. He sacrificed himself to stop Mahdis. If you can save him, do so."

Omeed nodded. "I'll take care of them. I promise."

Fakhira kissed Omeed's cheek and hurried away.

Chapter 38

Fakhira's bare feet slapped on the marble floor as she ran down the hall. Mahdis still had Santrice to use as a hostage against her. She worried over how to isolate Santrice to keep her safe as she hurried down the stairs. At a corner, she ran into a servant, causing him to tumble to the floor while the Waters kept her on her feet.

"Fakhira?" Amil stared up at her. Recent burns puckered the flesh of his face.

She crouched and brushed his damaged skin. "Did she do this to you because of Santrice?"

He nodded. "I kept it a secret as long as I could, but Mahdis came looking for you. "

Fakhira hated to ask him to risk more injury, but she needed help and had no one else to turn to. "She's got Santrice in my room again. Can you help me get her out?"

"I can..." Amil bit his lip. "I can sneak in through the window and sneak her out while you distract Mahdis and Zavin?"

"Yes." Fakhira took his hand and pulled him to his feet. "That would be perfect. Hurry. I'll wait for a count of one hundred."

With a firm nod, he squeezed her hand. "I won't fail her." He ran off.

As soon as he disappeared around a corner, she closed her eyes and wished Tahjis could be here to help her. Cyric, Radwan, or Jannat would be just as welcome. The moment she took care of Mahdis and Zavin, she'd go to Jashtel and see their bodies properly given to the Fires. Trimar and his lackeys would suffer for having them killed.

She took her time counting, stifling down tears for them. Later, there would be time to mourn. Now, she had to save who she could and stop Mahdis. When her count ended, she strode up the hall to the door of her own room and stared at it. It had been her sanctuary and prison, her salvation and damnation. The door, though, was just a piece of wood.

Raising her hand, she flung water forward, blasting the door in. She strode through it before the shards and splinters landed and settled, and noticed Amil using the noise to cover the sound of him opening the window. Mahdis sat on the edge of the bed, interrupted in the act of tying Santrice's foot to the bedpost. Both hands and the other foot had already been bound. Zavin leaned on his staff from a few feet away, watching. To Fakhira's surprise, he had her sword belted at his waist.

Mahdis sighed. "Of course you were lying."

"I'll handle her," Zavin said with a wave of his hand.

"No, you don't need to." Mahdis reached over and grabbed Santrice by the neck. Amil would have a hard time getting the girl free like that. "Remember our deal, Al-Kabar? You obey me and I let Santrice live. She would've had a nice life. Never going hungry, never forced to please a man, never fearing for her life. Aside from the sword you'd have against her neck, of course."

Fakhira had little time to act. She summoned Al-Kabar's confidence and squared her shoulders. "If you kill her, there's nothing to stop me from killing both of you. Which, of course, you know I can do."

Mahdis raised one delicate eyebrow. "No, I don't think you can. I think you want me to believe you can. You may be able to defeat me, but not with Zavin by my side. Your power, when countered by mine, is no match for true magic." She shoved Santrice aside and stood. "If you'd like to be crushed beneath our will, though, we can oblige."

Fakhira glanced from one to the other, taking the opportunity to check Amil's progress. He'd crept inside and hid behind a curtain. Tahjis would be proud of his stealth. "I think having me delivered to you already unconscious has made you underestimate my capabilities."

Laughing, Mahdis stepped into a wide stance and held out her hands. "Very well, Al-Kabar."

Zavin straightened and gripped his staff tight enough to turn his knuckles white. Though she'd never seen him work magic, Fakhira suspected he did it now. Using her water as a cushion, she dove to the side and rolled, putting a couch between them and her. Hissing and popping on the other side of the couch told Fakhira that her hiding place would be engulfed in flames soon.

She needed to get her sword. Though she'd managed against the rest of the Fire Dancers, she feared Mahdis might be right about Zavin. With the blade, she felt confident she could get close enough to cut him down. Then it would only be a matter of opposing Mahdis. The prospect filled her with trepidation and she leaned on Al-Kabar's strength to push her fear away.

Pushing down with her water, she flung herself over the burning couch and landed in a somersault. Her water swirled around her to cushion the blow and lashed out to knock Mahdis off her feet with a squawk. Fakhira plowed into Zavin's legs, sending them both sprawling. Stealing a glance at the bed, she saw Amil freeing Santrice's hand.

Zavin thumped Fakhira in the ear with his staff, drawing her attention back to him. Groping around his legs, she found the wrong sword first and squeezed hard, making him grunt. Heat seared at her feet. She wrapped her fingers around the hilt of her sword and jumped to her feet, ripping away Zavin's sash.

Dropping into a crouch with the blade held over her head, she scanned the situation. Mahdis lay on the floor still, flames billowing from her hand. Amil had one of Santrice's hands free. Zavin rolled to his hands and knees, a cocoon of yellow magic snapping into place around him. Not knowing what the cocoon would do, Fakhira chose to consider Zavin the greater threat.

Fakhira flung her water at Mahdis, throwing her body in its wake. Her water doused the flames and bowled Mahdis over. On her way past Zavin, Fakhira hit his outstretched staff and sprawled on the floor. She tightened her grip on her sword as she slid over the smooth marble, determined to keep the blade. Refusing to lose Mahdis either, she clenched her empty hand into a fist, causing the water to do the same around the Dancer.

Mahdis screamed until the water covered her mouth. Something hard hit Fakhira in the side. With her water holding Mahdis, she had none to protect herself. But Al-Kabar could take a beating. She rolled with the blow to hop on her feet and raised her blade in time to turn Zavin's staff aside.

His eyes widened as he saw the bed over her shoulder. "Dammit," he muttered. Hurrying away from Fakhira, he flung a hand out to send a crackling bolt of sickly yellow energy at Santrice. Without thinking, Fakhira swiped her sword at the bolt, catching it in midair and deflecting it to Mahdis. Though her blade affected it, the water did nothing to protect the Fire Dancer from it.

Fakhira watched as Mahdis curled her body around the spot where the bolt hit and fell to the floor, spasming inside the water encasing her. She glanced at Zavin and saw him freeze in horror, his mouth falling open.

"No," Zavin whispered.

Unwilling to give him a chance to recover, Fakhira closed the distance, sword ready.

"You— How? No one can—" His jaw kept moving without making words.

Fakhira reached him and swung her sword. It hit his cocoon and scraped yellow sparks off the edge, flinging them away. The near-miss jolted Zavin aware and he raised his staff. Sparks flew as Fakhira fought him.

Every swing of her blade hit his staff or his shield of magic. Though she spared little time for coherent thought, she suspected he refrained from trying another spell for fear her sword would throw it back into his own teeth.

As they battled, Amil and Santrice crept to the window and slipped out. Fakhira knew she needed an edge of some kind and skittered back to call her water from Mahdis's body. Not yet dead, the Fire Dancer wheezed and shuddered on the floor.

Zavin stayed several feet away and planted his staff, sucking in lungfuls of air. "You're magnificent."

Also panting, Fakhira held her sword ready. Water formed a suit of armor around her body, ready for whatever he might try. "You're on the wrong side."

"Maybe *you're* on the wrong side." The yellow crystal set in the top of his staff pulsed with a dim glow. "You're going to rule. Don't you think you'll need help? I'm highly experienced, in multiple ways. I've served the caliph and his wife for over a decade. I practically run the caliphate already."

Somehow, his words made sense. She already knew the job would be difficult, of course. Korval had said she'd be fine, but maybe he assumed she'd understand that she needed help. Something about this felt off, though, and she couldn't put her finger on it. "What about Mahdis?"

"A means to an end." Zavin dismissed the woman on the floor with a flick of his hand. "After all, without her efforts, the path to the caliph title wouldn't be cleared for you to now take it. Nothing and no one stand in your way now. I don't want it. I only want to serve the caliph."

Tension eased in Fakhira's shoulders as she listened to his words. Of course he only wanted to serve. Why would she ever have thought he wanted the title for himself? He'd served Korval Mahdis, and now he could serve her. She lowered her sword. "What do you think I should do about Trimar?"

Zavin smiled and stepped closer to her, then slipped around behind her. Where he touched her shoulder, she smoothed the water away to feel his warmth on her skin. "We'll kill him, of course. He's a fool and an irritant. He's forced his people to sacrifice for years so he could pursue petty little wars borne of what he perceives as injustice." His breath warmed her neck, delivering sensual pleasure and promising more.

Except she wanted that from Tahjis, or maybe Cyric. She barely knew this man. "We should go do that right away." Her voice sounded distant to her ears, as though someone else spoke the words.

"You've had a difficult day, Caliph Al-Kabar. Perhaps we should retire for the night and leave in the morning." He brushed his lips against her ear.

Fakhira's cheeks burned as she realized what he wanted from her. Though it seemed right, it also seemed wrong. "I should...I haven't bathed in days."

"I understand. You must feel very dry after your ordeal earlier. I'm glad Mahdis won't be able to do that to you ever again."

She turned and saw the Fire Dancer, weak and limp. To be on the safe side, she strode to Mahdis and plunged her blade into the Dancer's chest. Mahdis shuddered and went still.

"Come, let me draw you a bath." Zavin glided into the bathroom.

Fakhira watched Mahdis's blood stain the marble in a growing puddle and wanted to feel something. There ought to be a well of grief inside her, with guilt and relief. Instead, she floated on a cloud, content and...something else. A dark thing hovered out of reach. She frowned as she followed the sound of splashing water into the bathroom.

Zavin straightened from the tub, shaking water off his hand. "While you soak, I'll fetch you something to eat. Is there anything you'd like?"

"Lime." She remembered Tahjis presenting limes to her, bought with stolen coins. The thought made her smile. "Something with lime."

"As you wish." He bowed and left the room, his staff thumping on the floor.

Chapter 39

Fakhira pulled the shift off and settled into the warm water. She laid back in the large tub as it filled around her and stared at the wall. Her mind emptied of everything, reveling in the heat of the water. It rose to her chin before she turned the faucet off and dunked her head under to wash her hair. The Waters engulfed her.

Muffled voices whispered on the edges of her hearing. She strained to hear them. When nothing changed, she thought they might be in the room and popped her head above the surface. The moment her ears left the water, the whispering stopped. If the Waters needed to tell her something, they wouldn't have this difficulty.

The whispering began when she submerged again. Thinking the sword might help as it had done once before, she surged out and grabbed the blade, then pulled it underwater with her. It felt as if a fog around her mind shattered into a thousand sparks. Grief slammed onto her shoulders. Tahjis, Cyric, Jannat, and Radwan all had to be dead by now. Behrouz had betrayed her against his will. Korval had sacrificed himself for her.

Zavin had bespelled her, as he'd done to Behrouz. He'd made her forget everything that mattered for a short time. She'd let him do it because she wished she could go on without feeling any of it. That man was dangerous and needed to be dealt with. Though his goals aligned with her own for now, he'd dispose of her the moment he no longer considered her useful.

She broke the surface again, this time with her head clear. The sword could only protect her from magic she could see. The Waters could only protect her body. Her own mind and soul would have to protect her from insidious effects like this one. Stepping out of the tub, she called all this water to her command, leaving only a dry pile of sand and dirt behind.

The door to her rooms opened and she knew what to do. Setting her sword against the wall, she walked out wearing only water and tried to ignore Mahdis's body still lying on the floor. She struggled to keep her face pleasant when she saw Zavin carrying a tray of food for her.

His brow raised and his eyes roved over her body. Though the water distorted his view, he smiled the way Fakhira had seen Shahan watch Almiya on their way to the bedroom. But she couldn't afford to think of them now. "I expected you to relax longer," he said as he set the tray on her nightstand, "but I suppose you can take your bath with you."

She forced herself to laugh as though he'd told a grand joke. "The second I felt clean, I discovered how hungry I am." To play this part, she imagined Tahjis in Zavin's place and clamped down on a pang of anguish. Such pretense allowed her to stay still while he approached, his gaze never rising above her chest.

"I can help you with that. Come, let me touch you without this water between us." He took her hand and tugged her close.

When he bent to kiss her, she gushed water at his face. The liquid forced its way inside his mouth and nose while he shuddered with shock. She swept his legs out from underneath him and sat on his chest, pinning his arms with her knees while she directed the water with her hands. He thrashed and bucked for several heartbeats, then weakened and subsided. It took longer than she expected, and she left the water in his lungs long enough to be sure he wouldn't cough and get back up.

With him dead, she covered her face and wept. Twice in such a short time, she'd lost everyone and everything. The caliph's title couldn't warm her heart or bring Tahjis back. She'd settle for Cyric if he lived, though she couldn't imagine how that might be possible. Both men had been taken at the same time to the same fate.

When she'd been there long enough to feel wretched, something draped over her shoulders and she looked up through blurry eyes to see Santrice covering her with a robe. Tahjis's sister smiled at her and helped her move to the bed. They sat together for a long time, Fakhira still crying.

Eventually, the tears ran out. Santrice rocked her, humming a soothing melody. Fakhira rubbed her eyes. "I'm sorry. Tahjis is dead because of me."

Santrice nodded with a sad smile. "I heard Behrouz say something about Tahjis being hanged. I always knew he'd wind up into something so far over his head it got him killed."

She accepted it so calmly that Fakhira stared at her. "You're not upset?"

"Of course I'm upset." Santrice sighed. "It's been a week since I found out, and I've already mourned him. I wish we'd been closer, and that his death would tear at my heart for—"

"A week?" Stunned, Fakhira blinked and stared. "It's been a week since then?"

"Behrouz tried to seduce me. When I turned him away, he told me."

Although Fakhira had accepted he must be dead, she hadn't truly believed it. Hearing it this way shocked her too much to react. "I have to go make sure he's offered to the Fires properly."

"Yes, you should do that." Santrice helped her stand and offered her sand-yellow clothing. "I think these are yours. Amil brought them."

The bodies had been removed and Fakhira's water waited in a still pool on the floor. "This place will be in chaos." She threw off the robe and shrugged into her clothes. It didn't include her head wrapping, but did have her blue scarf. Instead of covering her face with it, she wrapped it around her hair. If anyone cared about her gender, too bad for them.

"It already is. The guards don't know what to do. The caliph and Zavin are both dead, so are all the Fire Dancers but one."

Fakhira took Santrice's hand and fixed her with a steady look. "I need to go to Jashtel. Can you handle things here for a few days while I take care of Tahjis? Omeed will do most of the work and make the decisions."

"Oh. Yes, I can do that for you. I think. Are you sure?" Santrice gulped. "I've only ever been a whore."

Fakhira wished she felt like laughing. "I'm sure that's given you plenty of experience with handling men." She grabbed her sword, then tugged Santrice out of the room and down the hall. At the front door, she stopped and cleared her throat. "I am Al-Kabar, and your new caliph. Because of the actions of my predecessor, I must leave for a few days to deal with difficult problems. I leave Santrice to act in my stead with Omeed's assistance. If either of them are treated poorly by anyone, I will find out who did it, and I'll cut off their heads."

She raised an eyebrow, daring them to argue with her or show signs of rebellion. One bowed in relieved obedience and the others followed suit. "Good. Make sure my words are known."

"I will, Caliph Al-Kabar," the first guard said. "Omeed and Santrice will be treated as if they were our mothers. Any man who lays a hand on either without permission will lose it."

"Let it be known that Caliph Korval died defending his people from a power-mad mage. He'll be mourned properly when I return." With that, she squeezed Santrice's hand and let go to stride out through the front doors. She had ideas about what to do with this palace and about how to manage her new caliphate. Korval had been right; she'd know what to do when she needed to.

Chapter 40

Travel through the tunnels with the Waters' help brought Fakhira to Jashtel in the late afternoon. She stood on the ridge overlooking the city and had no idea what to make of the sight. People left through the front gate in a steady trickle, pulling wagons laden with goods, but no one entered the city. Smoke billowed into the air from several parts of the city on both sides of the river.

With a shrug, she hurried down the slope. As she neared the line of people moving away from the city, she frowned. These people had none of the usual marks of merchants. She saw soot streaked faces, injuries, and subdued children. What she'd assumed to be goods turned out to be haphazardly packed belongings.

Confused, she matched the pace of a man trudging alongside a camel laden with too much blanket-wrapped baggage to carry him. "I came for trade. What's happening?"

"Revolution." He shook his head. "Been brewing for a while, of course, but I always thought it'd blow over. Every time someone stood up and opposed the caliph's little wars, they lost their head. Couple of days ago, rumors ran around about a rebellion and overthrowing Trimar. Figured it would be the same as it always is. Yesterday, someone blew up some of the caliph's buildings and started attacking city guards. Rebels popped out of the woodwork and it's nearly a war zone now. There's some rebels keeping the gate clear for people to flee, but otherwise, it's all a mess."

Stunned, Fakhira tripped over her own feet and had to stumble to recover. "What about the hangings a week ago?"

"Hangings? I didn't hear about any hangings. Best to turn around now, though, and go back to wherever you came from. There won't be trade in Jashtel for a while."

If there hadn't been any hangings, then Tahjis and Cyric might be alive, and the same for Radwan and Jannat. Starting a revolution against the caliph who tried to kill them sounded like something Tahjis might do. Fakhira stepped off the road and ran alongside it to reach the front gate. People called for her to turn back. She ducked through the gate, surprised to find the stench had been replaced by smoke and sweat, and scanned for the rebels protecting the area. When she spotted four older men in ragged clothes with battered swords, she hurried to them. On the way, she noticed more figures clumped around the gate in an arc, holding sharpened sticks and heavy pots.

"I heard you're trying to take down Trimar," she said to the four men. "How can I help?"

They looked her over, not bothering to hide their skepticism. "Can you fight with that?" one asked.

Fakhira let a laugh bubble up at the absurdity of such a question. "Yes. Where will I find the fighting?"

The man shrugged and gestured with both arms to encompass the city. "Pick a direction and go."

She nodded to the men and jogged past them. While she could spend the night hopping from fight to fight, she had a thought to do what she'd come here to do the first time. Dashing up the main road, she aimed for the palace. She reached a knot of men fighting, their swords and sticks clashing in the waning light.

Though she'd worried it might be difficult to tell who fought on which side, she found it simple when she came across the first group. Trimar's men wore the same uniforms burned into her memories in Aitrae Oasis. The rebels wore anything but that despicable maroon. All the rebels but one man wielded sticks, rocks, and other makeshift weapons. One man used a curved sword and fought with skill.

Fakhira's heart swelled to see Cyric still alive. In his current predicament, she thought that might change without her. Though his small team of rebels fought with courage and determination, Trimar's men had them outnumbered and outmatched. Before she reached the skirmish, one rebel fell and another took a serious blow to the leg. Cyric cried out as a sword sliced a gash across his chest.

She plunged into the small battle and cut down Trimar's men with wild abandon, desperate to save Cyric and his band of brave souls. Trimar's men stood little chance against her as she ducked and thrust and whirled among them. When she stopped, ten maroon-clad bodies lay at her feet.

The rebels, one checking on his dead friend, stopped to gasp for breath when the last of Trimar's men fell. "Whoever you are, thank you."

"I am Al-Kabar," Fakhira said as she swooped down on Cyric, who'd fallen to his knees. The injury, while shallow, would bleed him out if unchecked. She filled the wound with her water to keep him alive. She reached out and covered the other man's leg to keep him alive too.

Cyric hissed with surprised pain and gaped at her. "We thought you were dead."

Fakhira touched his cheek. "I thought the same of you. How did you escape?"

He grabbed her shoulder with a heavy hand, breathing hard. "Tahjis and his rat. We were able to get Jannat and Radwan out, and Tahjis decided he needed to avenge you by starting a revolution against Trimar. He said that's what you'd want, for the people to overthrow him."

"He's right." She looked into his eyes and saw affection that she felt in return. She would never love him, not the way she now knew she did Tahjis, but she would always care about him. "I'm fond of you, Cyric, and I owe you much."

He took her hand and squeezed it, his face twisted with pain. "I would wander the desert and walk through fire for you."

"I..." She sighed and groped for the words to explain what she felt.

"It's alright." He nodded as if he understood her difficulty. "I love you, Fakhira, but not the way most people mean. You're Al-Kabar, the champion of the Waters, and I'm your servant." When she struggled to respond, he clasped both hands around hers. "Tahjis loves you with all his heart. I saw it in his agony. I was upset at your death, and I'm cheered to see you alive. *He* was crushed."

It hurt her to know Tahjis had suffered so much for the past week. As much as she wanted to run and find him, though, she had more important things to do. He could wait. "Where will I find Trimar? Is he hiding in his palace?"

"As far as we know, yes."

"Is there a healer with the rebels?"

Cyric took her help to stand. "A lesser one, yes. This way." He and what remained of his men guided her through the city, giving some buildings a wide berth.

A few blocks away, as Fakhira helped Cyric with his arm over her shoulders, Jannat dropped into their path from an apartment balcony. "Al-Kabar," she squealed in surprised delight. Engulfing Fakhira in an embrace, she pressed a kiss onto her lips. When Jannat let go, she grinned. "For old times' sake."

Fakhira chuckled, sure it meant nothing more than friendship. She gave Jannat a once-over and found she'd settled into her role of warrior-woman. Jannat wore recovered armor with the maroon pieces and tassels stripped away and the leather and cloth cinched around her curves. No one would mistake her for a man, or for a helpless maiden.

Surveying Cyric and his team, Jannat tsked. Fakhira also thought concern flickered across Jannat's face when she saw Cyric's wound, but not for the other man. "Two injured, both bad. Bring them inside here." She grabbed a crowbar sticking out of a pile of debris and pulled, revealing it had been constructed to appear blocked while actually serving as a hinged door. Inside, sunshine filtered through cracks to create a hazy gloom.

"I can take them from here, Al-Kabar." Jannat took Cyric's weight on her own shoulders and surreptitiously rubbed her cheek against his. Cyric gave her a weak, pained smile in response and seemed pleased. "You should go and fight," Jannat said with a flick of her hand. "The longer you're in here, the more of these good people die and the fewer of Trimar's do." She pulled the scarf from her head to use as a bandage.

Seeing the rest prepared to take care of the other man, Fakhira nodded. Jannat would make a better match for Cyric than Fakhira could. "I'll see you again soon." She called her water to her hand and dashed out to return to her mission to find the palace. The faded, distant sounds of battle echoed in the streets and alleys from every direction. Hoping she remembered the landmarks well enough, she turned up the street and jogged.

Several blocks up and to the right, she ran across another knot of swords clashing. This group had more steel among them than Cyric's, and she dove into the fight from behind them. Her blade bit deeply and her power called the water from Trimar's men. When death again surrounded her, she stopped and took a moment to catch her breath.

"Al-Kabar!" Radwan's voice boomed louder than seemed prudent. Before Fakhira had a chance to turn and greet him, strong arms wrapped around her from behind and picked her up. Radwan let out a whoop. "You're alive! I knew it. Everyone else despaired, but not me."

Fakhira laughed and turned to hug him as soon as he let her go. "I'm glad to see you doing well." She sighed as she met his gaze, knowing what news she had to give him. "Behrouz—"

Radwan set her down and gripped her forearms. "I'll never forgive my brother for his treachery." He spat to the side. "But we escaped, and so did you."

"Don't be too hard on him." Fakhira returned his grip and met his gaze. "He was bespelled by a mage who's now dead, and I let your brother live after I defeated him. Caliph Korval and most of his Fire Dancers weren't so lucky."

"Oh, yes, the Fire Dancers." Radwan bobbed his head. Fakhira could see he preferred not to dwell on his brother for now. "Trimar's Dancers split, three for the rebels and four for the caliph. According to the ones that rebelled, they don't work well in even numbers for some reason, so you may have good fortune against them. My team came out here to loot supplies. Come with us and help. We'll take you back with us, to our pantry."

Fakhira shook her head. "I'm going to the palace. This will end when Trimar and his close advisors are dead, and not before." She squeezed his arm and pulled away. "Good luck, Radwan. The Waters watch over you."

"Now they do!" Radwan grabbed her shoulder. "You'll need a distraction. We'll come with you and do that. Come," he bellowed to his men, "we follow Al-Kabar to glory!"

His six men held up their fists in solidarity and Fakhira echoed the gesture with a determined smile. "I'm not sure how much of a distraction I really need, but you're welcome to join me. Let us sweep through these streets in a tide of justice." Her water surged to the ground and whisked her, Radwan, and his six men up the road. The men let out excited whoops and waved their swords in the air.

The eight of them blew through another small fight, hacking apart Trimar's men with ease and leaving cheering rebels in their wake. It happened again, and three more rebels hopped into the water to help the group clear a path to the palace.

Two blocks away from the palace, arrows flew at them. Fakhira saw them in the air and shifted the water to intercept the feathered shafts. Behind her, several men fell, surprised by the sudden shift. When they saw why she did it, a ragged cheer erupted at her back.

"I think they noticed us coming," Fakhira said with a laugh.

"I think we'll be the last thing they see!" Radwan shouted loud enough for Trimar's men to hear.

Fakhira ran up the road, her water flowing in front of her and deflecting arrows. Through the liquid wall, she made out a ring of Trimar's men on the ground behind barricades of debris and more men on the roof with bows. If she approached to fight hand-to-hand, she'd have to use the water as armor, leaving none of it to defend against the archers. She could bowl through with the water in front of her as a wedge to knock men aside, but that would leave these rebels and Radwan unprotected.

With a wave, she got her men to follow her behind a building for cover. "I can't protect us from the archers and fight the men on the ground at the same time. Ideas?"

"Protect us from the archers and we'll fight them for you," Radwan said. "Just like in Grev-Nol. You don't have to do everything yourself."

Looking to the rest of the men, she saw them nodding in agreement. "Alright." She clapped Radwan on the shoulder. "We'll rush them. Climb over the barricade, make a hole, and push through to the front door. If you can damage the barricade, do it. As soon as we're inside, hold the door while I hunt down Trimar."

Radwan and the men raised their fists and grunted in hearty agreement. They followed her around the other side of the building, then up the road. When they reached the barricade, arrows bouncing off the watery shield overhead, Fakhira stopped and let the men go first. They swarmed over the barricade, the first wave slowed by their enemy. In the midst of metal clanging on metal and the grunts and cries of men killing and being killed, she heard a rat squeak. Brumble sat on her foot, nose raised and whiskers quivering.

Fakhira's heart swelled. "Yes, Brumble, it's Al-Kabar. Get Tahjis. We're storming the palace."

The rat squeaked and scampered away. Fakhira crouched and scanned behind her, watching for any sign of her Rat. The sound of cheering echoed up a street to the right and she saw Trimar's men fleeing toward her. Radwan's men smashed a hole through the barricade, knocking Trimar's men aside with half a wagon.

Wanting to protect the incoming rebels from the archers, Fakhira looked up and made a decision. She blasted the archers with her wall of water, then called it back while they reeled from the impact and used it to launch herself to the roof. The water encased her body as armor as she kicked one man into another, knocking them both off the roof.

Two dozen men on the roof dropped their bows and rushed her with swords and daggers. Her sword guided her. She kicked and punched and spun and slashed through the small horde. Several more went over the side and the rest lay in pieces when she stopped to breathe. Stepping to the edge of the roof, she raised her sword above her head in victory.

"To Trimar's men, lay down your weapons and you'll be shown mercy," she called down. "Continue to fight and your body will be tossed into the desert to rot! I am Al-Kabar, and if you stand against me, you will die."

Around the palace, voices shouted in triumph. The jumbled noise shifted into a chant of her name. In the mess below, she couldn't see Radwan, let alone Tahjis or Cyric, and stopped trying to find them. Her sword jerked her body around in time to sidestep a billowing gout of flames. She saw a woman in a flame orange dress standing on the roof with her mouth twisted into a snarl.

"Impressive, Al-Kabar. But those are just men with metal." The Fire Dancer let flames flicker in her palms as her three sisters joined her. "You'll find us more of a challenge."

"Perhaps." Though she wished these women might be swayed by words, Fakhira charged them. They'd made their choice already.

Chapter 41

Expecting the Fire Dancers to be unaccustomed to physical fighting, Fakhira pushed her water out to assault them. The lead Dancer stood
her ground in the wave's wake while the other three staggered and fell.
Fakhira leaped at the lead Dancer, slashing her sword at the other woman's
body. The lead Dancer hopped aside and engulfed herself in flames. From
it, a sword formed, and she held it with practiced skill.

Behind her, Fakhira heard an achingly familiar voice. "Al-Kabar,
how about if you let us handle the rabble?"

She glanced back to see Tahjis hauling himself over the edge of the
roof. Three women in the orange and red of Fire Dancers landed beside
him, propelled to the roof by jets of flame. Fakhira's heart swelled to see
him in person. "What took you so long?"

"Some lunatic decided to attack the palace without telling anyone
first." He gestured for the Fire Dancers to proceed. "Ladies, after you."

Fakhira grinned and lunged at the lead Dancer. Her sword hit the
fire blade, flinging out a shower of sparks. Fire exploded around them as

the rest of the Fire Dancers rushed to battle each other. "You're on the wrong side," Fakhira told the lead Dancer as she shoved the fire blade away.

"You came here to kill my caliph." The lead Dancer launched a flurry of attacks, hacking over and over and pushing Fakhira back.

Ducking under a jet of flame, Fakhira whirled and saw Tahjis darting around the roof while the rest of the Dancers kept each other busy. "He's responsible for the murder of my entire family. The Waters have judged him and demand his death."

"*You've* judged him," the lead Dancer snarled.

Giving up on trying to change the woman's mind, Fakhira renewed her attacks. Where her water met the lead Dancer's fire, a sizzling curtain of steam rose. Something flashing in the light flew at the Dancer and hit her on the side of the head. Though the dagger caused no damage, it made her flinch and distracted her enough for Fakhira to kick her in the gut.

The lead Dancer grunted and staggered back, holding her stomach. Without hesitation, Fakhira leaped at the dancer, knocking her down. Agony seared her belly as the fire sword shoved past her water armor and into her gut. Fakhira cried out and surged up to aim her own sword and drive it down into the lead Dancer's chest.

She staggered up, ripping her sword out of the woman and clutching at her belly. Tahjis rushed to her side and ducked under her arm to support her.

"I'll be fine," Fakhira gasped. "Make sure she won't."

Tahjis let out a huff. "Shut up. The Dancers have it covered. Let me see. How bad is it?"

Fakhira gritted her teeth at the pain. "I just need a bathtub full of water."

"Stop hiding it and let me see." Tahjis pulled her hand away and sucked in a breath. "That's pretty bad. Anahita, stop messing around. We need water for Al-Kabar. Lots of water." He hauled her to the trap door in the roof. "I thought you were dead."

She met his gaze and forced a smile. "I thought you were dead too."

"I guess we're even, then. It's not acceptable for you to die now. So we're clear on that." He peered into the hole and nodded to himself in satisfaction, then he kissed her. He pulled away before she wanted him to. "Later, we're going to talk. And do other things." He grinned. "For now, it's clear below. I'll jump down and you follow."

She nodded and watched him swing down into the hole. Her water cushioned her landing. They waited for the two remaining Fire Dancers, only one of whom successfully held back her tears, then followed them up the hall. They slipped into a side room and one Dancer ran a bath in a large tub while the other stayed by the door.

"We need to find Trimar," Fakhira said as she stepped into the water without bothering to undress.

"We also need to find his son," Tahjis said. "While I've been here, I've learned a lot about them. For the past few years, Trimar has been trying to find a wife for his son. They go visit somewhere, then they come back and send the army to attack that caliphate. Rumor has it that the son can't keep his hands to himself. I suspect it's an act or excuse, designed to put a swift end to the allegedly diplomatic trip when they've got enough information about security and good places to raid."

Fakhira stared at him. "What makes you think that?"

Tahjis shrugged. "I hear things. One thing I hear is that Trimar's son likes boys instead of girls. Another I've heard a lot is how Trimar's got a cash problem. Seems like it should be because he's blowing money on wars, but that's not the case. His army is all criminals, and they take their pay and supplies from the places they raid, which means he doesn't pay much for either jails or an army. The caliph gets fifty percent and the soldiers get the rest, plus whatever women they want. So, he's got the biggest, best equipped bandit group in Serescine, and it's masquerading as an army.

"Fortunately, they met Korval's army head-on out there someone, and while they're pretty good, Korval's men managed to beat them and free those girls from Aitrae Oasis. Five or six dozen of Trimar's men came running home with their tails between their legs, and that's who we've been fighting for the past day and a half. They've got better weapons and are used to fighting, where we've got about four times as many people who want to be free and have no training. It's been an even match, give or take. Until now."

Fakhira sighed with pleasure as the water engulfed her. Though the tub still needed time to fill, she ducked under the surface and let the Waters do their work. She could hardly believe that the nervous, twitchy Rat she'd met by accident in Kamrik had become such a brave, capable leader. When the ache in her belly faded, she broke the surface again.

One question bothered her above all. "What's Trimar been doing with all his money?"

"Blowing it on us, mostly," one of the Dancers said. Fakhira remembered Tahjis calling this one Anahita and recalled hearing the name before, a lifetime ago. "He's been throwing money at us, and at guards and the staff. Bita didn't care, she'd do anything to keep her position as the Lead Fire Dancer of the caliphate. Some of us weren't so keen. We did what Bita told us to do because we had to. Now there are only two of us left. An even number."

Fakhira thought she understood part of Anahita's anguish. She also remembered Anahita's small mercy for Almiya. "I have only one Dancer in my caliphate. If I'm going to kill Trimar, then this one will be mine also. Omeed is a good Dancer. She'll work with you. Then you'll be three, and you'll oversee the largest caliphate in all Serescine."

"I don't care about the power, I never did." Anahita gave Fakhira a sad smile. "If I had, I'd be a dead body on the roof right now." She shook her head. "Darya and I will meet with Omeed, and if we fit, we'll be your Fire Dancers."

"Good." Fakhira nodded and climbed out of the tub, calling all the water to her. "I'm glad to know that's taken care of."

Tahjis handed her sword over. "What happened to Korval?"

"His army may have won that day, but he was abducted somehow." After Anahita gave them directions, Fakhira told Tahjis the story of her escape.

"That's disgusting," Tahjis said as she ended the story while they walked. "Pulling water from blood? And how Mahdis died. Ew." He shuddered. "Please let's just kill Trimar quick and leave him for the jackals."

335

Fakhira chuckled, too pleased to have Tahjis by her side to be upset by anything. They reached the wall Anahita had said would have a hidden door leading to the fortified inner vault she thought Trimar would have fled to. She stopped short of it and scanned the dead end hallway. The stonework had been painted along this corridor, with the short end wall in dark brown, the ceiling and floor in white and the two side walls in a peach tone. The brown drew her eyes but she saw no sign of a door.

"This is quality work," Tahjis said, brushing his palm over the stone wall. Brumble stuck her nose out of his shirt and climbed down his body. She sniffed at the bottom edge. "It's not in the end wall. That's the sign of a professional."

"Can you find it or not?"

"You wound me, Al-Kabar." Tahjis gave her a look of mock hurt.

She smirked. "This isn't going to be like the market, when I found the book despite your brilliant yet complicated plan, is it?"

"You may be the champion of the Waters, on track to become the first Sultan of Serescine in hundreds of years," Tahjis said. He pressed at the base of the wall and Fakhira heard a loud click. "But *I'm* the thief here." A trapdoor swung down, revealing a ladder descending into darkness. He grinned up at her and gestured to the ladder. "Thieves don't go first. Scary people with big weapons do."

"You think I'm going to be the Sultan of Serescine?" Fakhira rolled the title around in her head, trying to decide how she felt about it.

Tahjis stood and cupped her cheek with his warm, calloused hand. "You're the Al-Kabar, the chosen champion of the Waters. You've defeated a mage, Fire Dancers, even an army, and you think Trimar, or any other caliph, is going to stop you? They're all the same, Fakhira. They all need to be stopped. The time of greedy, power-hungry men leading our people is over. The time of the Al-Kabar has come."

She wrapped her arms around his neck and kissed him. Once, he'd been too shy or nervous to even look at her. Now, he held her close and returned her affection with interest. More than that, he used her name. When she pulled away, she smiled at him, her heart full to bursting. "You'll help, right?"

He grinned. "So long as you don't expect me to work very hard."

Unable to suppress a laugh, Fakhira shoved him aside and hopped down the ladder. When she looked up, she saw Tahjis following close behind. He'd always do that for her, always back her up, always keep her grounded. As she turned to face the reinforced doors, she knew that no matter how long their road might turn out to be, they'd walk it together.

Epilogue

"Do we need to manage this? It seems to me that Peshtir should be able to handle its own water issues. They didn't have a disaster while I wasn't paying attention, did they?" Fakhira tossed the thick report onto her heavy wood desk and leaned back in her leather chair. She pulled off the wire frame holding enchanted lenses over her nose and rubbed her eyes.

Tahjis sighed from across the desk. "Only if you count the new idiot they put in charge of the city. Thirty years ago, we would've gone and cut his head off."

"Thirty years ago, I still had my first sword." Fakhira set her glasses down and gazed through the window in her office. Rows of tall palm trees lined the street outside on a sunny afternoon. "Do you ever miss those days?"

"I miss getting up without making any noise." Tahjis stood with a grunt, his bones creaking. He waved dismissively at her desk. "Let it lie for a while. He might figure it out on his own if you make him."

"Or he might starve half his people."

"Bah." He clasped his hands behind his back and peered out the window. Brumble, her coat gray and thin, poked her nose out of his pocket and twitched her whiskers. "We should send Shadi to visit him. She likes to travel and cause trouble, and all her children are old enough to leave behind."

"Darius is only five," Fakhira chided. She braced on the arms of her chair to stand, her body protesting the movement. The Waters could ease those aches and pains, but she preferred to be reminded of her age. Forgetting could lead her to running off and doing stupid things. She stepped to her husband's side and slid an arm around his waist. His familiar musk greeted her.

He draped his arm around her shoulders and squeezed. "We have two other daughters and ten other grandchildren. They can handle him. Besides, she and her shifty lout should probably have some time together."

Fakhira chuckled and thumped him in the chest. "One of these days, Radwan is going to hear you call his son that and the boy will quit. Then I'd have to find another bookkeeper. Not to mention that he'd take Shadi and their children elsewhere."

Tahjis harrumphed. "Never trust bookkeepers. They know too much and can add big numbers in their heads."

"I seem to recall you being the one to suggest the match."

"I must have confused him with someone else."

"Then there was the wedding, where you—"

He kissed her, as hungry and passionate as the first time so long ago. When he broke it off, he rubbed his nose against hers. "What were we talking about? How much you enjoy being the Sultan of Serescine?"

She grinned. "Something like that. There may have been discussion of how much you enjoy *not* being Sultan of Serescine."

"I'm just an old street thief, not worthy to lick your boots."

Fakhira snorted. He still served as her master spy, though he no longer disappeared for days at a time to gather information or coordinate his network of informants and agents. "I'll never understand why you would ever think it's my boots I want you to lick."

Tahjis laughed, his weathered face crinkling along well-worn lines. Before he could answer, the door burst open and two young boys dashed inside. They thumped into Tahjis, forcing him to lean against Fakhira and take a staggered step. He whirled and swept Darius up in his arms.

"How many times do you have to be told to knock?" Tahjis's smile took the bite out of his scolding.

"Grandpapa!" Shahan, the older of the two young cousins, grabbed Tahjis's pants and jumped up and down. "Do the thing with the knife!"

"Easy, boys." Tahjis set Darius down again with a wince. "You'll break me in half one of these days."

Fakhira snatched Shahan's hand to divide and conquer the enemy. "Grandpapa isn't a show pony until after dinner."

Tahjis smirked at her.

"Sorry!" Shadi reached the doorway and leaned against the jamb, breathless. "They got away from me." She reminded Fakhira of Almiya so much she chose to believe the Fires had sent her sister back as her daughter.

"Boys, you were supposed to tell Grandmeer and Grandpapa that dinner is starting soon, not badger them for entertainment."

Fakhira ruffled Shahan's hair and shooed everyone out of her office. The warm wood floors creaked under their combined weight as they walked down the hall together. Her family waited in the large dining hall, a room big enough to feed thirty at once. She took her seat at the head of the sturdy table and watched with amusement as her daughters and their husbands and children scrambled for their favorite seats.

Tahjis sat beside her, as he usually did, and set Brumble on the table to roam freely. The rat lumbered to the nearest basket of bread and sat beside it, too old and lazy to bother bringing a roll all the way back to Tahjis's place setting.

Chattering filled the air as servants brought simple foods to be eaten with steel forks from wooden plates. Picking up the one concession she made to luxury, she brought the delicate glass goblet to her nose and breathed in the aroma of Tahjis's favorite imported red wine. Soon, she'd surprise her husband by handing the crown to their middle daughter. Their remaining years together would have no reports or paperwork or intrigue. Instead, they could visit Santrice and Amil and their brood. And they could finally be alone together as much as they wished.

As it should be.

Other Books by Lee French

Maze Beset trilogy

Superheroes in denim

Dragons In Pieces

Dragons In Chains

Dragons In Flight

Fantasy in the Ilauris setting

Damsel In Distress

Shadow & Spice (short story)

Al-Kabar

Spirit Knights

Young adult urban paranormal adventures

in the Pacific Northwest

Girls Can't Be Knights

Backyard Dragons (coming in 2016)

The Greatest Sin

Epic fantasy series co-authored with Erik Kort

The Fallen

Harbinger

Moon Shades

www.authorleefrench.com   www.myrddinpublishing.com

ABOUT THE AUTHOR

Lee French lives in Olympia, WA with two kids, two bicycles, and too much stuff. She is an avid gamer and member of the Myth-Weavers online RPG community, where she is known for her fondness for Angry Ninja Squirrels of Doom. In addition to spending much time there, she also trains year-round for the one-week of glorious madness that is RAG-BRAI, has a nice flower garden with one dragon and absolutely no lawn gnomes, and tries in vain every year to grow vegetables that don't get devoured by neighborhood wildlife.

She is an active member of the Northwest Independent Writers Association, the Pacific Northwest Writers Association, and the Olympia Area Writers Coop, as well as being one of two Municipal Liaisons for the NaNoWriMo Olympia region.

unique electronic & print books

FANTASY TITLES FROM OTHER MYRDDIN AUTHORS

Ross M. Kitson

"Make no mistake, Ross Kitson is an artist, and this novel is pure artistic excellence."

Prism series

Chained

Quest

Secrets

Loss

Broken

Connie J. Jasperson

"I found delight in her ability to both craft a compelling tale and create emotional involvement for the reader"

The World of Neveyah

The Tower of Bones

Forbidden Road

Mountains of the Moon

www.authorleefrench.com   www.myrddinpublishing.com